Captivating! This is a collection of original works almost impossible to put down. Ranging from futuristic fantasy, contemporary mystery, creepy horror and almost-sweet drama - you can immerse yourself in a treasure trove of compelling stories in eight distinctive voices. Such fun!

– *Shayla McBride*
Novelist

The intention of this anthology is to show the breadth of the human imagination. These authors stepped up. Their stories will not disappoint.

– *Marie Ginga*
Editor for MetaStellar Magazine

When I finished this book, the very next day I went out to my local library. I just had to read the rest of what's on Shelf 804!

– *C. Brian Moorhead*
Author

I love stepping into a candy shop – and that's why I love this story collection. So many flavors. Unexpected ingredients. All concocted by the feverish imaginations of eight very different writers. So don't hold back – indulge yourself!

– *Dana Norton*
Author

An Anthology

TALES
FROM
SHELF 804

an anthology

An Anthology

Tales From Shelf 804 published by Marie Ginga.

Cover art by Lucy A.J. Tew

ISBN 9798352141748

Welcome to Shelf 804!

Under the Dewey Decimal System, Shelf 804 currently holds a designation of "not assigned, or no longer used" – naturally, we were only too happy to lay claim to this rare niche of unoccupied library real estate. Step into a literary treasure trove that brings together the creative prowess of eight authors, spanning genre and style, as we populate our very own Shelf 804 with the thirty-two short stories collected in this anthology.

Each writer has engaged, in their own style, with four original prompts chosen by the group to inspire their writing. The result is an anthology as diverse as our imaginations. Join us on a journey that will transport you from a dueling piano bar in Denver, Colorado to the deck of a sailing ship worthy of Edgar Allan Poe; from the startling and unexpected world of 'the innerverse' to the gleaming, strangely quiet corridors of a moon colony.

Have fun discovering the hidden gems of Shelf 804. See if you can spot the prompts. Then take a minute and visit our Facebook Group, Tales From Shelf 804, where you can vote for your favorite story and chat with the writers. Take another minute to rate us on Amazon.

Respectfully,

Mike, Melody, Marie, Amira, Shayla, Brian, Dana, & Lucy

"We are, as a species, addicted to story. Even when the body goes to sleep, the mind stays up all night, telling itself stories."

– Jonathan Gottschall, The Storytelling Animal

THE CONTRACT

Writing Prompt

He'd never felt so ready for anything in his life. Once the contract was signed and the ink was dry, everyone who'd ever been an obstacle to his success was out of the way. He lifted his pen and out of the corner of his eye, something shifted.

"Well," she murmured, "what are you waiting for."

Stories

The Scrivener

By Marie LeClaire

Sabastian's fingers danced along the shelf that held a dozen codices owned by his friend, Pablo.

"You know how much I envy you your collection. Twelve volumes. A sizable number for our station," he said, referring to their mutual status as merchants.

Pablo's ire twitched at the implication that they were of the same class, but he let the comment pass. "Yes, Sabastian. It has taken me many years to collect them." He watched as his friend admired the spine of an illuminated bible.

"I beg you again," Sabastian continued. "Please let me borrow one of these masterpieces, to have it copied properly by the monks at the abbey."

It was a conversation they'd had many times. "You know I can't part with such a valuable possession, but you are always welcome to read them here, at your leisure."

"Yes, and I thank you greatly for that pleasure. But today my request is more of a business proposition than a favor."

"Indeed?"

"I propose that I lease the manuscript; that I pay you rent for the time it will take for the monks to copy it."

"It's an interesting offer, my friend, but what if there is loss or damage to my original during the process?"

"I will cover the original cost of the manuscript if anything should damage or destroy it while in my possession."

Pablo stroked his chin as he considered this new incentive. He didn't believe Sabastian could raise the money. "I am inclined to accept. When will you have acquired the deposit?"

"Splendid!" Sabastian reached into his jacket and offered a leather pouch with a letter to his friend. "I have it here."

A surprised Pablo took the letter and reviewed the agreement they had just discussed. It contained a written contract and an insurance agreement. He reached for the pouch. It contained enough silver to cover the lease terms. Reluctantly he waved a hand at his library.

"Which in my collection interests you?"

Sabastian knew exactly which one. He had perused each book of the collection before, in some cases sitting for hours in Pablo's library to enjoy entire volumes.

"I have always been drawn to this small one here." He removed it from the shelf. "Book of Night Hours. As you know, I often have fitful nights' sleep and I believe having a prayer guide for the quiet hours would allow me to spend the time in respectful devotions."

"And so it is. When would you like to take possession of it?"

"I have already consulted the Benedictine Abbot about scrivener services. He approximates a four-month process for the copying and binding. With a little extra persuasion," Sabastian gave a knowing tilt of his head, "they have agreed to start immediately."

"I see." Pablo rose from his chair and took the book from Sebastian's hands. He leafed through it cursorily then handed it back to Sabastian. "I have never read through the entirety of it, not being all that interested in nighttime prayers."

"I'm not surprised. Every standard Book of Hours provides ample attention to the spiritual needs of most people during the day." Sabastian accepted the codex with reverence. "I shall have it back to you in the absolute least amount of time."

After their goodbyes, Sabastian headed directly to the monastery on the hill.

***

The bells of St. Augustine Monastery rang before dawn. The brothers filed into the chapel for matins and then to the dining hall for porridge and dried fruit. Most of the scribes would pocket the fruit for later, when their focus would falter and the risk of error was greatest, usually just after terce prayers. The process would be repeated at the noon meal with a piece of bread or maybe a slice of cheese. If Prior Machello caught them though, it would garner them a solid strike on the back with his focusing stick. Any oil or crumbs on the parchment would eventually cause discoloration resulting in a reduction in payment if caught by the codex's commissioner.

Brother Silas was not like the rest of the scribes, devoted to the holy work of passing on God's word. On the contrary. He resented the work; resented the abbot; resented the brethren. Some days he resented God himself.

What possible offense to God had he committed at the age of five that his mother would drop him off, never to return?

The abbey had taken him in begrudgingly, putting him to work first as a houseboy then assisting with mixing inks and making parchment for the scribes. By the age of ten, he was copying hymnals for the local parishes. What started out as satisfying work, or at least better than scraping hides for parchment till his hands bled, quickly felt like servitude with long hours of standing, broken only by repetitious prayer and meals. Eye strain caused almost constant headaches. The material so redundant that it nearly crazed him.

In place of a formal education, the brothers had been sure to beat the fear of God into him as a child. He had grown to hate them all. Despite the abbot's refusal of classes, Silas had become fluent in the Latin, Hebrew and Greek of most codices and longed for the opportunity to copy something other than religious texts. Fortunately, he had developed a gifted hand at accuracy with unusual scripts which were more often scientific or historic in content.

This morning, Prior Machello approached him with the long confident strides of someone who perceived himself superior.

"I have a new project for you Brother Silas." Prior Machello began.

"Yes, Prior. I offer my services in any way God asks of me."

"A local merchant is requesting a copy of this codex." He opened a small book to expose simple pages.

"Are there no illuminations?" Silas asked.

"There appears not. And it looks to be a strange variety of Latin. You won't understand it but do your best to copy exactly."

"As always, Prior, I offer my best to God."

"Yes. Yes," Prior Machello waved him off. "Begin immediately."

Silas resented the assumption that he wouldn't understand it. That was Prior Machello trying to hold onto his fragile position.

Putting his attitude aside, Silas inspected the codex in his hands. *A Book of Hours.* How pedestrian. How many of these had he copied over the years. Tens certainly. His anticipation waned until he opened the front cover where the title was augmented. *A Book of Night Hours.* Well, he mused, that *was* unusual. Maybe this new project would keep his attention after all.

He got to work and soon understood the comments by the Prior. There were unusual words and phrases embedded in the text. Some were altered, some were completely unknown to him. It had kept his interest throughout the day, when he looked up and realized that he was alone in the scriptorium and the hour was quite late. He mumbled a few curses he'd learned from the Greeks and stumbled to his cell knowing the morning bells would come much too soon.

Dispensing with the usual evening prayers, he decided to invoke a new devotional using a prayer from the Book of Night Hours. He repeated it over and over as he invited sleep to come.

Just before dropping off to sleep, he was disturbed by a noise in his room. Generally noises, though rare, were confined to the occasional rodent getting at some of the straw that lay on the stone slab of his bed. This night the sound was different. A clicking jingle of things tapping together aroused his sleep.

He reached for his tinder box and struck a spark. In the dim light of the brimstone, he beheld a woman, if such could be said for the apparition that stood before him. In ragged dress, she swayed on skeletal feet, barely able to contain them in tattered shoes that matched the dress in poverty. The face and hair were those of a corpse long dead but its eyes showed a slight glow that was the most disturbing of all.

Despite his fright he addressed the thing. "Who are you and what do you want of me?"

She moaned as if struggling to speak.

"What curse do you bring upon me, I say!" Silas demanded.

When he reached for the cross around his neck, the vision vanished and he was left alone in his room wondering if he had dreamed it. Resorting back to the usual evening prayers, he eventually fell into restless sleep.

The next morning brought the same matins and porridge, the same procession to the scriptorium, but today Brother Silas felt an urgency in his chest as he approached his table. He recalled his recitation of the strange prayer from the night before. What was this book of night hours? And what of the strange dialect that appears woven into the text? With both apprehension and excitement he sat down to resume his task.

The bells that marked breaks in the work day now felt like an unwelcome interruption. An aggravation. When the day was finally over, Brother Silas was still hard at work.

"Brother," Prior Machello approached him. "It is time to rest. Go."

"Prior Machello, with all due respect, since I am scribing prayers for the night hours, would it not be prudent to do so at night?"

"That would require additional candle wax and an expense for the monastery."

"Yes, Brother Machello." Silas intentionally left off Machello's title. He knew it irked him. "But I also know that you received an extra donation, maybe a personal one, to expedite the process. No?"

The Prior's back stiffened. "As you will, Brother Silas, but work till dawn and be back here following the noon meal."

"In grace and gratitude, I thank the Lord for my opportunity to serve."

"Hmmph." Machello turned on his heels and left Silas alone in the scriptorium.

Silas refocused his energy then went to his task, carefully copying letter by letter. When he got to a word or phrase he didn't understand, he spent some time reflecting on its possible meaning. When he finished a particularly obscure line, he read it out loud.

"*Ad Dominum nocte sanctificationem meam*," he recited out loud.

"To the Lord at night I make my devotions."

Out of the shadows of the scriptorium moved a specter, the woman who had visited him in his cell. Tonight she had more body to her, less translucence. Silas was frightened but not as much as before.

"Who are you and why do you visit me?" he asked, tipping over his stool as he backed away.

"You call me," the apparition replied.

"I most certainly did not," he insisted.

The specter pointed to the codex. "Dark not night," she whispered as she slipped backwards and dissolved into the darkness.

"What? Wait." Suddenly, he didn't want her to go.

After a moment, he righted his stool, shook himself off and sat back down at the desk.

"Dark not night. What does this devil mean?"

He looked down at his most recent line.

Ad Dominum nocte sanctificationem meam.

To the Lord at night I make my devotions.

"Dark not night." He substituted the words.

"To the Lord at Dark I make my devotions." No, that wasn't quite right. He turned to the original. "To the Lord *of* Dark, of Darkness. To the Lord of Darkness!" Silas gasped. "Lord have mercy on my soul!" He turned the codex over to the front inside page. "The Book of Dark Hours," he whispered and blessed himself with the sign of the cross. How many hands have scribed this book assuming it to be a book of God? What was it a book of?

Sitting at his desk contemplating this turn in the translation, he began reviewing other points in the text where there had been an unusual reference or word not quite right. When seen with a new understanding, the book became clearly a worship of Darkness. The more he thought about it, the less distasteful this prayer book seemed. He needed to know more. The woman could tell him. He repeated the invocation.

Ad Dominum nocte sanctificationem meam.

Ad Dominum nocte sanctificationem meam.

Ad Dominum nocte sanctificationem meam.

Slowly, out of the shadows, the woman appeared with even more substance than before. This time he was not afraid.

"Why are you here?" he asked.

"You call me," she whispered.

"Are you the Lord of Darkness?"

"Angel of the Lord," she answered.

He noticed distinctly that her skin looked healthier, the rot had been replaced with flesh, the naked bones no longer visible. Even her clothing seemed to mend itself.

"Of the Lord of Darkness?" Silas asked.

She nodded slowly.

"What does the Lord of Darkness offer that the Lord of Lords and the glory of God has not already bestowed on me?"

"Grants wishes."

"You mean answers prayers." He said it as a statement.

She shook her head. "Any wishes."

Silas suddenly remembered all the beatings, all the hungry nights, all the unanswered prayers, every time the abbot struck him in the name of a God that, Silas now realized, had abandoned him.

"What must a disciple of your Lord do to merit such a gift?"

The specter raised her hand toward the codex and pages flipped over as if from a breeze. The book lay open to a page with a single line.

Detur voluntas pro anima commutatio.

"A wish will be given for the exchange of the soul," he read out loud.

He considered this then asked, "Must it be *my* soul?"

The woman shook her head. "You free it."

Silas spoke slowly as understanding dawned. “I must free the soul from its flesh?”

She nodded.

“Any soul?”

She nodded again and gestured back to the codex. Again, pages flew.

Sic recitans: Hanc animam devote offero tenebris. Suppliciter peto…

“Reciting thus: I devoutly offer this soul to darkness. I humbly request…”

When he looked up again at the specter, she was looking out the window at the first inkling of dawn on the horizon and slowly faded back into the last of the night’s shadows.

Brother Silas quickly copied a few more pages to satisfy Prior Machello then headed to his cell to sleep.

It was a fitful sleep as Silas repeatedly awoke recalling what the woman had said and thinking of all the times he had prayed that God’s wrath rain down on the abbot and brothers to no relief of his suffering. Could he do it? Could he take the life of another in the name of vengeance? That he did not know the answer to this question disturbed him.

He arrived back at the scriptorium after the noon meal and resumed his work. With heightened concentration, he scribed page after page, copying the unusual Latin dialect exactly. He dared not recite any of the words as he wrote, but he thought over and over about what the woman had said and what she had shown him. He couldn’t help but read the lines as he scribed. The codex described a ritual of worship for Mephistopheles, the controller of the Darkness. Page after page revealed in great detail the power wielded by this Lord and the indulgences granted to his disciples.

Silas prayed hard day after day for his God, Lord of Lords, to release him from the curses of this codex, but no relief came. Again, God had abandoned him. Then one night he came across the incantation again written in the pages he was scribing. Before he knew it, he was chanting aloud.

Ad Dominum nocte sanctificationem meam.

Ad Dominum nocte sanctificationem meam.

Ad Dominum nocte sanctificationem meam.

Sure enough, she emerged from the shadows. He stared at her. She still held the vestiges of a rotting corpse and yet, seemed somehow more pleasing to the eye. She might have been attractive in life.

"Are you an angel of the Dark?"

"Yes," she whispered.

"Will you show me the ways of the Dark?"

"Yes, mmmm," she purred. Her visage became cleaner, almost tangible.

"What must I do to garner the pleasure of your Lord?"

"Mmmmm," she responded and gestured to the codex whose pages flipped one leaf further.

The open page was only half filled with text. He ran his fingers over the letters as he translated aloud. "The bond to the Lord of Darkness is forever and eternal. No man nor God shall break the contract. The worship is one soul grants one wish."

He looked to the specter, "If I do this will the Lord of Darkness grand me any justice I seek?"

"Yeesssss," came the breathy voice of the specter.

He continued reading aloud. "*Signo juramentum sanguinis.* I sign the oath of blood."

He looked to the specter who nodded and purred, now nearly normal in appearance.

He transcribed this next page into the working copy and paused. He'd never felt so ready for anything in his life. Once the contract was signed and the blood was dry, those who had hindered his happiness would be out of the way. He lifted his penknife and hesitated. Out of the corner of his eye, something shifted. The specter was at his elbow.

"Well?" she murmured, "Why do you wait?"

With confidence, he gently sliced the tip of his finger and pushed on the flesh to elicit a large drop of blood. Dipping his quill into the droplet, he signed his name to the codex.

Brother Silas continued to scribe into the late hours of the night as he considered his next actions.

He needed to understand exactly how this new power worked. He needed to free a soul and make his wish. So, he planned as he wrote that the next night, when he was sure the abbey was asleep, he would leave the grounds to wander in the seedier part of town.

Silas soon came across an old man sitting in the gutter, mostly out of his mind and homeless. This would do. Silas approached the man.

The man looked up with hope at the monk. "Brother, pray for me for I am surely a lost soul," the man pleaded.

"Of course, my son. Let us pray together." Silas knelt down beside the man, his heart racing with fear and excitement. With a swift swipe of his penknife, he slit the man's throat.

"Hanc animam devote offero tenebris. Suppliciter peto...I devoutly offer this soul to the Darkness. I humbly request that Brother Machello be smitten with unremitting boils and rash for the remainder of his life and that the putrid smell of his wounds forces him into isolation."

He left the man in the alley where he had found him and returned to the scriptorium, where he copied a few more pages, before retiring at dawn.

The following morning, Prior Machello was seated quietly on the dais at the front of the scriptorium when Silas arrived after the noon meal. This repose was unusual for the monk, who typically walked the isles with stern dissatisfaction.

Silas couldn't help himself. Before he took his seat, he approached Machello.

"Good noon, Prior. I hope you are well today."

Machello squirmed slightly, then barked, "I'm quite well, brother. Mind your business and get to work."

"Immediately, Prior," Silas replied. He bowed as he backed away before turning to begin his work. As he passed his desk mate he whispered, "What evil irritation has befallen the Prior that we should bear the brunt of his temper?"

"Pray, I might have heard that the good brother has acquired an irritation of the skin that raises his ire," Brother Thomas answered without looking up.

Prior Machello growled from the dais, "It would be God's will for you to confine your attention to your work, brothers."

"Let us pray for him and for us," Brother Thomas added.

Silas pinched himself to avoid grinning.

Silas found it difficult to remain focused on his work. His mind kept playing out the events of the night, the current condition of Prior Machello, and the possibilities for the Abbot. It was three days before he could once again escape the monastery unnoticed.

He made his way to the other side of town, near the docks, where he knew drunks and maids-for-hire wandered the streets. He was soon approached by such a woman who was eager to please him for a coin and a prayer. He had never laid with a woman before and decided to take advantage of her offer. He felt some regret as he strangled her afterward, invoking the dark power.

"Hanc animam devote offero tenebris. Suppliciter peto...I devoutly offer this soul to the Darkness. I humbly request that Abbot Peter Matthias Benedict be stricken with unremitting pain in his joints such that he gets no rest and no relief."

Within days, rumors abounded about a sudden illness that struck the Abbot causing him pain and limiting his attendance at prayers.

***

Silas's copying of the codex was nearing its end. He wondered if his new power required that he be in possession of the actual manuscript. Reluctantly, he notified Prior Machello of his completion of the project.

"Good work, indeed, and quite fast. For your sake, I hope it is satisfactory work."

"I assure you, Prior, it is my best yet," Silas replied.

"Report back in the morning. I will leave the next task at your desk."

"Yes, Prior."

***

A week later, Silas was called to meet the Prior in the visitation area of the church.

"Brother Silas, this is Mr. Sabastian Cabot. He is the customer for whom you copied the Book of Night Hours codex. He wishes a word with you."

"Of course, Prior." Silas turned to face Sabastian, near panic. Did this man know of the true nature of the codex? Or was this just a grateful patron?

Sabastian began, "I wanted to thank you personally for your work. The codex has become a quick companion for my restless night's sleep."

"I offer my services to the Lord, Mr. Cabot."

"Yes. Of course. The devotion of the Benedictine monks is legendary and beyond reproach." Then, in another surprise moment, Mr. Cabot turned to Prior Machello and asked, "Prior, might it be possible for me to have a private conversation with Brother Silas?"

Machello was as caught off-guard as Silas. "Yes. Of course," he stuttered. "I'll leave you here. Brother Silas will see you out."

Machello closed the door behind him. Sabastian gestured to the two pews that lined adjacent walls. "Please, sit, that we might talk frankly."

Silas, still nervous, sat stiffly on the pew as Sabastian took the other seat.

"I admire the work that you put into the codex," he began.

"Thank you, kind sir."

"At the risk of intruding, I have asked the monsignor of your history with the order. He tells me that you did not come to your vocation in the traditional way."

"That is true," nodded Silas.

"You are now well beyond legal age and yet you stay? May I ask why?"

Silas eyed him. He answered cautiously, "Where is a scribe to be but in the monastic life?"

"And if there were an alternative?" Sabastian offered.

"I'm sure I don't understand."

"The world is becoming more literate and the demand for manuscripts of all kinds is steadily increasing. There are a few commercial scriptoriums but they are staffed with mediocre scribes at best. Everyone knows, there is no comparison to monastic reproductions."

"You have my interest," replied Silas. "Please speak frankly."

"I would like to open such a scriptorium, here in the city, and would like to offer you the first position if that is not offensive to your faith."

Silas was stunned. Was this the Lord finally relieving him from his bondage, finally answering his prayers. Relief washed over him.

"I dare say, Mr. Cabot, that the offer is not offensive in the least. It is, in fact an answer to my prayers. I have not felt at home here for some years."

"I understand. You can start as soon as the Abbot releases you from your vows. You can find me at the docks, Merchant's Building, office number eight. I'll leave you to your business."

Silas walked Sabastian to the outer doors where Machello was waiting. Silas hurried the departure before Sabastian could say anything more. "Thank you, Mr. Cabot, for your kind appreciation. Please give us the opportunity to assist you in the future."

Sabastian picked up on the tone.

"Thank you, again, Brother Silas." Sabastian bowed before stepping out onto the church stairs.

Prior Machello eyed him suspiciously. "What did he want?" he demanded.

"Simply to express his gratitude," Silas replied.

"Well, if that expression took the form of coins," he leaned towards Silas with a grimace, "it is the property of the monastery and is to be turned over immediately."

"Of course, Brother Machello. However, the gratitude was in word only, and a request that I scribe more for him as the opportunity presents itself."

"Indeed!" Machello backed off. "Return to your work then."

"Happily," Silas replied.

He headed back toward the scriptorium until he was out of sight of Machello, then took a circuitous route to the office of the Abbot, Monsignor Peter Matthias.

***

Silas arrived two days later at the office of Mr. Sabastian Cabot, Importer and Actuarial. He was still in the robes of the Benedictines. The Abbot, displeased at Silas's departure, had refused him any other clothing or belongings, save what was on his back.

"Brother Silas, welcome," Sabastian greeted him with a warm handshake. "I see you are still in robes. Are you still affiliated with the monastery?"

"Regrettably, Monsignor did not feel possessed to offer me any alternative clothing."

"I understand. I will have common clothes for you by this afternoon. Is your obligation to the order completely severed? Is there any further business you have with them?"

"Unfortunately, the Abbot was extremely unhappy about the turn of events and has terminated all ties I might have. There is no return for me."

"Unfortunate indeed to sour such relations but a great opportunity for you for a new life. Let me show you your work station."

Sabastian led Silas through the offices and down back stairs to the warehouse. "I'm afraid the only space I could carve out for the moment opens to the alley."

"I am ever grateful for the opportunity, Mr. Cabot. I assure you I will be happy here."

Sabastian led him to a desk and stool along a back wall with light from a large window.

"Have a seat. Try it out for height and comfort. I was only guessing at measurements."

Silas did as instructed, inspecting the meager supplies on hand. "I will need a few more items to provide you with the quality you are asking for."

"Not to worry. More things are ordered. They'll be placed here."

Sabastian circled around behind Silas, pointing out where future things would be in easy reach of the work surface.

Silas was listening intently, admiring his good fortune when suddenly he felt a constriction around his neck. It quickly tightened to an alarming breath-stopping grip. He grabbed at the cord frantically, unable to gain any leverage. The last thing he heard was Sabastian's voice.

"Hanc animam devote offero tenebris. I devoutly offer this soul to the Darkness."

Oscar-Worthy

By Dana Norton

My fingers flew over the keys and I finished typing with a flourish. I looked up at my client. "Let's make sure I have everything, OK?

"Staff meeting – check. Snarky boss teasing—check. Co-workers snickering—check. Verge of tears. More tormenting—check. And check. Is that it?"

"More or less." Her voice was low, and I had to lean forward to catch the words. "Maybe I've left out a tiny cruelty here and there, but that's the gist."

Madison Gaines sat on the edge of her chair. She looked to be in her early thirties, with a furrowed brow and a mouth turned down at the corners.

Nondescript-looking. Her thin dark hair was pulled back in a sloppy bun, her face devoid of makeup. Her brown pants were baggy, her tan sweater faded. In her lap, she clutched a very large black leather purse.

Her features, though, were distinctive: ski-jump nose, firm chin, deep-set eyes of a piercing blue. If she fixed that hair and didn't dress like the Invisible Woman, she wouldn't be bad-looking at all.

"OK, we'll make an appointment for next week and begin the work of writing the script. After that we'll do several sessions to practice and perfect your technique."

"But does it really work?" Madison asked.

"Absolutely," I assured her.

After she left, I leaned back in my chair and propped my feet up on the faux oak desk. Just another case for Role-Play, Inc.—Karina Sharpleton, Principal. And probably a pretty boring one at that. Oh well, a girl's gotta pay the bills. Especially when her husband is divorcing her and she will no longer have access to his lovely hi-tech salary.

"I still love you, Karina—but I just can't take it anymore," Daniel had said, when he first told me he wanted a divorce. "You criticize me twenty-four-seven: I don't make enough money, I snore like an asthmatic, I don't respect your mother, I need to grow a beard to hide my weak chin….enough!"

Daniel was exaggerating, of course. I'm not really that critical. All I ever tried to do was point out a few areas of improvement. Unfortunately, my husband didn't see it that way. Still, I was going to miss all six feet two inches of him: that sweet personality, shaggy dark-blond hair and big, soulful brown eyes.

Yes, I was still fond of him. We used to joke that all he had to do was crook a finger in that age-old "come-hither" gesture and I would fly into his lap.

Thank God I had my business to distract me. I started Role-Play, Inc. a few months ago, and I'm proud of the unique service I offer clients. Can't stand up to your boss? Role play with me and you'll be putting them in their place—and getting promoted, not fired. Tongue-tied during critical job interviews? A few sessions with *moi* and you'll blow away the competition.

We start off with the client describing the upsetting scenes that lay them low. Next we create a script that gives them a new way to handle the situation.

Then we role-play. Again and again. Until the client is Oscar-worthy.

My friend Melissa, a *real* therapist, didn't approve. "You're just putting a bandaid on a stab wound. These people need to dig deep, get at the *root* of their problems."

"Not *my* clients. Mine are in for the quick fix." And as an actor (between jobs) and a playwright (off-off-off Broadway), I know how to set up successful scenarios and conduct "rehearsals" until my client is letter-perfect.

If only I were that good at getting along with Daniel. Seriously, though, I'm at the point where I'm eager to part ways with someone who says he can't stand living with me.

So in three weeks I'll be signing those divorce papers. I've convinced myself that I've never felt so ready for anything in my life. Once they're signed and the ink is dry, my ex will be out of the picture.

I imagine the scene: I lift my pen to sign the papers but out of the corner of my eye something shifts. It's Daniel, turning to look at me.

"Well," he murmurs, "what are you waiting for?" And I don't see even a sliver of regret in those beautiful brown eyes.

So an intriguing client would be just the thing to distract me at the moment. Unfortunately, Madison Gaines' case was your run-of-the-mill, act-confident scenario. I could do it in my sleep.

We got down to it the following week. Madison, who worked at a marketing firm in downtown Boston, described a typical staff meeting.

Her boss, Amanda, was a know-it-all, late-twenty-something, who always looked "fabulous" and who had graduated from a school more prestigious than Madison's. She might start the meeting by proposing a new initiative. Then she would turn to my client. "Madison, do *you* have any suggestions on how to implement this? Maybe something more creative than your last idea?"

Cue snickering all around.

Cue Madison making the classic mistake, getting visibly upset. And like Pavlov's dogs salivating at the sound of a bell, her frisky, mostly fresh-out-of-college co-workers would bark with joy at the first sign of her distress. Then, of course, they'd tease some more. And Madison would wish that she were invisible.

So right off I had to teach her a cardinal rule: *never show you're upset.* Getting bent out of shape was exactly the thing that set her colleagues off. Instead, Madison needed to act like she was fine.

"But I'm *not* fine. Are you asking me to be phony?" Madison thrust out her pointy chin.

I looked at her, surprised. "Yes, I am. Have you ever heard of the expression 'Fake it 'til you make it'?" I picked up a pencil and began doodling in my notepad.

"So, your vaunted technique consists of asking me to be *fake*?"

"Oh, come on, Madison." Delicately I sketched in the witch's costume. "Ideally, of course, you don't want to even *feel* upset. But changing *feelings* takes time." I gave her my best, inspire-confidence look. "In the meantime, you have to pretend a little."

Madison frowned. She squinched up those lovely blue eyes.

"Moving on," I said quickly. "Let's talk about what you could *say* when your boss makes those remarks."

"So according to your moral code, it's OK to be a complete phony?"

Oh, God. I plowed on. "How about saying something very casual, like, 'I actually *do* have an idea. We've never done it before, and the novelty value alone—' "

"Never work," said Madison. "Is this the best you can come up with?"

Vigorously I colored in the witch's pointy black hat. "Why don't we put aside writing the script for the moment? Let's block out the scene. We can sit at the table by the window."

"Whatever you say." Madison sighed audibly, casting her eyes to the ceiling.

I walked over to the table. "Now, I'll be Amanda, your boss. I'll sit here in this chair and be slimy, like her. I'll cross my legs demurely and clasp my hands in my lap, looking all earnest and serious. Then I'll hit you with the nasty tease."

"That's not the way Amanda sits," corrected Madison. "I think it's important to get the details just right, don't you? Amanda *never* crosses her legs. And before she says anything mean, she always has this wicked gleam in her eye."

I jabbed at the witch's mouth, breaking the point of my pencil. I pushed away the pad. "Madison, listen. For the moment, let's focus not on my movements but on what I'm *saying*."

"So what's your degree in, again?"

I terminated the session early.

During the next couple of weeks, Madison continued to tell me how to do my job. Nothing I said pleased her. I tried to get hold of myself, but each time she left me feeling inadequate. Not something I often felt. I thought seriously about ending our relationship. I'd give her a refund and kick her out the door.

Things came to a head late one afternoon, a week before I was to sign the divorce papers. I had just had a particularly difficult session with Madison. Finally, she left. A minute later, Daniel waltzed through the door.

"Hello, Karina, my soon-to-be-ex." He looked cheerful, plopping down in the client chair. I looked away, so he wouldn't see the hurt in my eyes. Didn't he feel the least bit sad that in a week our marriage would be over?

"Hi, Daniel." I slumped down in my faux leather executive chair.

"What's wrong? You look like you just lifted five hundred pounds."

"I have. Or maybe a thousand. You wouldn't believe my latest client, Daniel. She's paying good money for my advice, then criticizes it at every turn! She makes me feel like a complete jerk."

"I'm sorry, Karina. I can imagine how you feel." Daniel was looking at me intently.

For some reason his sympathy rubbed me the wrong way. "How would *you* know how I feel? I'm telling you, if there was an Academy Award for Most Critical Person Ever, she would win hands-down."

"I would hope so," Daniel said quietly. "I hire only the best."

I bolted upright. "WHAT??? Are you saying…*you hired her to consult me?"*

He nodded. “Isn’t she great? Lucky for me, she was in between acting jobs.”

“I don’t understand. Why?”

“Can’t you guess?”

“No, I can’t. Why would you want me to feel constantly browbeaten?”

“So you’d finally understand what it felt like being married to you.”

I gaped at him.

“Go ahead,” said Daniel.

“Go ahead *what?”*

“Go ahead and criticize. You were going to, weren’t you?”

“No, I wasn’t! But now that you mention it—how *dare* you play this trick on me?”

“I’m sorry, but I *had* to show you how you made me feel.”

“Can I help it you’re so sensitive, Daniel? By the way, it wouldn’t hurt to talk to a therapist about it.”

“Karina, you’re doing it again! Can you stop being critical for just one second?”

“I’m not criticizing, I’m *suggesting.”*

Daniel gave a bitter laugh. “Suggesting? Are you kidding? You’re bossy as hell.”

“You’re acting like I’m some kind of witch.”

“If the pointy hat fits –”

“Damn it, Daniel! If you don’t like me the way I am—”

“And if *you* don’t like me the way *I* am….” He sat back in his chair. “Look—the best thing for both of us is a divorce.”

No! Suddenly I realized what I truly wanted. And divorce played no part in it.

I took a deep breath. “Okay,” I grudgingly admitted, “maybe I *was* a tiny bit hard on you.”

“A *tiny bit*? You put me down night and day.”

I jumped up. “Go to hell, Daniel!”

“Karina, if you don’t stop playing tough guy, we don’t have a chance.”

I was winding up with a clever retort—then clamped my lips shut. Did I hear right? Was Daniel saying we *could* have a chance?

But I was a “tough cookie,” as my grandfather used to say. “Daniel. Let’s get this straight. No way am I going to turn my whole personality upside down and inside out for you. A few changes—maybe. But not overnight,” I added hastily.

“I doubt very much you could change enough.” Daniel looked down at his feet, but not before I caught a pleading look in his eye.

That was all I needed. I didn’t feel so tough anymore. “Please—can we try one more time?”

“I don’t know.”

“Daniel?”

Yes, Karina?”

“Maybe we could do some role-playing?”

He burst out laughing. “Oh, Karina,” he said softly. “I always *did* love your sense of humor.”

The Bride of Chelsham

By C. Brian Moorhead

The Bride of Chelsham had been docked for almost three weeks when Josiah Ward approached the harbormaster. Josiah hadn't selected the vessel specifically. He was unaware of the nature of its previous voyage, or the rumors about it that had spread among the sailors' taverns since it had docked. All the harbormaster told him was that the Bride was furloughed, and thus currently available.

Josiah found the Bride easily enough from the harbormaster's coarse description of its figurehead. The bow's rough wooden carving jutted over the dock, displaying the upper half of a woman with seaweed-green hair, and a whalebone corset but no chemise. Her outrageous proportions could only have been carved by a man who hadn't clapped eyes on his subject matter in months. Josiah resolved not to let it distract him. He asked the mate sitting on the dock permission to speak with the captain.

Josiah found Captain Marite in his quarters, poring over letters. He was the very image of a sea-captain—salt-worn complexion, full beard, pipe in his teeth. His maroon overcoat hung on the back of his chair, while its matching tricorn hat sat on his head. He tipped it to Josiah as he approached the desk.

"Welcome aboard, sir," said the Captain, "What business have ye?"

"Yes, well, I certainly hope to do business." Josiah said. "I'd like to hire a boat for a voyage."

"Ye've a destination in mind?"

"I do. You see my father, Bartholomew Ward, signed on about nine years ago, but he... never returned. And he couldn't've just run off and left the family. Harbormasters up and down the coast all confirmed that his ship never returned to any harbor, and there's been no trace of the rest of the crew either."

"Oh, I believe you." The Captain doffed his hat in reverence. "I lost a brother to the sea meself."

"I'm sorry to hear it, sir."

"That's *Captain*."

"Captain! Right, of course. But you understand then, what it's like." Josiah produced a journal and handed it to the captain. "I found this jammed in a wall at Parva Manor. The manor was the last house my father worked on before the voyage, and he told me before he left that I should try to get their business. I'm sure he hid it there for me to find! There are maps and charts in there, some of my father's business records, and these other funny diagrams I didn't understand. But the maps show a course that doesn't match the one the captain registered with the port authority! Why, this map here even shows a planned landfall in the Rookery Islands, despite there being no harbor! I'm convinced the ship was never found because they searched in the wrong place."

"Sounds sensible to me. So ye wish to sail for the Rookery Islands then? Find what became o'yer father?"

"Yes, exactly!"

"A voyage that long won't be cheap." The captain never looked up as he spoke. "I think we have the ready provisions in the hold, but most o'me crew won't sail to the Rookeries without an advance. There's strange tales come from that place."

"Well…" Josiah hesitated "my father's assets included several thousand pounds, and shares in a lumber mill which has since prospered. I'm the sole inheritor, but the bank needs proof of his passing before they'll disburse it."

"So ye can't pay the advance with it." The captain was still flipping through the journal as he spoke. He flipped to the last page – star charts, Josiah thought, and some mathematic scribbles. His eyes widened, his face blanched, and his pipe fell from his teeth as his jaw quivered.

"A widow galley's mark!" the Captain whispered.

"Beg your pardon, Captain?"

"What ship did you say yer father sailed on?"

"It was the Auricula."

"Auricu— !" The captain snapped the book shut and thrust it back into Josiah's hands. "I can't take this contract! You'll have to find another ship."

"But why? What's wrong—"

"You get that thing off my ship now!"

"I'm… sorry, sir—Captain."

That evening, Josiah ruminated over supper at the local pub, still puzzling about what had put the Captain off so suddenly. He was deep in thought, and barely noticed as Chester Greystone approached his table.

"Ward, I've a crow to pluck with you." Chester was a reedy, bespectacled man in a fine suit and waistcoat, barely older than Josiah himself, yet he spoke with the authority he felt he deserved as Josiah's creditor.

"What's the matter?" Josiah wiped his mouth and turned to face Chester. "I dropped off this month's payment yesterday morning. Haven't you received it?"

"I did. But your good faith as a borrower is in question."

"What? Why? Because I spared a shilling for broth and biscuits?" Josiah gestured to his bowl, and Chester glanced at it before locking his gaze back on Josiah.

"Not that. I've heard from the harbormaster that you met with Captain Marite about signing on as a privateer."

"What?! A privat… ?" Josiah nearly choked. "Oh, sir, don't slander me! I'm a carpenter, not a pirate! You can go back in the morning and ask him yourself."

"Ward, don't play the dunce with me! I know as well as you do that ships carry carpenters in their crews. And you know as well as I do that contracted privateer vessels have their crew's lists sealed. They wouldn't tell me if you had signed on."

"I didn't know that!" said Josiah. "Heck, I didn't even know the Bride of Chelsham was a privateer vessel!"

"So you did meet with Captain Marite then!" Chester leaned in and narrowed his gaze, a hungry grin creeping across his face.

"Wha—I, well, I did, but not to become a privateer! I spoke with Captain Marite regarding… well, the circumstances of my father's disappearance." Josiah produced the journal again. "Here, take a look at these charts. I had shown them to the Captain to see if he could shed some light on any of it."

"Ward, we offered you that loan on significantly more favorable repayment terms than a man of your means should merit." Chester wasn't looking at the journal. "And we did so on the strength of your reputation for reliability in business dealings."

"And my father's life savings, sitting in your bank as collateral." Josiah added.

"At the end of the week, the senior bankers will meet to discuss whether this constitutes evidence of Acting in Bad Faith, and if it justifies recalculating the terms of your loan." Chester glanced at the journal with a sneer. "You may present your arguments then."

Late that night, Josiah lay awake, unable to sleep, stomach churning. For the past year and a half, he'd been living meagerly, working long hours, scrambling for clients, and pinching his pennies to ensure he covered his expenses. Just one more year or so before it was paid off. Another four years, and the statute of limitations on his father's will would expire, and he could officially reclaim the family home. His home! He had almost made it through, and now this?!

Josiah lumbered out of his bed and into the kitchen. It was small and cramped, with little more than an iron stove, small table, water keg, and a pantry shelf, but it was the best Josiah could afford. He cursed his father for his negligence. What had he hoped to find on that voyage that couldn't even wait until he'd finished paying off the house?

A cold breeze blew in from a small window, carrying a distinctive smell of ocean. Josiah chastised himself for dishonoring his father's memory as he turned to close it. His current predicament wasn't his father's doing. He could still hear Chester Greystone's ultimatum in his ears. *At the end of the week, the senior bankers will meet.*

Josiah put his candle down on the table as he retrieved a pitcher of water and a glass, hoping to settle his stomach. *Acting in Bad Faith.* He could still smell the ocean, despite having closed the window. *Significantly more favorable repayment terms*, he had called them. Bah!

"Significantly more favorable than debtor's prison, perhaps." he mumbled to himself.

"Why, yes," a voice behind him said. "I certainly expect so."

Josiah spun around. Between him and the candle, a large mass had suddenly appeared, but it was too big to be a person, and the room too dark to see anything but a shadowy outline. It smelled as if it were made of seaweed and sawdust. Josiah walked around it with caution. As he approached the candlelit side, he realized that it was indeed a person—an impossibly large woman.

She sat on both of Josiah's chairs pushed next to each other. Her hips were still wider than both seats together, and she was taller seated than Josiah was standing. A man's tricorn hat rested atop her head, pinned to her hair as a lady's hat might sit on a normal-sized woman. Around her shoulders she wore a man's overcoat that fit her like a shawl. It was fastened by a brooch at the collar, as her outrageous proportions gave her no hope of buttoning it. Under the coat she wore a whalebone corset and shift but no gown. Her legs were too long to fit folded under the table as a proper lady ought to sit, and so her bare feet, the like of which no cobbler in Chelsham had ever shod, were propped up on a stool.

Josiah took a gulp of water and threw the rest on his own face. When he wiped his eyes clear, the woman had not disappeared to wherever dreams go when one awakens. She was lifting the candle to light the lamp hanging from the ceiling beam – something Josiah needed the stool to do but she managed without rising from her seats.

"Are you still interested in discussing business, Mr. Ward?" The woman asked. Her voice was a basso profundo that Josiah could feel in his own chest, but it was unmistakably a woman's. "I expect to make you an agreeable offer. More favorable than debtor's prison, I assure you."

"Wh—who are you?" Josiah managed to stammer out.

The woman blinked, as if expecting to be recognized.

"Were we not properly introduced?" she asked. "My apologies. The Bride of Chelsham, at your service."

"The Bride of—!" The figurehead! Josiah hadn't seen the resemblance before in the dim light, but now he recognized that this woman was the ship's figurehead statue, the very same face and figure from the bow of the Bride of Chelsham, somehow come to life! It seemed impossible, but what other explanation was there for what Josiah saw before him?

"Now then." The Bride took the pitcher from Josiah's hand, and held it as a lady would hold a teacup. "Earlier this evening, your creditor Mr. Greystone was at the docks, laboring under the delusion that he could forbid my crew to do business with you."

"What? Well, he... does hold a fairly large promissory note in my family's name."

"Irrelevant. Maritime law grants a sailor certain rights regarding his affairs on land, including forbearance of any pre-existing debts. This has prevented the Greystones from selling your family home in the years since your father's disappearance. As his sole inheritor, however, you would be able to waive the forbearance and authorize such a sale on his behalf, if persuaded."

"How do you know all this?"

"Mr. Greystone declared such to us this evening. At full volume. My crew have a word for men of his character that a lady does not repeat."

"He—then all that about him accusing me of bad faith was all a bluster! Why I bet that senior bankers' meeting is just a pretense to try and pressure me into signing away the house!"

"Yes, several harsh truths have come to light tonight," The Bride's gaze drifted off as she spoke, "among them that Mr. Marite had defaulted on our privateering contract. This, coupled with his refusal to hear your proposal to the Rookeries, and his neglect to hire a proper shipwright, have finally demanded that I discharge him of the office of Captain."

Josiah only now realized that the Bride's tricorn and coat-shawl were the very same that Captain—Mister—Marite had worn that afternoon. He wondered how exactly the soul of a ship "discharges" its own captain.

"But to the matter at hand." The Bride produced a large map from under her shawl and spread it out on the table. "I will need that journal of yours to be sure, but the Rookery Islands are roughly twenty days out from here. Assume a similar length return journey. We currently have almost three months' worth of provisions in cargo," the Bride glanced up at Josiah's pantry, "— plus any that you have here on hand, should allow us six weeks at the destination to discover what we may."

"I—I don't know how much you heard from Greystone, but I won't be able to pay the advance."

"I am not requesting an advance. You aren't sponsoring the voyage, Mr. Ward, I am proposing that you sign onto it. A shipwright typically draws a salary of £69 annually, plus food and rum rations."

"A shipwright? Me?"

"Yes, a shipwright is as vital to a ship's needs as the captain is to a crew's, and my own such needs have been neglected. You are a carpenter though, are you not? Have you apprenticed?"

"Of course. I completed my apprenticeship under my father, and I've practiced as a journeyman for the past nine years."

"Capital!" A grin beamed across the Bride's face. "A trained hand at last! How often have you worked on ships, or in shipyards?"

"Never. I've always worked on houses."

"Oh. I see." The Bride's expression fell. "Well, the navy still would accept you, I suppose. Can you operate a bilge pump?"

"Well, I've been shown how."

"Can you patch shot holes? I took an enfilade last spring and the previous patch was," the Bride ran a hand along the side of her torso and winced, "unsatisfactory."

"I've patched plenty of holes in roofs to keep rain out," said Josiah, "though never while under live cannon fire, I admit."

"And can you—", the Bride paused, and her hands grew restless around the pitcher of water. "—holystone, Mr. Ward?"

"To repel water damage? Sure, I've polished down Madame Parva's widow's walk every spring."

"Oh, Mr. Ward! That will do!" The Bride shifted uncomfortably in her chairs and lifted the pitcher to her mouth, in a vain effort to conceal her blushing. "That will do indeed, sir!" Finally she produced another parchment and slapped it down on top of the map. “Very well, I propose £18 for the three months, plus a speculation if the voyage runs long and a share of any treasure or valuables recovered from the Auricula.”

“Say, why do you come to me with this offer?” He looked at her suspiciously.

“You have information I need in that journal regarding the Auricula’s last known coordinates. And besides,” the Bride said, “you and I both lost a family member to that voyage. The Auricula was a dear sister of mine.”

The room fell silent, and the two of them shared a moment in solidarity at each other’s grief.

“But to business. If these terms are agreeable to you, Mr. Ward, we can set sail as soon as you sign the contract and gather your belongings.” The Bride pulled a feather from her tricorn and produced an inkwell. “The contract includes a forbearance request to Greystone Bank, as well as authorization for the harbormaster to collect any personal effects you leave behind and store them in port authority until our return. Unless you prefer to carry rent on this room in your absence, in which case I can draw up a new—”

“No! No, that won’t be necessary. Port authority will be fine.”

“Does that mean you accept the proposal? Are you ready to depart?”

Josiah grinned. He’d never felt so ready for anything in his life. Once the contract was signed and the ink was dry, everyone who’d ever been an obstacle to his success was out of the way. He lifted the quill, and out of the corner of his eye, something shifted.

“Well,” she murmured, “what are you waiting for?”

Josiah turned. He saw nothing behind him, but a new, malignant odor had now mingled with the Bride's natural ocean musk. He turned back to the document before him and signed.

"Capital! It shall be waiting on the harbormaster's desk when he arrives in the morning. Now then, to work." The Bride snapped her fingers and gestured at the door to Josiah's bedchamber. "Your new mates here will help you gather your things," said the Bride. "As I mentioned, bring any food you have here, lest it spoil before you return. And all your carpenter's tools, of course. But do make haste, please, for it is already nearly one o'clock and I intend to be out of view of shore by sunrise."

"My new mates? What do you —?"

Josiah turned, and saw two figures in the doorway. There he saw the source of the new, foul odor — slowly staggering toward him, with empty footlockers in hand, were the pale, drowned corpses of Captain Marite and Chester Greystone!

The Quantum Belt

By M.J. Cote

James regretted every day since writing that stupid letter to Harry's girlfriend—the one that caused her to break up with Harry and turned him from his best friend into an arch nemesis. It was now Harry's life's ambition to make James's life as miserable as possible. Funny how a stupid practical joke in college ten years ago could have started it all.

The doorknob clicked open as he entered. What was he doing visiting a psychic, anyway? He was a professor of astrophysics at Harvard and was about to be tenured. He was here because Harry was trying to ruin his life again. Harry had recently become an administrator in the computer lab. Coincidentally, yesterday James received notice from human resources that they'd had a complaint. A close colleague of his who had inside information let him know it was about a salacious email he'd sent to a coworker. Of course, he hadn't done any such thing; it was Harry trying to ruin his life.

James's career was in the balance. A colleague thought a counsellor he knew might help and advise on how best handle the *delicate* situation. So, he came to see the counselor. Apparently, Clara of Clara's Clairvoyance, was both a counselor and a mystic.

He thought about going home, but what the hell, what did he have to lose?

His visit brought him to a dimly lit room, sparsely furnished with a worn sofa, and several tables piled with books. It looked much like what he expected of a psychic. She sat at a table with the crystal ball in a candlelit room laced with shadows. Uncertain but resolved, he took a seat across from her and after exchanging brief introductions, he explained his situation: "I'm in trouble for something I didn't do."

"I see," she said, listening intently.

"I'm sure they'll fire me. I have the weekend to figure out what I'm going to do. Can you help?"

They chatted for a bit. She said she'd been a pilot for one of the first jets to fly from earth into space and back. She also told him that in a past life he had been reckless, with *joie de vivre* and died in a plane crash. For that reason, in this life, he lived a conservative life, safe, and boring. It was supposed to convince him that she had real psychic abilities. But he was a scientist and didn't believe her.

James examined the woman as though she were his final hope. She wore thick-rimmed glasses and dark purple robes. Her hair was tied up in a bun and her face covered with thick makeup. She looked vaguely familiar but he couldn't put a mental finger on who she might be.

"Tell me how I can help with your… stalker?"

"He's not exactly a stalker."

"He follows you and tries to undermine everything you do, right?"

"I guess."

"That's the definition of a stalker, James." She thrummed her fingers. "I'm a fortune teller. What makes you think I can help you with that?"

"My colleague said you were also a counselor—"

"My mystic abilities might help."

"How?"

"I could look into my crystal ball and see if there is anything you could do that will lead to a happy life."

"Anything. Right now my life is damn miserable."

"Or maybe something in the stars could help—astrology—that sort of thing."

James was ready to leave, frustrated with this last-ditch effort. He didn't believe in any of this rubbish.

After watching him fidget, she said, "I can offer something."

James brightened. "Some advice?"

"Let's call it an unusual alternative. But you need to understand what I offer is irreversible. There is no guarantee of success. Many turn it down after reading the contract."

"Why?"

"They're afraid to even look at the *Quantum Belt*."

"Quantum Belt?" He'd heard of the Kuiper Belt, but never a Quantum Belt.

She reached behind, opened a drawer, and extracted a set of documents. "I recommend you read them carefully. If you're interested, sign it, and we'll go from there."

The night sky was cloudless. James bent over his quark-field reception telescope that he'd brought out onto his back porch. He scanned nearby stars. Not there. He felt certain Clara was offering him a mission to a newly discovered planet. She was involved with SETI, flown jets into space—this "mystic thing" had to be a coverup. His best guess is that he would be traveling to a new star system—never to see Harry again.

At first, he thought the belt had to be around a neighboring star, where a planet might exist. Then he tried for one near the closest black hole. Perhaps the Quantum Belt might make more sense near an event horizon where virtual particles snapped into and out of existence. He repositioned it, then squinted through the eyepiece.

Nothing.

At least nothing his telescope could find. He thought to locate the planet on his own, to examine it before accepting. But after fruitless searching, he decided he had nothing to lose.

He called Clara and told her he was ready to sign then made his way back to her shop. He'd never felt so ready for anything in his life. Once the contract was signed and the ink was dry, everyone who'd ever been an obstacle to his success would be out of the way. He lifted his pen and out of the corner of his eye, something shifted.

"Well," she murmured, "what are you waiting for?"

How many wished they could do what he was going to do tonight? "Where am I going?"

"I can't tell you *anything* until you sign the contract," Clara replied.

He hesitated. The pen still had not touched the paper. He'd been tricked too many times in his life. He read the important part one more time: *The Quantum Belt will change your life.* That's precisely what he wanted.

"You'll be the first to sign the contract. I hope you read it carefully."

He hadn't. He didn't care what it said. "What I can't understand is how you discovered this Quantum Belt.

You're not really a psychic, are you?" He could see her face flush.

"Sign the contract. Otherwise, I'm bound to secrecy."

He smiled and signed.

***

I buckled the belt and looked around the mystic's shop.

"What do you see?"

"Well, I was standing here, then I thought I was sitting down, all in a fraction of a second. Whatever this thing is doing—it's weird."

"Excellent—that would be the quantum field taking effect."

I am James or at least I thought I was. Turns out there are many of me. Turns out, it was an *actual* belt not something in the constellations. You know, the kind you wear around your waist. It had a small circular buckle that held some sort of complicated circuitry.

"Why the gut and not the brain?"

"Your gut, as you call it, is your solar plexus and is the largest part of your neural system outside of the brain. It affects your mood and bridges your perceptions."

"What's supposed to happen?'"

"You'll see for yourself. Everyday events are superpositioned the same as in the quantum world, this nerve complex instantly selects one event of many. The belt dampens this biological response. It lets you see the real world—the quantum world. You see, our world is a set of interlinked events from which we select those we want. The quantum vision you will develop will let you see things that might have been, are, or could be. So be open to those possibilities but be careful not to bump into objects like walls."

"Why?" What was she talking about?

She grimaced and pressed her lips together before answering. "You may end up quantum tunneling to a different time-place."

"Time-place? Are you serious?"

"It's well known to scientists that time is not separate from space. When you move, your action takes you from one space-time area to another. Radioactive particles, for example, quantum tunnel to escape through what should be an inescapable barrier."

"I don't understand."

"Try to roll a marble up a hill without enough force. You'd be surprised to find the marble on the other side of the hill—but it happens. The marble will quantum tunnel over. It's a random effect but happens constantly and regularly, but our neural system normally filters it out."

My jaw was six inches off the floor. She had to be kidding. "How's all this going to help me get rid of my pariah stalker?"

She looked at him strangely. "You *did* read the contract, *right?* What made you think it had anything to do with that?"

Damn—he should have read it. He'd only glanced at it and read what seemed important. What had he gotten himself into?

"Seeing the truth of things might help your situation. I don't know how and I made no guarantees."

"I thought you were a spacecraft engineer and I was going to some new planet where I could start my life over again."

"Really??" Her face contorted with incredulity.

"Suppose I want to back out."

She shook her head. "There's no backing out. Once the belt is on, the changes are irreversible."

What the heck—things couldn't get any worse.

I went back to work and walked straight into Donna's office, our human resources director; except there were two of Donna. One, who told me I'd have to leave, and another, who said she'd uncovered Harry's involvement.

From this point, things started getting *really* weird, if they weren't already strange enough.

I quickly backed out of the office and went to find Harry. He arrived at his cubicle, at the same time I did. We looked at each other. He sat and I sat. I got up—he got up. This was bizarre. After a few minutes, I decided to confront Harry, feeling confident the belt had changed my future. I could pick the future where Donna had uncovered Harry's devious deception.

He and I walked over to the kitchenette at the same time. I stopped because I didn't like the way he was mirroring my every move. He stopped at the same time. My shoulders slumped, his slumped. What was going on?

When we reached the office, we spoke. And I mean *we* spoke.

"I hear Donna let you go," we both said, together.

This was insane. We both ran out of the office and I decided to walk home and call Clara. She'd given me her number to report on my progress.

"Quantum entanglement," she said. "From what you've told me, you and Harry are linked. You never noticed before wearing the belt. Sometimes such entanglement happens in one or more superpositioned events like the two that you saw in Donna's office—one where you are fired and the other where Harry is let go."

"Which happened?"

"I don't know. Whichever you picked."

"Well, Harry seems to think it was where I got fired and I think the other way round."

She was silent for a moment. "You may be stuck in a Schrödinger uncertainty cycle."

"A what?"

"I hadn't planned on this. Explaining it won't help. I need you to go back to HR. That's where the split started, right?"

"And do what?"

"See what happens and call me back."

"But!" The phone line went silent. That's how I found myself staring down at Donna, again. Not just one Donna—ten of her.

I blinked. It was like seeing ten ghosts all doing slightly different things while sitting in the same chair. I had no idea what to do. I'm not even sure I knew how I knew there were ten of her, but there were. More disturbing was that I was now aware of ten different pasts that led up to today.

Which was real?

Harry mirrored me again and entered her office at the same time. He had a smile and a frown. I assumed the smile was in the event where Donna prepared to fire me, and the frown was where he got caught.

"How did this all start?" all ten Donnas asked at once.

"I played a prank on him in college."

"What kind of prank?" Ten Donnas faded into two. I wasn't sure why.

"I wrote a stupid love letter to this other girl and signed Harry's name. She left him. I tried to find where she'd gone and to explain it was just a prank. But she'd disappeared." Two Donnas coalesced into one. I understood now—I had selected this event. "Harry's blamed me ever since."

"You ruined my life!" both Harrys shouted, the one who got caught, and the one who didn't.

My mind started short-circuiting. I was feeling horrible about the prank, but I didn't know which "Harry" to address. I couldn't deal with this.

I knew I had to remove the belt.

I ran out of the room and headed home. Once there, I yanked the belt off and bent over with horrific pain streaking up my spine. I didn't care how painful it was, I was glad it was off. I lost my balance and hit the wall—hard—and found myself on a sidewalk.

I didn't know where I was. This must be what Clara meant by quantum tunneling. I ran down the street and threw the belt away in some dumpster. Panicked and not knowing what to do, I pulled out my cell phone and dialed Clara.

"I had to remove the belt."

"You signed a contract."

"I don't care."

"I don't think you understand, James."

"The whole world has changed."

"No—you changed. The belt changed your neural system. It can't be undone, ergo the contract. The world is the world. It's the way it is. Our brain and neural system select from the quantum nature of things we observe. The belt compromised your ability to filter out the inconsistencies. But science has proved, time and again, that objects become entangled. People are objects. So, we become entangled. Events that surround us are more often superpositioned than not. Our neural system filters out all but one event. Our perceptions are wave-like with everything regularly fading in and out of consciousness."

"And you tell me this now."

"The key points were all in the contract," Clara said, sounding annoyed.

"I don't care about the damned contract!"

"We knew we couldn't change things back—that's why we had you sign one. We included details on what might and might not happen."

"I'm like this—forever?"

"All I know is that the belt released your neural system from its normal filtering capabilities. I don't think it will—"

I hung up.

I threw my cell phone against a tree—and I didn't. I decided to choose the event where I did.

She was right, I could see things fading in and out. I blacked out for a split moment then my awareness would sharpen and cycle like this over and over. It was like watching a movie. It was horrible. If I focused on what was happening rather than the flickering, things appeared normal. But I couldn't live like this.

I ran back toward the office, having decided I would select a different set of events— then I saw Harry. He sat crying on a bench, head in his hands; he looked up at me pleadingly; and simultaneously lay dead from a self-inflicted knife wound. All three things at once, superpositioned one over the other, as Clara called it.

I shook my head. This was too creepy. I pulled myself together and hid behind a tree and watched. Eventually, I picked the "Harry" who was crying. I wanted to know why—why my foolish act, so long ago, had affected him so deeply.

Before I could approach him, Clara came walking down the street and sat next to Harry.

"Abigail?" he said, looking up surprised.

"I go by Clara, now."

I knew she'd looked familiar when I first met her.

"What are you doing here?" asked Clara.

"I need to speak with James, face to face. I was walking to his apartment when I saw you. I'm so sorry for what happened?" He looked like a beaten dog.

Her eyes melted into the saddest look I'd ever seen. "I'm sorry I left, but I had no choice."

"You had no choice because of James' prank?" Harry pressed his lips together and they trembled just a little. I even felt sorry for him. "It wasn't me and it wasn't true."

"It had nothing to do with why I left." She put her hand on his.

Her statement flummoxed me.

"I'm still in love with you," said Harry.

"Stop that," she replied and pulled out a tissue. "How can you be in love with me when we haven't seen each other in years?"

That was when the weirdest thing happened. I blinked and I, James the astrophysicist, was Harry talking to Clara.

"I left to work on a highly secretive project. One that could change the world."

"You dumped me for that?"

Clara stiffened, unsure what was happening.

"Earlier, you said James and I were entangled."

She sat back. "James?" she almost whispered.

"James, Harry, I guess I'm both."

She clasped her hand across her mouth and looked me over.

"I still love you. I think I loved you both as Harry and James. That's why I did the prank. That's why I looked until I found you." I shrugged and gently took her hand. "I was looking for you. How do you think I came upon your project?"

She stood. "I'm sorry, Harry, or James. I'm not in love with you."

"Are you married?"

"To my work." She looked like she was in such pain, having to say what she had said. I could tell from her lying eyes.

"I *am* your work—and I will continue to choose the option that keeps me close to you, forever, until you can love me back."

Demonology

By Melody Friedenthal

The demon was only fifteen inches tall. At that diminutive height she was easy to overlook and easy to underestimate. Avery made the first mistake several times but subsequent to his first encounter with Mavka, he was careful to show a certain petrified level of respect.

He didn't know where she'd come from, but her manifestation at his bedside one night (after an evening of heavy drinking and heavier boasting at O'Connor's) was sufficient to elicit a rather immediate and painful sobriety.

Her skin was leathery and ruby-red, the color attenuating to a paler tangerine on her winglets. Avery was surprised to see that her appearance matched the sermons he'd been subject to. And she made Avery the usual offer, one which he had read about in a double handful of stories, but had never given credence to.

The impossibility of it all was offset by the attractiveness of Mavka's offer. So much so, he was unable to focus at work. His mind was roiling with possibilities and not a little fear.

It had been a month of relentless pounding.

Carly got the promotion Avery was pining for. Sami beat him, 6-1, at tennis—and smirked about it for days. Penelope's lawyers were cleverer than his own, and she got the vacation house, the Mercedes, and the children. Hamid just proclaimed "past performance is not a guarantee of future results" when Avery called him, sweating, about his mutual funds' nosedive. And Frank-the-louse managed to abscond with the back strip of Avery's turf by erecting a fence a yard over the property line, and professed innocence when Avery protested.

A nice round-up of current events. Avery wondered when the next shoe would drop—what miserable thing would happen today? As the month came to a close he became closely acquainted with his Scotch bottle.

So Mavka's proposal had its attractions, even when he was sober. The next visit—or maybe it was "visitation"?—was the following week. Same offer.

She visited often, and each time Avery came a little closer to acquiescing. His initial response had been laughter but the light show that erupted from her barbed tail was impressive, and he discovered that photons *hurt*. A lot.

With his bank account spiraling downward and his debt spiraling upward, Mavka offered freedom from financial worry. But even more alluring was her promise of retribution.

"What exactly happens if I sign?"

Mavka smiled, but without any joviality. "Carly will not be able to take that promotion."

"She's already got it," Avery protested.

"Offered and accepted, yes. But you'll see, she won't be in a position to fill it. In fact, she won't be able to do any job at all."

Avery froze. Then, considering that prospect, he relaxed. Yes…

"And Sami?"

"Can't play tennis if you've got two broken arms," she smirked.

"And Frank?"

"The fence will burn down, and it will burn again if he tries to replace it."

Avery was almost afraid to ask… "What about my ex-wife?"

Mavka's eyes narrowed. "Do you really want to know?" Upon consideration, he did not.

"I want the Mercedes back!"

"Sign and it's yours."

So, he had to give up his soul—big deal.

"Ready? Just sign here," she purred.

He'd never felt so ready for anything in his life. Once the contract was signed and the ink was dry, everyone who'd ever been an obstacle to his success was out of the way. He lifted his pen and out of the corner of his eye, something shifted.

"Well," she murmured, "what are you waiting for?" A man who chose a car over his children was already seven-eighths hers. Her winglets rustled.

Avery picked up the quill pen. Inked his name, exhaled, smiled.

It was his last voluntary action, ever.

Decomposition

By Lucy A.J. Tew

December 2019

The ski-trippers had descended, and Saturday night at Denver's Rock-Keys Dueling Piano Bar was in full swing.

"Oh, classic... we danced to this song at our wedding, remember, babe?" Tim struck a few chords on his keyboard.

Mel shrugged. "Must've been your other wife. *Titanic*'s a piece of shit and *we* all know it." She gestured to her half of the bar, which cheered.

It was a basic dueling pianos game: two pianists, two tip jars, two halves of the house. You want your pianist to play something from the request jar, you tip. The only way she stops is if somebody tips the other pianist and *he* picks a request. Makes the audience feel like they're on a game show and forget that they're giving away money.

Melanie and Tim Daley had put their own spin on it as the only married dueling-pianist team in Colorado – that they knew of, anyway. Half an hour into tonight's first shift, Melanie had a full fishbowl of requests and about $250 in tips; slow business for the Dueling Daleys.

A girl with long braids had reached Melanie's jar. Mel smiled and reached for a request slip. Then the girl's hand landed on Melanie's wrist, and she had a split second's deja vu.

"How about an original?" the girl suggested, before walking away again.

Melanie stared after her in delighted shock, but was stopped from shouting Padma's name by the roars of her half of the patrons, begging her to put the tip to use and stop Tim. She punched up the chords and lyrics to "We Didn't Start The Fire."

February 2020

When Mel got up the courage to ask Padma out for a real catch-up, she chose the Rock-Keys, before a shift. Neutral territory with an easy out. Most of their once-close friendship had been carried out in occasional phone calls, semi-frequent texting threads, and bursts of swapped Instagram memes, ever since Melanie and Tim had married right out of college, and Padma had moved to Los Angeles.

"It's kind of *Hallmark*, you know?"

"What's Hallmark about it?"

"The 'Dueling Daleys' stage an argument through their pianos, then reunite and share a movie-musical kiss in front of a hundred of their closest barflies, three times a night?" Padma shrugged. "It's fun, just… kitsch."

"Yeah, well. It's what everybody likes," Melanie picked up her drink, something with peppermint schnapps and a cherry liqueur she could *feel* giving her a hangover. She avoided meeting Padma's eyes by scanning the bar; Arthur and Mike were mid-set onstage.

Padma wasn't letting it go. "But nobody ever notices that it's an act?" she asked. "Not even the regulars?"

"Dueling piano bars don't have *regulars*," Melanie pointed out. "We're a tourist stop. We even have minor name recognition at some of the resorts. Everybody's apres-ski stop."

"Sounds like it's been… a good move."

Heat rose up Melanie's neck. "It's a bar gig."

"Hey, you're performing. More than what I've been doing with my degree," shrugged Padma. Her eyes moved somewhere behind and above Melanie's shoulder, and her smile twitched. "And there are those of us who have gotten along by just being savants."

Melanie felt Tim's arms slide around her.

"Who's a savant? *Moi?*" He played the air keys in front of Melanie's face. "I dabble."

"A dabbler who's becoming a professor." Padma lifted her drink. "Congrats."

"I told her about the Boulder job." Melanie looked back at him, and he didn't quite meet her eye.

"Oh, yeah," Tim shrugged. "Well, I'm just a guest lecturer with private lessons."

"Still, it's awesome," Padma replied with another tip of her drink. "I may need the name of your contact in their music department, I'm having shit luck finding jobs here."

"You'll find something," Melanie assured her.

"I may try that gay bar in Littleton again," Padma shrugged with a smile. "The manager seemed interested."

"Ooh, is she cute?" Tim asked.

"Not as cute as my first true loves! Reunited, at long last," sighed Padma with affected drama, as she pretended to reach longingly for both Melanie and Tim. Mel smiled.

April 2020

Melanie was scrolling Pinterest with only the barest attention. The novelty of having time to herself had worn off around the sixth straight week of Duke canceling their Rock-Keys gigs. That now-weekly phone call was the only semblance of a routine that still existed in the lives of the Dueling Daleys.

"I'm just saying, lockdown is the worst. I *just* moved here and I can't actually go out. I don't know *anyone* in Denver." Padma's voice burst tinnily through the speakers of Melanie's laptop.

"You know us," Melanie offered, pinning a photo of a mason jar craft to her 'Apartment Ideas' board, and then immediately unpinning it.

"It's not like I actually get to spend any *time* with you, though. Even pre-lockdown," Padma added.

"Sorry. We get busy during ski season." Melanie clicked over to FaceTime, pulling up Padma's video. Padma was sitting at a table, working on a puzzle. "Plus I think we all passed around COVID at the bar in February. We're getting antibody tests next week."

Padma put her chin on her fist. "I know. I'm just cranky. I thought moving here was going to be this great new start for me, and for *us*—I don't know, it's just a mess, Mel."

"No shit." Melanie blew out a breath and asked carefully, "What do you mean, for us?"

"Just—we never acknowledged how stupid that fight was, back then. And I feel like we let it get in the way," Padma shrugged, going back to her puzzle. "It put us on a hiatus."

Melanie's breath caught. "Hiatus?"

Padma set down a puzzle piece, hesitating. "Don't make me say it. You know we haven't been as close as we were in college."

Melanie clicked back to Pinterest. "We just haven't lived together since then," she said. She chanced a glance at FaceTime. Padma's expression hadn't changed, so Melanie added hastily, "Hey, I just mean – you've always been my number one, okay? I know we've both been busy, but if you want a new start for our quarter-life crisis or whatever, then I think that sounds great."

Padma was quiet for a second. "What's Tim doing?"

Melanie shrugged. "On a video call too, in the bedroom. A lesson, I think."

"What are *you* doing?"

"Pinterest. Hard seltzer. Ritz crackers." Melanie picked up the can and jiggled it.

Padma was quiet for a moment. "So… are you okay?"

The question alone brought a lump into Melanie's throat so quickly, she nearly slammed the lid of the laptop shut. Since moving to Denver with Tim five years ago, she'd had exactly three local friendships – her bar manager, Duke, and two of her neighbors who had ultimately kicked Melanie out of their running group for being unable to commit to a marathon training schedule. She hadn't minded any of this when it felt like she and Tim were scrabbling to build a life together. Then Tim had gotten his first teaching opportunity, the weekend seminar that had led to the long-term position in the university's music department, and something had changed.

Melanie had tried to ignore it, but she'd felt Tim pulling away from her, as if he too sensed the tectonic plates of their marriage shifting beneath them. She couldn't see why, when she'd done exactly everything she should have done, breaking off her college flings (*fling* – just the one) and settling down for the serious work of being happily married. Then, before Melanie could figure out what she ought to do to salvage her relationship, Padma had arrived, and no matter how hard Melanie may have tried to ignore them, those long-lost feelings were back – somewhere between deja vu and an imaginary parallel universe. In that universe, Mel hadn't walked out on the first person who'd said she loved her.

"Melanie?" Padma asked.

"Yeah?" she said, in a passable imitation of her normal voice.

"Hey, what ever happened to *Hummingbird*?"

Melanie blinked in surprise. "I've—still got it. Somewhere. On my old hard drive, maybe?"

This was a flat-out lie. Before that day in December, she hadn't seen Padma in person since the courthouse wedding after graduation—but Melanie had never been able to let go of the EP they'd started together. It was like a lifeline, tied all the way back to a time before Mel had met Tim—before she'd chosen *this* universe, instead of the parallel one where she and Padma might have had more than just a single night with too much wine and truth-telling.

In any case, Mel couldn't think about that – not now, when there was *nothing* else she could do for a distraction. But the truth was, Melanie had ensured that every note, every voice file, every photo of every chord chart from their EP was preserved, traveling across shifting storage clouds, hard drives, and USB sticks. The unfinished project sat on her desktop even now, in an unnamed folder that sported a transparent image of a hummingbird for its icon, camouflaged with the digital wallpaper. You'd never know it was there, if you weren't looking for it.

June 2020

"What do you mean, you're booked?" Melanie asked incredulously. "What bars that aren't *this place* are booking *anything* right now?"

Tim shrugged. "I didn't say it was a bar, I just can't do this next week." He gestured around the cramped back office of the Rock-Keys, where they were trying to keep their argument as quiet as possible. Smaller crowds and more open windows meant a serious loss of privacy these days.

"You already missed last week's show," she told him, lowering her voice. "What, Jenna can't get enough of you? She needs you *so* desperately in Boulder?"

"She wants me to do a guest seminar with her classical summer intensive students, and she's paying," Tim said. "Duke's not going to fire us. We're the only people he's got left except Arthur, and you can do the show with him."

"Yeah, I'm sure his husband will be delighted when we make out onstage," Melanie snapped.

Tim looked unamused. "Not *our* show. Just the normal version."

Melanie's head swam with a million possible retorts —including that she wasn't as stupid as Tim seemed to think she was. She knew there were no summer intensives happening in person at the university. Jenna, on the other hand, had shown no qualms whatsoever about meeting Tim in-person for his many "online teaching evaluations" from the last semester.

There was a sharp knock on the door, and they both pulled their masks back up. Duke appeared, his permanently red face just visible between his white buzz-cut and the surgical mask slung under his nose. "C'mon, you two, showtime!"

Melanie caught Tim's eye, willing him to just read her cues so they could finish this discussion. "One sec, okay—"

"Hey, Duke," Tim said, pulling the door open further, "I hate to do this to you again, man, but I gotta do something in Boulder next Friday night."

Duke frowned. "Again? I don't know… honestly, we're struggling to get folks back in here."

"But you can reschedule with them, *right*, babe?" Melanie asked pointedly.

"Oh—totally," Tim sighed. "No worries."

"Well…what's it for?" Duke asked slowly.

"It's this mentoring thing I do in their music school," Tim said. "Some of those kids are better than me! One's just a freshman, and he's already winning awards—well, he *was*, pre-COVID."

You manipulative creep. Mel scowled behind her mask as Duke shrugged his huge shoulders and smiled. "Oh, I guess it won't hurt if you go and help the kid out." He clapped Tim on the back. "But you're gonna have to make it up to me, Timmy. Now do me a favor, you two, and don't play that goddamned Billy Joel song, even if it's on the request ticket. Art did it three times already and if the gals behind the bar hear it one more time, *they're* gonna start a fire."

August 2020

"Wow. I am… so sorry. What a fucked-up thing to do," Melanie said into her AirPods.

"Honestly, the thing I'm angriest about," Padma sniffled, "is that now *we* can't hang out. And she wasn't even the one who *told me* she got it. I found out from an Instagram story."

"That's awful, P, I'm sorry. But we can push our plans. Just take care of yourself." Melanie had come to a stop mid-run at the end of her block to take the call, and was now ambling slowly in the direction of the apartment building. "How are you feeling?"

"How do you think I'm feeling? I have fucking COVID and I got *dumped*," Padma wailed.

Melanie laughed, not unkindly. "I'm sure you'll pull through on both counts. You always do, right?"

"I am an indomitable fortress," Padma whimpered, sniffling again. She'd stopped crying, though – Melanie could tell. "You're lucky you're not doing this whole thing alone. Give Tim a hug for me."

"Yep. Will do," she replied, coming to a stop just before the driveway. Melanie studied the cartoon of the snow-draped Rockies on the side of the U-Haul, contrasted with the background view of the summertime peaks in the distance.

Four of their neighbors – compensated with beer and pizza and the promise that this would be the worst item they had to deal with—loaded Tim's upright piano into the back of the truck.

October 2020

Padma leaned against the balcony railing, staring down at the street below. "I can't believe you let me bitch about my problems for all this time and never said anything about what was going on."

"I'm sorry," Melanie mumbled. She was perched on one of the two tiny chairs the balcony fit. "I just… wanted it to be okay."

"No, Mel," Padma said, "Not just this year—which has definitely sucked. But you said this Jenna bitch wasn't even the first time? That he—I mean, in college, too? You *married* the guy."

"I know," Melanie laughed miserably. "I know, I'm an idiot."

"*Stop* saying that," Padma snapped. She looked unsettled, upset, and turned back to gaze at the evening skyline of Denver. It hadn't snowed yet, but it would, soon—there was a particular autumn-cold smell in the air.

Melanie looked down at her feet, poking out from under the blanket she'd cocooned in. "I'm not brave like you."

"Do *not* start that gays-are-so-brave BS," Padma warned.

"That's not what I'm saying," Melanie said, stung. "I'm saying—I have had way too much time to think about myself, lately."

"So…?" Padma prompted.

Melanie hesitated. "So… okay, so, I've only ever thought I wanted what I was *supposed* to want. And I was so happy when I got it that I just took it and figured I couldn't possibly want anything else. Meanwhile, you actually *did* what you said *we* should both do."

"And set my whole life on fire," Padma clarified. "Three cities in four years and *no* albums, no deals, nothing to show for it."

"It's not just the music stuff." Melanie stood up and leaned on the railing beside Padma. She started to go on, but Padma stopped.

"Hang on," she said firmly. "I'm not your escape hatch out of a shitty time in your life, Melanie."

Melanie pulled up short. "What?"

"I know you, Mel. And I love you, you're—my *best* friend," Padma raised a hand between them, palm out. "I'm *not* an escape hatch. You can't burn me like this again."

Melanie's stomach dropped.

Padma turned and went inside. She picked up her bag and coat, hastily pulling a mask from her pocket and slipping the loops over her ears. "You are smart, talented, and—" she paused, straightening up, "—one of the most incredible people I know. I have loved you since we were eighteen years old. And the messed-up thing is, a year ago, I would have given *anything* to hear whatever it was you were just about to say. But I am not here to fix whatever you think is your problem. You're smart enough to figure it out for yourself."

And she left, the door clicking shut behind her.

December 2020

The last meeting to sign the divorce papers took place on a cold morning before a forecasted snowstorm. Weitz & Crenshaw, P.C., was a nondescript beige box of a building halfway down York Street, overlooking the duck pond in Denver's City Park. It was all rather anticlimactic, actually, and Mel found herself sitting out in front of the frozen pond a short while later, grateful for the mask that was hiding her tears – and providing a bit of extra protection from the cold. Seeing their married life evaporate in a few strokes of a pen had been much more of a shock to her system than she'd expected. And now, what was left? Melanie looked around at the gray-and-white midmorning gloom of the leafless park in the middle of the city. She had no plan, now—no way forward—nothing that would guide her to what was coming next.

It had taken a long time—too long—for her to realize that she'd never felt so ready for anything in her life. She'd told herself that once the papers were signed and the ink was dry, everything that had ever been an obstacle to her happiness would be out of the way, for good…

She lifted her gloved hand, just as something shifted in the corner of her eye.

"Well, what are you waiting for? It's freezing out here. You need a ride, or what?" Padma was wrapped in a bright red puffer coat, two scarves, a mask, and a hat. She stamped her feet to fight off the cold.

Melanie stared at her. "I screwed up," she said, shaking her head. "I totally screwed everything up."

"Nope," Padma cut her off. "You're improvising." She hooked her arm through Melanie's and pulled her onto her feet. "It's an original."

When The Ink Dries

By Shayla McBride

Jason Little had never felt so ready for anything in his life. Once the contract was signed and the ink was dry, everyone who'd ever been an obstacle to his success was out of the way. He lifted his pen. Out of the corner of his eye, something shifted.

Well," a female voice, throaty and low, murmured, "what are you waiting for?"

He blinked. What? Was it…no, no, couldn't be. They were done with each other, that was the deal. He didn't want to see her again. She could be so mean…

He stared around his office: the new carpet, the fancy real wood desk. He was alone, wasn't he? Only a faint mist writhing in the corners. His belly cramped. *Ignore that.* Fussily, he tapped the papers together. Frowned at his new toy.

Somehow, the solid gold and green lacquer pen had looked better on the website than on his big new desk. The thing looked kinda…cheap. Like a working girl playing trophy wife. And if he wasn't impressed with the pen, why would his pigeon be? And if his pigeon wasn't impressed, would he sign? Had he jeopardized the whole deal for this shiny toy?

The fountain pen was 18K gold, engraved with classical Greek motifs. Whatever that meant. Classical Greek motifs? The idiots in his life wouldn't know classical Greek from a comic book superhero.

The pen gleamed like a gold bar. Hell, a gold bar might've been cheaper. He ran one index finger along the oversized, engraved barrel, flicked the broad 18K gold nib. The pen wobbled in a half-circle, came to rest with the sharp, gleaming tip pointing at him.

Bad omen? Good omen?

"Make your own goddam omens," he muttered, giving the stupid thing a dismissive flick.

His pigeon should arrive in ten minutes. Sign the papers—maybe he'd let him use the million-dollar pen with the figure of a club-wielding bodybuilder on the barrel. Classic Greek somebody, his butt cheeks draped in a…yeah, a lion's skin, paws and all, but who gave a fat rat's?

Certainly not the soon-to-be Duke of Deals, the Prince of Ponzi, the Sultan of Scams! Once the ink was dry, victory. Everyone who'd ever laughed at Jason Little, sneered or taunted or bullied him, anyone who'd given him a noogie, a wedgie, a bloody nose or a black eye, anyone who'd tried to kick him to the curb or throw him under the bus (more than once, literally), they'd all be silenced. No more a loser like everyone in his family, like damn near everyone he knew. He'd be the winner. And nobody could stop him. Nobody!

Jason rubbed his hands together as he snickered with glee. When his laughter faded, the silence had become oppressive, the air tainted. The odor had a sharp, acrid tang, like a fire-scorched slaughterhouse. The pale mist obscuring the far corners of the room had grown. Shit, shit, shit! Was she here? What pit had she slithered out of? Why? He'd had it all under control! He spun the chair sideways and eased down onto the platform. Peered over the desk.

"Go away," he ordered, shooing at the fog with nervous hands. "I'm a very busy man. You got no part in this. We're done, remember?"

The mist pushed across the new carpet, its leading edge undulating heavily like an oil spill. Flashes of light flickered under the milky surface, poison greens, livid reds, putrid yellows. A sly chuckle wheezed.

The mist grew nearer, the chuckle closer. Jason's spurt of anger was stillborn, overcome by a cold fear that fogged his mind. He'd paid his dues, done everything she'd demanded! No way could she ask for more. But that didn't mean she wouldn't.

"I've done everything." He tried to keep his voice level. So undignified to sound like a six-year-old spotting her first snake. "Every last thing you asked. Even the shit that made me puke, I did what you wanted! Now I get my reward, right? Right? That was the deal, the promise!"

The mist crawled onto the platform, twined up his legs, making the little sucking sounds he'd come to hate. The sounds took on a mocking tone as the mist belled out around him. Mottled snakes darted in and out of the mist, scales of rotting green and dead black.

Snakes? Oh, no! It really was her! She was the worst of them all, with her fanged mouth and her bulging eyes blazing savage red. Still the white flesh grew, the skin curving around the obscenely voluptuous figure coalescing in front of him. Atop the head, the snakes swayed back and forth, fangs dripping yellow poison that sizzled as it landed.

"My new carpet," he wailed, seeing the charred holes.

Another phlegmy chuckle rose in the air. "Little mister Little and his little concerns..."

Acid rose in his throat. He coughed. "Please...please, no...go away...you can't..."

"I can't what, baybee?" Pure menace. "You gonna tell me what I can or can't do?"

"I t-take it back," he said through a constricted throat, "I mis-spoke. You can do anything..."

"Course I can. Silly little Jason Little," she sing-songed, twining her damp arms around him, pushing her thighs into his chest. She tossed her head back to keep the snakes at bay. "You and I both know I can do anything I want. And you'll do anything I want, too. Or do you want to go down another size or two?"

"No! Not that. B-but we had a deal," he croaked.

She bent, showed her fangs. "Deals are made to be broken, silly man."

He dodged a snake, heard the poison sizzle on his jacket. "You promised..."

"Tsk-tsk," she murmured, her dead eyes staring without pity, "so naïve. After all you've done for me, all those bodies, all the blood and screams, all the begging you didn't listen to, how can you be so trusting? Didn't your dear, drunken mommy teach you deeds speak louder than words, huh?" Her arms tightened. "And if that fat whore didn't, how about your own life, baybee?" She smiled. Humorless. Hideous. "Maybe you need a reminder."

His bones creaked, new pain flared. Terror tore through him. "No, no, not again! You said you were done! You said you'd never—"

"Fool." Tighter, tighter! "Oh, quit with the howling. You can stop it, if you want."

"H-how?" Every joint, every bone ending, burned with a blowtorch fire. "How? Tell me, I'll do it!" He groaned as the pain ebbed and she laughed with triumph.

"Simple. When he walks through the door, kill him."

"My pigeon? Kill my pigeon?" He shook his head, fought the urge to hold his jaw so his head wouldn't come loose. "I thought I was done killing for you."

Another moist chuckle. He cried out as she raked her claws across his skull. When he blinked open his eyes she filled his sight.

"When he comes through that door," she hissed, "little Jason Little, tiny Jason, little man, *my* little man, you will kill him. Or you'll wind up so small you'll be able to stand under your pretty new desk." Her grip tightened. He couldn't stop a whimper. She giggled. "Just imagine being two feet tall. Where'd you buy your suits, huh? C'mon, all you gotta do is kill him. No biggie, how many times you done it? By now, you shouldn't be so delicate, baybee."

"Why," he choked out. "Why him? He's not all that bad—"

The extravagant pain eased. Her mouth smiled; the cold eyes stayed dead. "Cause I said so. All you need to know."

"But…" He broke off with a cry as new pain poured into his knees and elbows.

She grinned. "You're down an inch already, Jason baybee. Want more?"

"No!"

"Good boy. As a reward, I'm gonna tell you a secret. Your soon-to-arrive guest may talk about his so-noble concern for families and children and for precious lives unborn, but," her eyes went colder, something he'd thought impossible, "he never saw a preschooler's ass he didn't want to fondle. And explore, you get my drift. You need details?"

"No. No, no. He's a p-pedophile?" Images of his mother pushing him into her clients' sweaty, grasping hands overwhelmed him. He blinked, desperate to not let the tears flow.

"Active and getting worse every year. Age no barrier, he loves them all. Until they get to fourth grade. Or if they get pregnant? Right-to-life goes right out the window."

"He's a dead man." He flicked a stare into the soulless eyes as a thought entered his disordered mind. "Hey, hey. What if you're not telling…uh, if your information is uh, incorrect? What if it's maybe somebody else? Wha—ow!"

"You questioning my judgment?" She shook her head slowly. The snakes writhed, one lunging forward to attempt a strike. She brushed it back. "Sides, would I lie to you? Something this important? C'mon, baybee, you're hurtin' my tender feelings." Her dead eyes narrowed. "He's parking his Maybach now. Be here in six, seven minutes. See this?" She picked up the pen, twirled between her claws. "The perfect weapon."

"That thing cost twenty large!"

"He'll go out in better style than he deserves, then."

"The body! What'm I supposed to do with it? All sorts of people might know he's coming here."

Her lip curled. "Why would he tell anybody he's coming *here*? Far's the body goes, I'll take care of it. With pleasure." She licked her lower lip. "Wanna watch?"

He shuddered. "No, thank you. Once was enough."

"He's on the stairs. You got four minutes. He's such a whale he's gotta haul himself up. Maybe he'll have a heart attack and you'll be off the hook."

"I'm never that lucky. With that much blubber, tell me: how'm I gonna kill the whale with a six-inch fountain pen?"

"In the eye, silly, right smack into the eye, deep as you can go."

"But that might not kill'm right away. He's a big man, he could flatten me before he croaks."

Again the purple tongue caressed her lower lip. A trail of spittle gleamed. "Ooooh, make my day. I love 'em still breathing."

Jason's mind was a chaos of emotions ranging from fear and disgust to impotent fury. His stomach roiled and heaved, sending a jet of acid into his throat. He coughed, trying to speak, as she informed him the pigeon was in the hall, leaning against the wall trying to catch his breath.

"Hope he makes it in here," she muttered, the words half drowned by the snakes' hissing. "He needs to die where I can see every putrid drop of his blood."

Something personal there, Jason thought. Very personal. "What's he done to you?"

"My bosses, not me." The snakes hissed in unison. "Need to know, and you don't. But I'll drink his blood like it's the finest Amarone money could buy."

He pushed the image away and concentrated on the unfamiliar word. "Amaronay?"

"Spectacular Italian red." She pointed to a recyclable grocery bag against the far wall. "I even brought Sweet Baby Ray's BBQ Sauce. The low sugar version."

He pushed that image away, too. But the sound of bones crunching still erupted from his memory. He shuddered, concentrated on the pebbled glass of the outer door. There was no shadow: where was his precious pigeon?

“He’s leaning against the wall,” she said, putting a snake’s head between her lips and sucking the venom. “Hm. Might be having second thoughts.”

Jason couldn’t stop the whimper. “He can’t. He has to sign, everything depends on it. He. Has. To. Sign!”

“Poor little Jason Little,” she snickered. “so easily upset. Don’t get your knickers in a knot.”

“Easy for you to say,” he said bitterly. “Everything rides on this. Everything! I’m the one with blood on his hands. I’m the one who had to—”

Her claws dug into his throat as she lifted him so they were eye to eye. She set him on the desk top but kept digging into his larynx as he whooped and gurgled.

“I’d rip your throat out now,” she said in a homicidal whisper, “but you’ve got a job to do for me so I’m gonna let you live. How long is mostly up to you.” Her eyes slitted as a brisk knock sounded on the outer door. “Don’t fuck this up or it’s you who’ll get the Sweet Baby Ray’s.”

Perspiration dripped down his temples. And his ribs, his back, his thighs. He couldn’t feel the desktop beneath his feet. She straightened his silk tie, smoothed his lapels, wetted one fingertip with her swollen purple tongue. His stomach flipped.

“I’ll smooth my own hair, thank you,” he said.

“I was gonna wipe the blood off. But it’s not too bad.”

“If you ruin this deal—”

“Bet on it, baybee.” She lifted him down to the floor, did one last smoothe-pat on his shoulders. *Tsk-Tsk.* “Try Head and Shoulders, dude.”

Another tattoo on the door. She snapped her fingers and the door opened. The pigeon, preening in an iridescent bespoke suit that had probably nauseated the tailor and now only exaggerated his bloated belly, swaggered in. He looked around. Sneered.

"I had to wait," he said with a peevish scowl. "I don't like to wait." He sniffed, peered at the carpet. "Smells funny in here. Something burned?" He laughed. "You running an illegal cremation service here?"

"Welcome," Jason said, standing up straight on his platform. The bloated belly was level with his shoulders. "Please, have a seat." He motioned to the chair in front of his desk.

The pigeon shook his head. "I'm a busy man." *An important man.* "I don't have time to waste." *You're a waste of time.* He snapped his fingers. "Papers?" *You worthless insect.*

Jason hid his anger and smiled. "If you wish to sign standing up, that's perfectly fine with me. I have everything ready for your review and approval."

He picked up his twenty-thousand-dollar gold pen. The barrel was cold and uneven against his fingertips. It really had been too big for his hand when he'd ordered it and, thanks to her, was even bigger now.

"Not sure this is in my best interest," the pigeon said, pushing the guest chair aside and bellying up to the desk. "I think an adjustment in some of the details might be necessary."

Jason smiled again. Friendly, warm, confident. "Well, take a look and point out the areas you're not happy with." He pushed the papers across the mahogany. "We'll see what we can do. But any change will affect your amazing return, of course."

The pigeon leaned his hands against the wood and bent down. Muttered as he read the words to himself. Looked up.

"Sign now," Jason said, putting his focus on forcing obedience. Hoping the monster was using her magic.

For a moment, eyes flickering uncertainly, the pigeon hesitated. Then shrugged and pulled out a gold pen. Jealousy flared in Jason's mind. It was the one he'd decided not to get: too expensive, even more so than the authentic Greek mythology extravagance. The pigeon saw his expression, smirked. With an even bigger smirk, he scrawled his signature and tossed the obscenely expensive pen down.

"You can keep it, you want," the pigeon said, nudging the object across the desk. "I got plenty more."

"How very nice for you," Jason sneered.

The pigeon looked up at the sarcastic comment.

Smiling, smiling, smirking, Jason plunged his own thick-barreled pen into the pigeon's left eye. He scrambled across the desktop as the fat bastard roared and fell back, grunted as he pushed it in deeper, deeper, his bloody palm flat against the greasy forehead. The pigeon writhed on the carpet—ruined now, he'd need a new one —and convulsed. Once. Twice.

No more.

"Take that, you pompous asshole," Jason said, wiping his hands briskly on the pigeon's lapels. "And death to all pedophiles."

"Uh-huh," she said, delving into the mist around her feet. Opening the shopping bag, she pulled out the bottle of barbeque sauce.

"Not now," Jason said, his throat burning at the thought of what she planned for the pigeon.

"Fresh. Gotta do 'em fresh. You know how I like 'em fresh. Or even kickin'."

"Yeah, yeah. But not on my carpet. And not him. He signed the paper, now he's gotta have a natural accident so nobody questions the deal."

"Not him, huh. Okay, have it your way."

"Damn straight I'm right." He puffed out his chest. "I'm the man, now, I'm—"

"Little man," she said with faux regret as she floated toward him, "you haven't learned a thing, have you? Still the innocent boy shoplifting bags of chips and tins of snuff." She shook her head. The snakes drooped, twined in pairs and trios. "Such a futile little life, baybee."

"What're you talking about? I got the deal. I'm the man now!" He strutted around the desk and hopped up onto the platform. "The Prince of Ponzi! The deal's done and I'm—Hey! Hey! What the hell you doing?"

"What's it look like, little man?" She squeezed the bottle again and barbeque sauce jetted onto his face and throat. She tossed the bottle over her shoulder. Her other hand swept around and grabbed him just under his jaw. She scooped up the pigeon's fat, gaudy pen, shoved.

He couldn't breathe, could barely think. The pain was a cold, living presence filling his body. He shook his head in wonder and confusion. Everything he'd done, all the ruin, the deaths, the atrocious acts he'd committed. The faces rose in front of him, faces as he'd last seen them, eyes wide in shock, mouths open in accusation, blood flowing. All at her behest, every deed, every life. And this was the thanks he got? His reward a pen—that pig's pen! —in the throat?

His chest heaved in futile effort. The pale, cold mist rose before him, hazing everything. He was traveling on a blurred cloud of noxious white, whirling with sickening speed. Fire jetted up his arm as something ripped at his flesh. His scream came out a gurgle. From far away, he felt the brush of the monster's hot breath, heard the monster's voice.

"Always had a taste for them little Cornish game hens, baybee."

Spirit on the Border

By Amira Loutfi

Shahinaz waited by the gates to the border crossing to the Sacred Valley, the hours ticking by slowly. Pressed against the gates was a crowd of her people—the Orebi—and some foreigners. At dusk, when the street lights turned on, she could feel the arrival of spirits. Or maybe it was one? She looked about—she could hear something that felt both near and far at the same time. It had a bell-like chime but without an actual sound. Isn't that what people said about spirits? No one else seemed to have noticed. She composed herself, trying to suppress her curiosity. *Even if it is a spirit*, she chided herself, *it's none of my business*.

Shahinaz's family lived only about an hour beyond the border by bus. But she usually waited much longer than that for the border authority to let her through. *I can't even visit home,* she said to herself, *without being reminded of how much they hate us*. The ambiguous wait by the border was just one of many infrastructural tools the ethnic competitors of the Orebi used to aggravate them.

She could hear someone in the crowd speaking Ereni, the language of the imperialist tyrant who had pitted the ethnic groups of her homeland against one another. Others in the crowd spoke Ereni also, but with a Cutathi accent. It almost sounded like a separate language but Shahinaz knew better. The crowd that gathered by the border was always made up like this—natives of the Sacred Valley waited for hours without any communication of when they'd be let in. Sets of foreigners, be they citizens of Eren, Cutath, or any other nationality, would be allowed to pass through within minutes.

Shahinaz could pick out the foreigners not only by their accents, but also by the way they dressed. One man silently pushed past her. Shahinaz guessed he was foreign not only because he'd just arrived, but because he also wore a brand of shoes that she'd only ever seen in foreign movies.

Even more obvious were those decked out in religious accoutrement. Shahinaz knew exactly what faith tradition and myth each symbol was associated with. Occasionally she'd see some of the foreign women covered from head to toe in dark veils with only one eye and traces of the flesh around it exposed. Others announced their pious intentions by wearing rosaries, cheek powders, and red hair dye. Neither the Orebis nor their ethnic competitors could ever match the foreigners in matters of religious zeal.

Shahinaz stretched on to her tiptoes, peeking between the crowd. A group of young officers on the other side of the gates waited lethargically. What was it like to get paid to siphon off friends from enemies at the border? They made it look boring.

After a few minutes, the gates opened and disturbed the demographics of the crowd. A third of them went inside. Only Orebis remained. Shahinaz had witnessed the process over a dozen times that day. She wondered what it was like to come and go to the Sacred Valley as a pilgrim.

They always looked so excited and purposeful. While she and her brethren, one of only a few ethnic groups native to the valley, had no choice but to suffer the caprice of their foreign-backed competitors. She examined the remaining Orebis glumly. Some of them had been waiting even longer than herself—

"Did they just open the gates?"

"I think some people just went through!"

"Oh, yeah! The crowd shrunk, for sure!"

Turning, Shahinaz saw a group of young women, speaking with alarm and energy, their accents thick with a Cutathi twang. The girls' cheeks were flecked with blue powder—a symbol of self-annihilation in the Sacred Valley. Shahinaz was a short girl, but these were even shorter than her—perhaps by two inches. Clearly they had not seen the non-Orebis pass through.

It was a miscommunication. One that Shahinaz could easily help clear up... but a part of her resisted. Even though she was relatively talented in the Ereni language, her interactions with its native speakers always left her feeling stupid. Ignoring them was the best way that she could preserve her pride. Besides, the border *was* controlled by a proxy group of Eren. And Cutath was Eren's strongest political ally.

Serves them right to get punished by the policies of their own people. With that thought, Shahinaz's breath caught in her throat, and her chest got tight.

Am I punishing them if I ignore them? The realization hit her like a wave. A lump formed in her throat and her eyes watered. She felt a pain unlike any she'd felt before.

I should help them, she said firmly to herself, *even if they do think they're better than me*. It felt bitter, but far better than her original instinct. *The border authority is unfair to Orebis, but that doesn't mean those Cutathi pilgrims ought to suffer along with us.* She breathed deeply*, it still hurts, but at least now I'm going to be kind.*

She turned to the girls again, careful to tilt her chin slightly upward lest they think themselves superior. One of them returned her gaze with curiosity, and her bitterness softened.

"The officers will let you through," she said to them, "just show them your Cutathi passport." And she called out for the other Orebis to make way for them.

The girls expressed their thanks with exuberance and Shahinaz was surprised to find herself affected by their blue-flecked happiness. As they passed by her, each one gave her a smile and a small hug. There were four of them. No... five. There were five of them? They all looked like the typical baby-faced Cutathi, with the little button nose and round cheeks. Except for the fifth one. Shahinaz wasn't sure about her.

Even without her help, Shahinaz knew the girls would've figured it out eventually. But there was still something really satisfying about showing kindness to citizens of the wealthy and powerful Cutath in their moment of confusion and helplessness.

The border authority allowed Orebis to pass at random times. Sometimes only once in a day and sometimes two times. And some days none at all. The only way to find out was to wait outside. After the Cutathi girls had gone, the Orebis waited for several more hours until the officers received orders to retire. There would be no more passage through the gates that night.

A lump formed in Shahinaz's throat, but it was one she'd felt several times before. It was one less day to spend with her family in the Sacred Valley.

The crowd dispersed and the place got quiet fast. Shahinaz bought a shawarma and soda from a vending machine down the road and sat on the curb. She selected a dark spot, a few paces away from a weak street lamp. She took a bite and felt the relief of the bread, meat, and pickles in her mouth.

"I can't *believe* they did that!"

Shahinaz flinched. She thought she was alone. She looked about for the source of the voice. It spoke Ereni with a Cutathi accent.

"I almost went with my Cutathi girls," it said. "But I couldn't."

"Who is there?"

"Me."

Shahinaz gaped. Under the street light, a cloud of dust and smoke spun together and materialized into the figure of a woman. She had a stocky build, round cheeks, and a smile that didn't seem proportional to the rest of her face. Shahinaz was startled, but then it struck her. This was the fifth girl.

"You're a—" Shahinaz said breathlessly.

"Well—" the creature seemed about to argue the point. Instead it said, "I just wanted to thank you for helping my Cutathi girls get across the border tonight. It was unbelievably kind of you." The speech of the creature didn't quite sound like speech. And Shahinaz realized that that was the soundless bell-like chiming she'd felt earlier that day.

"What are you doing here if you already went through—."

"I *didn't* go through!" the woman cried, "And I think it's because of guilt! I felt *guilty* that my crowd was able to go through and yours couldn't!"

"No, don't feel guilty." Shahinaz said. The sudden emotionality of the strange woman frightened her, "I was happy to help them."

"Of course you'd say that." The creature growled, her eyes moved in a manner unlike that of a human woman, "But I know you struggled to make that decision. It was me who whispered to you about punishing the girls—". The creature's chiming voice stopped abruptly, before it blurted out, "*If you have a hard time getting across tomorrow I'm going to go bonkers!*"

"No" Shahinaz stammered, she was so startled all she could say was, "...It's fine."

"Fine?" The creature snarled, practically lunging at her, "*They're being unfair*! What gives *them* the right to block *you* from visiting *your* family?" As she continued, her appearance as a woman morphed slightly. Her skin ripped like cheap fabric and from between the tiny tears little strings of smoke escaped.

Shahinaz gasped, dropping her sandwich. She began to recite an ancient incantation against evil.

"Stop that!" The foreigner snapped. She examined her own body, and saw what was happening, "Ok, I can see I'm scaring you." She sighed, calming, and sat cross-legged in front of Shahinaz, almost touching her.

"I can't make massive changes to Ereni policy," she said, "but I do want to reward you for having a big heart," and she smiled intensely at Shahinaz, who did not feel comforted by it, "I can write you a deal with no strings attached. I can—" and out of the darkness, she pulled out a sheet of parchment, an ink glass, and a quill pen.

"I can make magically binding contracts. Just tell me what you want the most."

"What? Why?"

"Listen. The first thing you're getting is hassle-free passage through the border from now on until you die. That includes your traveling companions." She smiled triumphantly, and slapped the parchment between the two of them, as though there was a small table there. It floated between them, straight and stiff. As the creature scratched away at the parchment, Shahinaz could see a faint outline of her handwriting floating into the air like smoke.

She looked up, "If you could have anything else, what would it be?"

Shahinaz thought about it. She'd love to have the freedom to travel back and forth between school and her home like the foreigners did. But the spirit was already giving her that. After a few more moments, she realized she'd also love to be perfect at Ereni. No. Not just Ereni.

"I wish I knew every language in the whole world," she said, "perfectly."

"Good one," the creature excitedly dipped the quill and wrote.

When she lifted up the parchment, Shahinaz could see it sizzling with a life of its own, the text dancing with sparks and smoke. At the bottom was a thin straight line. A space for a signature.

"This really is a magical contract," Shahinaz said, flooded by a feeling of excitement.

"It is."

Shahinaz had never felt so ready for anything in her life. Once the contract was signed and the ink burned through, anything that had ever been an obstacle to her happiness would be out of the way. She lifted the quill and out of the corner of her eye, the foreigner shifted again.

"Well," she murmured, "what are you waiting for?"

BOOKS

Writing Prompt

Her nose was in a book, as usual. Trying to get her attention would take more than just a call from the bottom of the stairs.

Stories

Disaster on the Hasan Family Starship

By Amira Loutfi

Raabi'a tiptoed out of the sleeping pods of the Hasan family starship, *The Uniter*, with a teal-colored blanket and cream pillow in her arms. She peeked into the control room. Along its walls were air vents, screens, wires, and command lines blinking and beeping for attention. Tacked to every bit of bare space was university memorabilia. "Galaxy University or Bust" one banner read. She spied her two brothers in there, Mi'shaar and Thaani. They looked deep in conversation, examining a data set together, their low voices murmuring amid the bings and boops of the busy room. It was the perfect opportunity to sneak past. She held her breath.

Once past the control room, she exhaled nervously. It seemed like her brothers hadn't noticed her. She slinked toward the vacuum tube at the end of the corridor. She shoved her blanket and pillow through the hatch and snapped it shut, glancing about herself with the excitement of a young criminal. The vacuum sucked away her cozy gear with barely a sound. She then crouched near the hatch, pulling her knees into her chest, and stretched the rubber over her entire person. It sucked her up and spat her out onto the second level of the ship.

Over the past week, and thanks to the guidance of Mi'shaar, she'd become comfortable aboard her family's giant starship. The layout was pretty straightforward and the vacuum transit system had become second nature to her. The top two levels included starship controls and living facilities. The bottom three levels carried *The Uniter's* powercore, its data center, engines, safety features, and extra repositories of fuel, oxygen, and the like. Raabi'a felt that she knew enough to get around.

Raabi'a gathered her things and ran down the hall, a trill of laughter bursting from her chest. It felt like a jail break. She stuffed the bedding through the next vacuum hatch and repeated the same process, reaching the second storage level. Around a bend she saw her final destination. Another hatch separated the hall from a vacuum tube that would send her out to the escape pod. Her parents had warned that the escape pod was only for emergencies, but Raabi'a had begun to spend every free hour she had there.

The pod was only loosely connected to the Hasan family starship, by a robotic arm and a piece of tubing. The tubing was probably not strong enough to secure the pod to the ship if the arm ever broke. It was designed that way, obviously, in case passengers ever needed to escape.

The escape pod was the quietest part of the ship and had also proven—so far at least—to be a good hideout. Mi'shaar and Thaani still hadn't discovered the indulgent manner in which their little sister was using it. She wanted to keep it that way. Once inside the escape pod, Raabi'a held her breath again, listening for her siblings...

Nothing.

Good.

Raabi'a wrapped herself in the bedding and grabbed a book from a large pile. Each book was a near-perfect copy of a historic relic created from *The Uniter's* morphing tray. It was incredibly accurate, too—down to the last bit of foxed, yellowed fibers of their pages. It even granted them a slightly musty smell.

Sometimes she read them, sometimes not. Raabi'a would thoughtlessly add books to the pile and ask the morphing tray for another one. *The Uniter* would produce a similar piece of literature in a minute, which is exactly what Raabi'a expected it to do this time. But instead, the tray beeped. Raabi'a sat up to look at it. There was a message on its screen. It appeared to have run out of creative materials.

What? No. But it was true. She read it again.

It said that the only way it could generate another book for her was if she returned at least 200 pages back into the tray.

With a sigh, Raabi'a flopped back on the cream pillow. The books she chose were from other planets and peoples, but they were all similar in content and most came from a similar time period. She fumbled through the pile until she found one she hadn't read yet. Raabi'a rolled in her blanket and studied the title and the author's name—

Midnight Magic Academy by Tiffany Brian Tuft - Part 1 of the Romance Rejecters Saga.

It featured a beautiful young female on the cover surrounded by dark birds and purple lightning. The blurb on the back boasted a handsome teenage male as the antagonist. The pile was full of books like this. She suspected the male would fall in love with the girl on the cover. She considered it for a moment and cracked it open.

It only took a few pages before she was riveted. She already wanted the boy and girl to fall in love. No—she was *dying* for them to fall in love. She wondered which one of them would do the rejecting that was proposed in the saga's title. The thought made her shiver in excitement.

This brief happiness was interrupted by a muffled shout. It was her name.

The shout came again, "Raabi'a!"

She sat up again, sighing. It was Mi'shaar. He was probably trying to share some new educational experience with her. She looked around. The pod had large navigation windows through which she was quite visible. From the second level of *The Uniter*, anyone could see her lying there.

Raabi'a shimmied herself into one of the curved repositories along the side of the pod. It hid her completely from sight.

***

Thaani, the middle Hasan child, quickly observed a mismatch in enthusiasm between his elder brother and little sister. Raabi'a was the youngest of their family and it was her first time coming with them to university. It would also be her first time away from their desert home planet. Their eldest brother, Mi'shaar, was thrilled to take her under his wing. Not only was Raabi'a his little *sister*, whom he had sworn to their parents he'd protect, but she had also been accepted to the same training program he'd attended for the past three years. Mi'shaar was brimming with pride and excitement about her education.

Thaani thought that Mi'shaar's pedagogical enthusiasm might be too much for his protégé. Watching him try to teach her was kind of funny. But he also hated to disappoint Mi'shaar whom he felt was a great elder brother. And besides, Raabi'a *should've* been interested—she'd chosen the starship hardware program herself. Thaani thought her sluggishness was odd. Regardless, he wasn't surprised when she became harder and harder to find aboard *The Uniter*.

A week into their travel, Thaani noticed another odd thing. Holding a couple of data sets, he sought after Mi'shaar and soon found him in the internal control room, checking coordinates and travel routes.

"Mi'shaar, when did you last go out?"

"I haven't since last cycle." Mi'shaar said without looking up. As a starship mechanic, Mi'shaar would float out to *The Uniter's* exterior to maintain the powercore and other equipment essential to the ship's safety.

"There was a drastic change in ship pressure only a few minutes ago. The controls aren't saying what it is." Thaani flicked a holographic data table over to Mi'shaar, who steadied it in his hand.

"I don't know what this means," Mi'shaar said, "but something might've gotten loose. I'll go check." He suddenly perked up, dropping the data set which faded into nothing, "Where's Raabi'a?" he asked, "We can go check the exterior together! It'll be a great learning experience for her!"

"Last I saw she was reading in the sleeping pod." Thaani said. He bit his tongue to hold back a sarcastic comment about Raabi'a's eagerness to learn. Instead, he summoned a few more screens and a command line. Numbers and graphs continued to form and shift on the tables.

"Raabi'a!" Mi'shaar called, but he knew it would take more than a call from the control room of the starship to rouse her if her nose was in a book. He would have to go get her himself. He disappeared, the *tak tak tak* of his footsteps gradually quieting as he made his way to the sleeping pods. Thaani could hear him calling Raabi'a's name again.

Mi'shaar returned. "She wasn't there," he sounded disappointed.

"The data still says nothing," Thaani said. The screens disappeared as he flicked them into the air. "Let me know what you find." He sauntered down the steps to the kitchen. "Do we have any more of that date paste?"

"I hope so," Mi'shaar called after him. "I'm gonna go nuts if we ran out already."

Thaani laughed as he grabbed a tray of mesh cutlery, "I know," he said, opening a cupboard. Crammed into the small space were about three dozen food trays and stiff pouches. His finger thrummed across the row of labels, "it's the only actual nutrition—"

The Uniter shook with an aggressive shudder and a wuthering boom, the force of which threw Thaani to the kitchen tiles in a sprawling mess. The cutlery sprayed out of his hands. He could hear things crashing around him.

"What was that?" Mi'shaar yelled from the control room.

Thaani was stunned for a moment, sitting on the floor of their kitchen. The explosion had also thrown all thoughts of date paste out of his mind. When his wits returned, he jammed his wrist controls, flicking through multiple levels of data tables that appeared before him.

"What does it say?" Mi'shaar screamed as he leaned into the kitchen, his dark eyes furious.

"It still isn't saying anything," Thaani cried. Mi'shaar disappeared. Thaani could hear the sound of the terminal capsule opening. "What are you doing?"

"If you don't know what to do, then I'll do the one thing I can think of!" Mi'shaar cried. "I'm going to switch out *all* of the hardware in use!" He yanked his space suit out of the overhead compartment, and violently jammed his left foot through the leggings.

A second low boom shook *The Uniter* with a violence equal to that of the first. Thaani's data tables dispersed as he flew through them. Mi'shaar rolled over the control room floor, fighting to get his suit on. For a moment, the Hasan brothers accomplished very little. Both yelled one thing or another. Dozens of irrelevant data sets exploded into the room as Thaani fell over the threshold back into the control room. Mi'shaar jumped about in a panic that barely allowed him to fit his space vest over his head.

In between the floating screens, something moving on the floor of the control room caught Thaani's eye. It was a delicate space fork from the cutlery set that their parents had gifted them only a week before. One of its teeth had curled. The middle tooth sparked and released a faint trail of smoke. Thaani stood up and approached it, breathless.

Is this what was killing them?

He picked up the little space fork and stood before the capsule where his brother violently fumbled about with his harness. "Mi'shaar," he said, "it's oxygen. It's gotta be an oxygen leak—"

Mi'shaar stopped to look at the little fork, "...yeah," he said, "But what busted it? And how?"

Then, Thaani dropped it, jerking his hand away. It had become too hot for him to hold.

On the floor of the control room, the shape of the utensil started to deform and bubble. A small flame appeared on it and a thin trail of smoke curled into the air. The brothers both stared in terror, their black eyes round. Oxygen was dangerous.

"We should be dead by now," Mi'shaar said, "But *The Uniter* must be correcting it."

Thaani said nothing as he vigorously worked the controls, drawing up every piece of information he could. More and more data sets and graphs appeared until the two brothers were surrounded by floating screens.

"Here!" Thaani screamed, "Our left side oxygen tank blew out, but it looks like you're right. *The Uniter* is correcting the gas leak with decompression and nitrogen. Are you sure you checked the oxygen tanks on your last outing?"

"Of course I did." Mi'shaar said, looking perplexed, "Everything was completely fine. Including both sets of oxygen tanks."

Thaani watched as Mi'shaar pulled off his suit jacket and refastened it. In his haste, he had thrown his arm through the collar and gotten the rest of his person tangled up in his harness in a manner that was almost comical. Thaani would've laughed, but the troubled look on his brother's face stopped him.

"I'm going to go fortify this ship," Mi'shaar said angrily, "starting with the oxygen, then all the other life-support systems. When you figure out what happened, hit me."

Mi'shaar looked angry as he reattached his jacket over his vest, successfully this time. He was responsible for the hardware, after all. The young man was probably ashamed of himself. Thaani was about to say something kind, but he was instead distracted by something on the top Mi'shaar's head. He swatted his brother's curly hair, releasing a dry cloud of maroon-colored dust.

"Why is there sand on you?" he yelled.

The two looked up. More grains of sand fell dryly onto Mi'shaar's face. He jumped back, and another faint cloud fell to the floor.

He muttered an array of expletives. Thaani was breathless in shock. The look he received from Mi'shaar suggested they were both thinking the same thing.

"Why is there *sand* coming out of the ceiling?" Mi'shaar asked nervously.

Sand was destructive to all types of machinery, including starships. This was common knowledge. Their desert home space-faring facilities possessed powerful fortifications against sand. And they worked well enough that Thaani had never heard of more than a few specks of sand getting in. And he'd never heard of a starship with a speck of sand on board. Let alone a steady trickle like what he saw just then.

He and his brother gazed up and down in consternation. From the ceiling, a soundless string of earthy colors continued to fall. On the white floor of the control room, a dry splattering of sand slowly grew.

"Could it be a sand shifter? One from home?" If it were a sand shifter, the small splatterings of sand would slowly start to coalesce. Thaani rubbed the sand with his toe. It didn't *feel* alive...

Mi'shaar gritted his teeth, "I'm tempted to just tell you that *that's impossible*. But it does explain how we had an oxygen leak.." His face was grim and serious as he thought.

"There must be another explanation," Thaani said, "if this is really a sand shifter then that would mean that it was stowed away on *The Uniter* for at least a week? That can't be."

Mi'shaar went quiet for a moment as the sand trickle continued to fall. The floor between them was increasingly covered in earthy tones. He heaved anxiously and through his head back. Finally he spoke.

"*It could be.* A shifter could've been hiding in our defense system," he said grimly, "*The Uniter's* shield is old and obsolete... and I almost never check it. There's no reason to. But if a shifter was hiding up there then it makes sense that a few living grains would eventually get whirled into the hardware of our life-support chassis. We have vents and valves that work the oxygen up there."

The brothers looked at each other, frowning, serious. A few small piles formed in the center of the deck.

"It's a sand shifter then," Thaani said, "...and now they're moving."

Several small piles of sand began to roll about rhythmically, glimmering in dull shades of gold and magenta. They moved slowly and aimlessly on the control room floor.

"At least it's gathering here, right in front of us," Mi'shaar said, "We can start to contain it."

Mi'shaar and Thani had battled sand shifters before—each young man sported multiple scars from their encounters with desert-dwelling monsters at home. They were particularly familiar with sand shifters—a relatively common creature. One could be removed safely if handled with proper skill and circumstances allowed. But the brothers also knew that a shifter could be fast and deadly when angered.

"There's no open desert to release it into, Mi'shaar." Thaani said nervously.

"I know—" Mi'shaar said, "but all I can think of now is to gather it."

A little dune was rolling towards the kitchen. He gently kicked it with his foot. It rolled back to join the others. Little sand hills continued to move about the control room floor. Thaani caught a few with the sides of his feet, too, nudging them towards the center of the floor.

An idea struck him.

"The garbage shoot!" He said, "First we gather it all together here, and then guide it through the halls using the vacuum transit system. When it gets angry enough to start attacking us we can suck it into the garbage shoot and then release it into space. What do you think?"

"I *think* we'll be dead." Mi'shaar snapped, "The garbage shoot doesn't just release stuff into naked space like that. It'll just sit there and then come right back up. *It's sand.*"

"But you can use the ax from Baba—"

"We'll be dead by level three!" Mi'shaar cried, "You think we can handle this beast for five levels?"

There were about a dozen little piles now, the largest was the size of Thaani's heel. He felt like he was playing soccer with the small dunes. And the two brothers danced about the deck as they continued their nervous conversation.

"We can survive until level three at most—" Mi'shaar began, "And on that level," he paused as he kicked a relatively large sand hill, "*The Uniter* has a polymorph tray. We can generate a water tank to hose this guy down. Once he's mud, our problem is solved."

"The polymorph tray!" Thaani cried, "why didn't I think of that?"

"Because we never use it," Mi'shaar said, "but I think it's pretty simple. It has an old-fashioned interface, but you can figure it out."

Thaani tensed as he saw the largest pile roll towards the kitchen, its dust and grains swirling in small clouds about its body. He dived onto the floor in front of it, using his entire upper body to block it. Heavy pockets of sand slapped him painfully—but Thaani was relieved to see it slowly move back to the center.

There were three piles of that size. And yet the sand trickle from the ceiling continued to fall. It was only getting bigger.

"We need a shovel." Thaani cried. He was referring to one of the large traditional shovels from back home that were used to control large sand shifters and similar problems. But of course, they had nothing like that aboard *The Uniter*. There was supposedly no need for it.

"The shifter piles are getting too large!" Thaani said. He found himself bracing against the onslaught of another large pile that threatened to seep into the crevices of the command line. Thaani rushed for it.

"Catch this—" Mi'shaar said.

Thaani paused just long enough to catch a giant piece of curved hardware that came flying at his face. It was bigger than him, but he caught it well. Grasping the large curved piece, he swung it in a broad swipe at the misguided dune. The beast heeded the move and turned back to the center of the floor. Thaani took a split second to look at his new tool. He was holding a door. The hinges were torn. Mi'shaar was holding one, too. He had somehow managed to pry off two large doors from elsewhere on the ship.

The shifter piles finally approached one another in a glitter of gold, tawny brown, and warm magenta, rising into a whirlwind, blending together in a scratchy, noisy flurry. All the brothers could do was stare, grim and tight-lipped. When it finally settled into one pile, it was the size of Thaani and Mi'shaar together.

The two paced carefully about the creature, observing its movements. It slid over to the other side, heading for the kitchen.

The brothers stood side by side in front of the kitchen and held the two doors adjacent, creating a curved half circle. The giant sand pile slammed into it and once again turned around.

"The trickle's done!" Thaani shouted, "Let's move it!"

The sand shifter had grown to be twice the size of the two young men. In spite of this, the brothers' teamwork wielding the two doors proved incredibly effective. They succeeded in the first part of their plan. Guiding it through the vacuum tube to the lower level—then down the hall to the next transit hatch. They were getting close to level three and the key to their salvation—the polymorph tray.

In the hall just before the last vacuum tube, the shifter started to show signs of resistance. It wanted to seep into the wall. The brothers, of course, stopped it.

It tried again.

They stopped it again.

The beast stopped moving for a moment, appearing as a motionless hillock of sand, the crest of its dune nearly touching the ceiling. The brothers watched with bated breath. Out of the hillock, a row of rocky-looking stalagmites formed and solidified. It was the first sign of violence. The stalagmites were sharp, and the beast began to thrust them about in a stabbing motion, its movements propelled by tumbling waves of sand. The brothers dodged successfully, but it left dents and deep scratches all about the corridor.

They had only a moment to breathe while the shimmering earthy monster recollected itself. It was apoplectic. It formed more stalagmites and twisted around as though looking about itself. The large sand wall turned and towered menacingly over Thaani. The desert youth somersaulted across the room in a flash.

The shifter chased him in a violent fury. Thaani dodged skillfully, but the earthy monster appeared to have also learned. It twisted and turned quickly and kept close to the young man's heels.

Thaani realized it was an opportunity to guide it once more. Mi'shaar was clearly thinking the same thing. He was holding the hatch for the vacuum tube open, yelling something.

Thaani dove into it, yanking the vacuum tubing over himself. He was sucked out of the room. He landed on the next level down of *The Uniter* and sprung up immediately. He covered his face as a large pile of sand came flying through the tubing after him. The passage through the vacuum tube had disoriented the furious beast. It was just a sand pile again, its dusty clouds needed time to settle. Mi'shaar quickly joined in the sand pile and they both clambered out while the beast was stunned.

But they were on the third level—and almost had their secret weapon. Thaani raced towards the polymorph tray.

The monstrous dune reformed its sharp tools and sliced towards Thaani again. He dodged, but not quickly enough. A rocky stalagmite sliced through his left leg. He gasped in pain, and gawked at the shifter. It was collecting itself again, but had left a nasty imprint of the blow on the corner of the hall where Thaani had been a second before. The ship was damaged, deeply.

"We're gonna die!" Thani cried. If the walls caved in, they'd be dead in a second.

"The water tank!" Mi'shaar screamed as he stood over the shifter pile. It was starting to form sharp parts again. Using one of the doors he'd torn off the ship, Mi'shaar swiped and cut apart the creature. The creature was so furious at this point that there was no fear that it would scatter and seep away. It was angry and wanted blood. The monster coalesced quickly, forming another large dune.

Thaani crawled up the morphing tray command line, wincing and leaning on his good leg.

It was a new device for Thaani. He stared at the screen. His brother was right. The morphing tray was as old fashioned as a piece of technology could be. It was physical, not holographic, and connected to the wall by an arm. It had a dun-colored schema, a pitch-black command line with a blinking green rectangle, and a keyboard with raised square buttons that he had to punch in with his fingers. He quickly figured it out.

He punched in a command for a water tank, and the device beeped. He stared as the device continued to... do nothing. Instead, its interface asked for more creative materials. Thaani glanced behind himself. Mi'shaar and the golden monster engaged swiftly. Thaani turned back to the screen in horror.

"It's not working." His voice cracked, "Mi'shaar! It's all... out of juice!"

"What!"

Thaani looked back at the morphing tray's command line in disbelief. "It says all its creative material has been used up over the past hundred and forty hours on... foreign books...? The Maryam & Ahmed Magical Meet Cute duology..? Elves and Lovers..? The Twelve books of the Romance Bears on Mars..." The list went on and on. There were hundreds of similar products listed on the morphing tray's screen. A sense of doom crept into Thaani's chest.

"How could that happen?" Mi'shaar screamed.

"It says we have to feed it back at least 200 pages of—

"

A rock slapped Thaani in the face. Blood filled his mouth. He tried to dodge, but in his injured state he was too slow and found himself covered in trickles of blood. He wasn't sure how it happened, but an excruciating pain in his side suggested he'd broken a rib. When he turned to see the beast behind him, but found that he was not under attack. The corridor was full of angry clouds of sand that contracted into solid rock and then scattered into dust. This amorphous rocky cloud-thing chased Mi'shaar, close on his every move. The few rocks that had injured Thaani were collateral.

Thaani thought that this could very well be the end of them both. He was aware that his brother, no matter how skillful, would not be able to keep ahead of the sand shifter for much longer. They were trapped. And when Mi'shaar got tired, the beast would get him. And then it would seek another opponent. He didn't see a way out, and he was starting to get dizzy.

Thaani was so affected by his injuries that he barely understood what happened next. In the midst of the withering whirlwind and crashing rocks, his brother landed in front of him. Mi'shaar grabbed him and rolled him across the floor against the other side of the hall. Thaani hit into the wall and was stunned.

Mi'shaar screamed, "The escape pod latch!"

His brother had deposited him beside the hatch leading out to the escape pod. His brother dove towards the hatch. The sand shifter was right behind him, just as it had chased Thaani earlier. But this time it was Thaani who slammed the latch. It sprang open and curly-haired Mi'shaar dove through, followed immediately by the beast.

Thaani dragged himself up to gaze out the window into the escape pod. The sand shifter was once again disoriented and had once again become a large lifeless pile of sand. It clearly did not enjoy the pneumatic pressure of *The Uniter's* internal transit system. Thaani didn't see his brother. But he could see that the vacuum tubing that connected the escape pod to the ship was already destroyed.

Mi'shaar reappeared in his space suit, flying through the exterior of *The Uniter*. He was wearing a thin emergency helmet and carrying the giant ax from their baba. He perched on the arm that held the pod to the rest of their ship, raised up the ax, and lurched forward to strike at it with all his strength.

The pod shook gently. In a minute the hinge had come loose. Mi'shaar held on to his harness as he swung to the side of the arm, and began alternating between aggressively hacking at the thing and using his hands to yank the nuts from the bolts.

Through the window, Thaani could peer into the escape pod. The sand shifter was slowly waking up. Thaani gaped through his bruised and swelling face. In the center of the pod was a pile of books.

Was that all the polymorph material?

It had to be. He knew he hadn't seen all those books before—and there was no way any of his siblings had brought them on board from the home planet. It was a very *large* pile of books.

Through the large translucent windows of the escape pod, Thaani could see lumps of dust and sand begin to race about in another whirlwind. As the force of the sands grew, it yanked pages and bindings off of the books in the pile. The books tore apart, their yellowed pages of various size flung about, circling and slapping against the interior of the pod soundlessly.

Thaani suddenly realized something. *Raabi'a was addicted to romance novels!*

***

Inside her cubby, Raabi'a was getting to a really steamy part in her book. The boy and girl were about to kiss. *Finally!* She was absorbed, and would have remained so, but something didn't feel right. A little bit of shaking was normal for the escape pod, since it was only loosely connected to the ship. She had always rolled with the waves, unperturbed and undistracted from her reading. She didn't mind how cramped the cubby was, but she felt that the pod was shaking more violently than usual. She put the book down, feeling both petulant and curious at the same time. It was the loud scratching, slapping, and whirling that finally inspired her to act. She slid open the cache door and saw what looked to be an earthy whirlwind.

A sand shifter? In the pod with her?

That didn't make any sense. She reached her entire arm out of the cache and grazed the side of the whirlwind with the tips of her fingers. What resulted was a horrible burning sting. She looked at her hand to see the tips of her fingers covered in paper-thin lacerations, forming tiny beads of blood.

Her heart sank. She wrenched herself out of her hiding place. The sand continued to whirl about, so she pressed herself against the window of the pod avoiding its touch. She looked up at the home ship. As clear as ever, she saw the two faces of her brothers—Thaani and Mi'shaar. Thaani was inside *The Uniter*, on the third level. His face was covered in dark red mud and he was hunched over, holding on to the sides of the window as though he could barely stand. Mi'shaar was in his space suit, clinging on to the arm that connected the escape pod to *The Uniter*. He held the giant ceremonial ax from home, the one that the nomadic peoples used in rituals. And he was using it to hack away at the final cords that remained on the arm that connected the escape pod.

Raabi'a and Thaani both screamed, waving their arms, and slamming their respective glasses. It was no use. Mi'shaar didn't hear either of them. He was determined, and he was not the distractible type. The last few strands that held the arm together were coming undone.

In one more moment, Mi'shaar had completed his task. Raabi'a watched as her eldest brother finally lifted up his head. He clutched the ax under his armpit. Then he turned around. His eyes met Raabi'a's, and his face slowly transformed into one of horror. A painful lump formed in Raabi'a's throat. She stared at both her brothers in silence as the pod slowly floated farther and farther way. And the sandy beast continued to rage.

Hot Date With a Book

By Shayla McBride

Her nose was in a book, as usual. Trying to get her attention would take more than a call from the bottom of the stairs.

But…one last try. “Pizza! Your favorite, with pepperoni.”

Silence.

Louder. Could he hide his desperation? “Get it while it's hot!”

“Uh-huh…”

Resentment swept through him, darkening his vision. The stairs suddenly seemed to stretch up into a moonless night, only the single light gleaming off her pale hair like a distant star. An unreachable star. His free hand tightened into a fist. Slowly, silently, he pounded it against his thigh.

“Going, going, gone!”

“…a minute…”

The damn books. Her damn books. No more conversation, no more laughter. Glances once warm now only a quick, uninterested flick of her eyes. Now only the bent head, hair curtaining her face as if even looking away from the false world she inhabited was preferable to reality. The reality they once shared. Now fantasy consumed her, her conversation one way as she murmured to herself phrases she found delightful, her trills of laughter for the hidden amusements on the page.

"Just got it from Enzo's, best in the world!"

"Mmmm…"

So many books. Stacked on each stair tread, three, four, five, six of the damned things. In all, nearly a hundred. Plus the stacks on tables, the couch, the hutch, the kitchen counter. Next to her bed, some dogeared, some still in their packages yet to be devoured. She would finish one, sigh, and pick up another. Her satisfied sighs used to be for a different reason.

"Stop it. Not tonight, I can't put this down, it's so interesting…"

He swallowed, razors in his throat. That had been the final put-down, the one that broke his heart and almost destroyed the will to hang in there. His leg hurt, a dull throb from knee to hip that matched the throb in his temples. He put the container down at his feet, picked up a book, methodically ripped out the pages. They twisted from his hand, blanketing the floor. He grunted as he emptied the first, the second, the third…

"Sure you won't join me?"

"When I finish this…"

Another flutter of pages. His feet were covered by drifts of ragged-edge paper. His breath was as ragged, loud in the stillness. Still he reached – the fifth stair step now, he thought with savage satisfaction – and grabbed another book, ripped the cover off, then pages and pages and damn her and her damn books…

"Last chance! Join me!" Sixth step, half way. Would she meet him half way? "C'mon, give the real world a chance!"

"This is the real world, silly…"

"You're gonna regret it, I promise you!"

"…Uh-huh…"

With a flourish, he tossed the pathetic last pages into the air. Watched them slip-slide onto his feet, down the stairs, out of sight. Made a sound he didn't recognize, between bitter laughter and a defeated sob. Another man he could've fought, could've defeated. A book? Paper and ink and dreams? Never.

Not bothering to mute his steps, he descended the stairs, picked up the container. Removed the cap.

Poured the gasoline on the steps, the walls, the paper. Flicked the lighter. Turned away as the flames blossomed and snapped. Papers shriveled as the flames leaped from step to step. He stifled a shrill giggle.

He had a date with a pepperoni pizza.

Familiar

By Lucy A.J. Tew

"May!"

I lean on the bottom step as I wait for her to respond. I try to listen for some indication or sound of movement—a door opening, or water running—but nothing. My dork-a-saurus best friend is somewhere up there, probably in her bedroom, *probably* working on something for school. Again. Her nose in a book, as usual. Trying to get her attention is going to take more than just a call from the bottom of the stairs—it always does when she's in the zone. Nonetheless, I call her name again, just in case.

"May!"

May isn't May's real name, by the way. It's just a nickname, and mine is June, or sometimes it's Junebug. Neither of us have birthdays in May or June (we're both Scorpios, of course), and after all this time being best friends, I honestly can't remember how we got in the habit of calling each other these names anymore. She just started calling me Junebug, so I've always called her *May*, even though it's a little hard to pronounce with my accent. May never makes jokes about the way I say her name, though. Anyway, my point is, *May* just suits her.

It's a personality thing—hard to explain.

"May! Maaaa-aaaay," I sing-song, loud as I can.

No response. I roll my eyes and give up, setting off quickly and quietly up the carpeted stairs. At the top, I poke my head around the doorway of May's dad's office. I'm extra careful as I do this, not wanting to be noticed in case he's working, too. But there's no sign of either of them. He's probably at work or in the yard, which is just as well, because he and I get along about as well as oil and water. We've quite literally disliked each other from the first instant we met, even though I was really young.

It's a personality thing—hard to explain.

He once went ballistic at *me* when May accidentally left a set of fully washed bird bones on the bathroom sink. He completely refused to listen when May and I tried to explain that it was part of a spell we'd been casting. He didn't care—or he didn't listen, which is basically the same thing, and May got grounded for two weeks, even though *nothing* happened, good or bad. The spell flopped (not enough rosemary), but nobody got listeria, or whatever bacterial misery he was shouting about.

As this memory surfaces, however, I decide to check the bathroom next. May's been going through an *experimental* phase, hair-wise. I'm her best friend in the world, so you'd have to put me on a torture rack to get me to admit this to anybody, but her latest home dye job (a flattish black) and attempt at cutting her own hair has her looking a little less *Teen Witch* and a little more *Teen Wolf.* But I can't blame her—I do most of my own self-care routines, too, and I've definitely let my anxiety win before—and I haven't even had the year May's had. After all, my mom left so long ago I don't even remember her. May's got tons of memories of her mom, but now most of them involve hospitals, and chemo, and hospice care. I honestly don't know which version of not having a mom is worse—probably hers.

Which is the whole reason I'm even here, risking the chance of May's dad seeing me and giving me the nasty looks he probably thinks I don't notice. It's like he just can't stop himself from implying I'm some kind of filthy animal, just for existing in his plush carpeted paradise. He's had it out for me ever since he found out where my mom and I lived before I got fostered. Classist asshole.

For the record, May's mom never used to treat me like that—she'd hug me like I was her own kid, just like May. I was there in the room when May said goodbye to her, too – because that's what you do for your best friend, and someone who treats you like their own kid.

Okay, now I'm just making myself sad, especially walking down this hall full of old family pictures and photos of May's mom. I shake myself. Where the hell is my best friend?

"Ugh, *May!*" I groan, louder than ever as I see she's not in the bathroom. I march straight down the hall to her bedroom door, which is slightly ajar. I shoulder it open so I can stride inside with a dramatic flourish, which always makes May laugh.

She's curled up on the cushion of her window seat, where she keeps all her stuffies and the soft fleece blankets that people insist on giving as presents to other people they don't know very well. Usually, when we hang out in her room, the window seat is my spot, or we squeeze in together—but she's been spending a lot of time perched here lately, reading *The Practical Witch's Guide.* Her mom gave her that one, I remember. She used to love that May was into witchy things, and had never given up believing in magic.

"Hey!" I snap, and May startles, finally looking at me. Her face lights up like a Fourth of July sparkler, her frown of concentration evaporating when she sees me.

You know what? All the people at school who are snotty and awful to May will never get to have *this* moment—which sucks for them, because having a best friend who looks at you like *this*, just because you walked into a room, is the best feeling in the entire world.

"Hi, Junie," she says happily, beaming as if she hasn't heard me yelling for her all the way through the house – which she probably hasn't. *In the zone,* I think.

What a dork-a-saurus. I narrow my eyes and twitch my long tail, then dart forward and leap up onto the window seat beside her. I butt my head hard against her knee and pretzel myself sideways, landing with a *flump* in my favorite patch of sun and rolling over to show her my soft, tiger-striped belly.

Murder at the NAA

By Melody Friedenthal

I was leaning back in my office chair, eyes closed and with Kissy-the-Kitty purring gently in my lap, when I heard an odd, indistinct sound. It rose to a minor crescendo before cutting off abruptly. It seemed out of place among the usual clankings and ventilation noises of this, the fourth sub-basement of the National Antiquarian Archives. I sat up, alert, and peered around my office, wondering where the sound had come from.

"Office" was a misnomer—I had just a corner of the floor to call my own, no permanent walls, just a six-foot high partition to separate my personal territory from that of my colleagues. Most of my teammates had desks in this first room, too—at least the human ones did. The felines owned the entire space, of course. We humans were archivists, conservators, catalogers, historians, and researchers. The cats interned as mousers and comic relief, and like interns everywhere, were paid in munchies.

From my desk I could see through the wide entryway into the small workshop where examinations and repairs were done.

Beyond that was a door leading to the humongous storage area of the repository proper, at least one floor of it. Stretching out for almost half a mile, it contained rows upon rows of archived books, ephemera, images, records, maps, diaries, manuscripts, and government documents. All those items were stored in a vast array of telescoping bookcases, display cases, shelving, work tables, and supply racks. I walked these corridors daily, in awe of this treasury nestled deep under the city's streets.

Some minutes passed and, when the odd sound didn't repeat, I mentally shrugged and took another sip of the day's first mug of chamomile tea—or, as Aub sniffily denigrated it—"an herbal infusion." The archive was climate-controlled but not for the benefit of the living, so I drank hot tea all day to keep warm. My right-hand desk drawer contained an assortment of teabags, loose tea leaves in tins, and an infuser or two. On top of my desk was a mug-tree. In addition to the mug I was currently using—a black-and-gold mug with the "NAA" logo —I also had a cream one embossed with a Little Green Alien, and a hand-thrown over-sized one that Zinka had given me for my birthday three months earlier.

While reviewing the requests and work orders that had come in overnight, I petted Kissy, who expected it as her due. She rubbed her head against my chin and purred. Black-haired and sleek, her left front paw was white, a pattern shared with her sister, Hissy-the-Other-Kitty. Hissy was just as sleek, but pearl-gray. They were aptly named, although I don't know by whom. Hissy was probably off somewhere hissing at an archivist or stalking shadows, but definitely letting everyone in eyeshot know she was of the tribe of tiger.

Which reminded me: I checked the paper calendar on my desktop, and called out, "Hey, Laurel, your turn to change the litter box."

I kept the kitty-calendar on paper because the cats officially didn't exist and electronic records could be hacked or accessed by management. Immediate management was Clarence Pericles Aubrey and that bow-tied recluse rarely left his office upstairs on the third sub-basement. When he did though, he was as silent as Hissy on her little padded feet, so the rest of us tried to keep a lookout for him, warning the rest of the staff when he shambled out of his (enclosed) office.

One time Aub unexpectedly showed up at my desk and asked about the curious notations on my calendar. As straight-faced as I could, I told him it was a period-tracker. Momentary confusion turned to rosy embarrassment and, mumbling, he retreated back upstairs to his lair.

Laurel didn't respond. Maybe she hadn't heard me – or maybe she wasn't in yet? I leaned out and peered down the row of cubicles: no Laurel. She'd been with us only seven months. Since I'm the group supervisor I'd sat in when Aub interviewed her. She arrived wearing a navy-blue linen suit, white blouse, and small pearl earrings. Her brown hair had been up in a demure bun. I could see Aub thinking "*professional.*" Her credentials were excellent and she was well-spoken, so Aub and I agreed she'd make a good replacement for Gaston, who'd retired. Sixty days later, when her probation was completed, she came in with purple hair, a nose ring, a punk skirt, and thigh-high black leather boots. Aub was never the same.

I worked for another hour, updating the database. Kissy wandered away. Then I went through the two doorways into the actual repository, the overhead lights turning on automatically one by one as I penetrated further into the stacks. When I reached Aisle 15, Rank B, Case Two, I cranked the handle that sent that shelving unit sliding on its tracks, compacting the rows on one side, and dilating them on the other, like an accordion. This feat of engineering maximized the usable space for collection storage. The more modern setup upstairs was controlled electrically, but on B4 and B5, it was still manual cranking all around. I sighed; the upper-body workout cut down on the need for a gym membership.

I needed the safety ladder to reach the specific storage slot. After retrieving the requested portfolio, I returned to my desk to review it before sending it upstairs to the anonymous patron who had called for it. Well, he, she, or xe had to sign for it, but credential checking was the purview of the Upstairs team. For those of us who worked Downstairs, every patron was an anonymous ghost.

Walking back to my desk, I passed by each of my teammates' cubicles and noted that I was still alone on B4. Was today a holiday I had forgotten about? To my embarrassment, that had happened once when I was first hired—oh-so-many-years-ago. The first couple of weeks went well, but nobody mentioned to me that the staff had the Friday before Labor Day off, in addition to the regular three-day weekend. I had come in first thing in the morning and worked for several hours before I realized something was amiss. On the Tuesday following the holiday my teammates had a good laugh at my expense. To add to my chagrin, I realized I could have avoided the cost of a full day of baby-sitting.

A few minutes later, the elevator doors opened and Laurel exited. Today her hair was half orange and half hot-pink, and her earrings were silver unicorns. She looked a little frayed around the edges.

"I was looking for you—you've got kitty litter duty this week."

Not her favorite thing, she being a dog person.

"No, I don't, Rachel," she snarled at me. "Zinka was supposed to do it last week but she was on vacation so I did it for her. We exchanged weeks."

"Okay," I agreed. "Have you seen Zinka, then? It's been very quiet down here. I haven't seen Val or Marty yet today either."

"No clue." She shrugged, dropped her tote on her desk, and went over to one of the work tables. I knew she was restoring a seventeenth-century Book of Common Prayer. She brought it back to her desk and, picking up a magnifying glass, set to evaluating it.

Where was everybody else?

At eleven thirty Val arrived. "Second damned flat tire this month!"

"Oh, that sounds expensive. Did you see Marty on your way in? Or Zinka?"

"Nope to both. I tried calling Zinka to tell her I'd be late because we were supposed to work together to catalog some colonial clay pipes, but she didn't answer." Val dropped his stylish European backpack on his desk and went to grab some coffee. I knew not to get between the man and his coffee. His accent was most apparent—and most delightful—when he talked about roasting beans.

Marty, who never took the elevator, came out just then from the stairwell next to Laurel's desk. His t-shirt read "Live Long and Prosper" and matched his russet hair. He was carrying a flat box. I could tell from the logo that it contained donuts, so I inferred he'd just come down from street level. He opened the box and offered me a donut. I chose a chocolate-glazed one, took a bite, and mumbled my thanks.

"Marty, I hate to say this, since I accepted your donut-bribe, but you really need to be here on time."

He smiled brightly and held out the box to Laurel.

Zinka didn't show, nor did she call in. There was no cell coverage in the sub-basements, so we each had land-lines on our desks. The only phone call that came in that morning was from Aub, who was checking up on a supply order. Trying to balance the demands of friendship against HR department policy, I hesitated, then phoned Zinka, but no one answered.

I had lunch by myself in our kitchenette, still wondering where Zinka was and growing a bit concerned. I barely tasted my tuna-on-rye. Done, I went into the ladies' room and took care of the kitty-litter myself, refreshing the cats' water bowls, and refilling their food dispensers with their favorite fare; also tuna-flavored.

After lunch, my next task was to retrieve a file of rare early American manuscripts attributed to one of the founding fathers. Those holdings were archived one floor down, in the fifth sub-basement. I took a cart with me to save myself from having to carry a heavy box. I put my tablet on its shiny steel top and headed for the elevator, where I flashed my electronic badge past the magnetic card reader. It chimed, I entered, and pressed the button labeled "B5."

The only sounds I heard on B5 were the cart's squeaky wheels and the hiss of the ventilation shafts. Or maybe it was Hissy, who might be planning her leap onto my head from the top of a storage unit at that very moment. One could never tell. I kept my head down.

The database record said that the file I needed was in Aisle 56, which I knew was at the opposite end from the elevator. I was puffing a bit by the time I got there, passing by what seemed like endless beige walls. Arriving at the designated aisle, I cranked the control handle at its endcap so I could access the right storage space. I double-checked my tablet: five cases in, and seven up from the floor.

As I cranked, the rows to my left slowly compressed. I idly looked up at the opposite wall where there hung an oil painting of some previous Chief Archivist, and I absently wondered what he had done to be exiled down here.

After all these years I knew subconsciously how many times I needed to crank to fully open an aisle. So I was surprised when the steel shelving unit came to a halt prematurely, without the full compaction I expected.

I cranked in the opposite direction so I could see what was obstructing the works.

And in the aisle just to the left of my target, I found Zinka, her torso compacted, in the aisle that would not. I recognized her blouse, with its red and black embroidery, one of several she'd imported from her birth country. But there seemed to be more red than I remembered… and then some part of my brain noted the small pool of congealing blood on the concrete floor around her.

Hissy was also at the far end of that aisle, her ears lying flat on her head, and her back arched. She hissed at me.

***

I stared stupidly at Zinka for a few seconds. I think I whimpered. Then I ran all the way back the way I'd come, gasping and thinking inanely that I shouldn't have had that donut. When I finally arrived at the elevator, I slammed my fist into the call button. The electronic sign above the closed gray metal doors signaled "1"—ground level.

I watched in frustration but the indicator didn't change. I ran to the stairwell and shouted up for Laurel. There was no response. I'm sure her nose was in a book, as usual. Trying to get her attention would take more than just a call from the bottom of the stairs. So I panted my way up the stairs, hauling myself up the spiral and grasping the handrail in a death-grip. Bad choice of words!

I stumbled onto B4 and called out, my voice squeaky and panicked. Laurel and Marty rushed in together from the workroom. I didn't see Val anywhere.

While I was trying to catch my breath, I remembered the odd sound I had heard that morning. My heart skipped a beat… I realized that it might have been Zinka calling for help or screaming in fear. An accident? Impossible; it took real, sustained effort to turn those cranks. But, if not an accident…

And then it occurred to me—none of my teammates had an alibi…

Grandmother's Library

By Marie LeClaire

With a trembling hand, Elaina turned the last page, conscious of the time. She knew she was cutting it close but she could feel the wind on her face and the refreshing coolness of the water, and she hadn't been able to put it down.

> Sukara stood at the edge of the cliff, peering down intently into the clear blue of Yokama Bay. She waited anxiously as the sun glistened off the soft ripples of the water's surface. She knew Rem was hot on her tail. Then she saw it. A flash of light coming from the sandy ocean floor. At that instant, she leapt off the cliff, gaining as much distance as she could from the rocks before straightening out her body, raising her arms together over her head and tilting herself down towards the sea.

She had heard the jeep crest the hill just as her toes left the cliff's edge. She wished she could see the look on Rem's face. A good imagination would have to substitute. She allowed herself a slight smile as she inhaled deeply. She hit the water like a guided missile, knowing exactly where her target was.

The fishermen on the shore gasped when they saw her sailing through the air. No one dives from that height. Almost no one. They instantly recognized Sukara. Her graceful silhouette was unmistakable, just like her mother's, and her mother's before her. But what was she after today? Here? Another clue? Some launched their boats to wait by the wake of concentric circles identifying her point of entry. They watched as her rippling image searched the ocean floor thirty feet below.

It was almost ten minutes before she broke the surface again, letting out a long whistling breath that echoed off the cliff. It was the siren's song of the Ama, fabled Japanese pearl divers. Held high in her fist were a half dozen gold coins.

"She did it! She did it!" the fisherman called out. They jumped and danced in their boats, some tumbling into the water with excitement. Finally! The boon this little village was hoping for.

Back on shore, Nako sat with a net stretched out over his lap, a darning needle frozen in mid-stitch and eyes fixed on the bay. When Sukara breached the surface, he jumped up on his rickety legs and began to dance. He turned to Yuiko. "Go to town. Run. Tell everyone. Sukara has found the treasure. Bring food for a feast."

Crowds gathered quickly, hundreds of people bringing food and music. A team of young men dug a fire pit on the beach while women pampered Sukara with sweet-smelling blossoms and cool drinks. Everyone in town was there, except for Rem and his crew. He had been spotted at the top of the cliff, watching Sukara fall through the air, but he hadn't dared circle around to the beach. He knew he was not welcome.

When the feast was ready, Sukara wound her way back to the clifftop and graced the crowds with a celebratory dive, this time dressed in the traditional white garb of Ama. This dive was purely for show. The crowds

> went wild and rushed her even before she could get out of the water. She had brought good fortune to the village and touching her would bless them even further. The village would prosper once again and Sukara was glad she could be a part of it.

Elaina exhaled a long whistling breath as she closed the book and maneuvered her wheelchair onto the lift that gave her access to the upper shelves. It traveled in tracks secured to the walls both horizontally and vertically, and traversed the entire library collection of four thirty-foot-high bookcase walls. Using the electric control pad, she made her way to the book's assigned spot and was tucking it in place with trembling hands when she heard her grandson call.

"Grammy, it's time for dinner," Harold called up the stairs. His voice echoed off the large, wood-paneled foyer. The library was just at the top of the staircase but if her nose was in a book, as usual, trying to get her attention would take more than just a call from the first floor. He didn't understand what was so compelling about those old books. Sometimes Grammy would talk as if she had lived the stories herself. Why didn't she enjoy the home theater they had put in or the cozier TV room on the first floor? The terrace and gardens had been modified for her wheelchair and family would gladly take her anywhere she wanted to go. Yet she insisted on her books, spending hours behind the library's closed door.

When she didn't come out to the landing, he headed up the sweeping main staircase. Elaina was settling the lift back at floor level when he opened the library door.

“There you are, Gram. Dinner’s ready.” He walked over to assist her off the lift. “I don’t know what you see in all these old books.”

She nodded and smiled weakly, which was the best she could do since Parkinson’s had taken the use of her vocal cords.

Harold rounded the chair and started pushing her to the elevator that would take them to the dining room. “Hey Gram? Is your hair wet?”

She smiled again. At least she could still read.

Regret

By Dana Norton

Looking back, *I wish to God* I hadn't done it. It will haunt me for the rest of my life. Still, at the time, it seemed absolutely necessary.

Let me tell you why I was driven to do what I did. I wonder what you would have done in my place.

***

It was a cold, blustery evening in January. Half-frozen, I hurried up the curving, crushed-shell walk to the front door of Isobel's two-story cottage.

Emotionally, I felt nice and warm. I was looking forward to a fun evening with Isobel, and at the moment my life was going well. At twenty-five I was thrilled to be on my own, living in a charming New England seaside town. I had a great job and a close circle of friends. Best of all, I had met a really wonderful, sweet guy a year ago, and we were planning to get married in the spring. It looked like I was finally putting my nightmarish past behind me.

Lights twinkled through the frost on the quaint lattice windows. Isobel's home was surrounded by lovely woods, which gave her lots of privacy and no neighbors within a mile. Inside, I knew, the living room hearth would be blazing. Her home seemed to be opening its arms to me, saying, "Come in. Here you will be safe and warm."

I banged twice with the nineteenth-century brass knocker, and a few seconds later Isobel appeared in the doorway.

"Hey, Jen. Come on in. I have good news!"

"What is it?"

"Later," said Isobel, with a maddening smile. "I'll tell you after dinner."

"Tell me now!"

"Sorry." But she didn't look it. Her expression was almost sly. "I'll serve my news with the dessert."

Isobel was my best friend, but she could be irritating. How like her to announce that she had a surprise, then tease me by withholding it! One minute she could be sweet and supportive ("I'm so sorry you had a rough day, Jen"). The next, she could be insensitive, even taunting. Like she did with one of our friends at a gathering two weeks ago.

"Michaela, you hardly eat anything when we get together." Isobel had pointed this out with several people around. "If I didn't know better, I'd think you had an eating disorder."

Actually, Michaela *did.* And thanks to Isobel, a lot more people found out.

So why did I like Isobel so much? Maybe because she fascinated me, with her quick wit, her knowing attitude and her arresting looks. She was never boring. Deep down, I suspected my biggest reason was something different. Because of my disturbing past, I had almost no friends growing up and was incredibly lonely. But Isobel seemed to really like me. She was *my* best friend – I only hoped I was *hers.*

This evening her look was "I-really-don't care" artsy. She was a few years older than I, tall and slim, with dark hair that flowed over her shoulders like a river, wavy and wild. Her eyes were the palest blue. She was all in black—wide drawstring pants with a soft, oversized hand-knitted sweater. Completing the outfit was an antique necklace of irregular turquoise stones, huge, textured silver hoop earrings and the longest scarf I had ever seen, its frayed black and white strands almost kissing her bare feet. Next to her I always felt dumpy and ill-dressed. I also felt quite inferior as a writer: she was published; I was not.

But writing was not Isobel's only talent. This evening we sat down to a five-star, home-cooked meal of salmon-and-leek pie and arugula salad, accompanied by a bottle of sparkling white wine. After the meal, like the upper-crust characters in an old English novel, we retired to the drawing—I mean, living—room to take our coffee.

"So Jen, here's my news." Isobel dropped with a flourish into the most comfortable armchair. "I'm writing my first novel! The first three chapters are done. My agent is going to look at the draft and send it along to publishers."

A novel? Isobel had made her name writing a couple of very successful cookbooks. Why was she switching genres?

"With a novel you can do anything you want," she said, reading my mind. "Cookbooks are *so* confining. But a novel, well, you can make up the whole story. Use whatever ingredients you want. Best of all, you can do anything with the characters." She took a sip of her coffee and leaned forward. "You can even base them on people you know."

Isobel was looking at me so intently. Why?

"I'm going to read you the first three chapters. Of course, since you haven't published anything yet, I'll have to take any feedback with a grain of salt."

And rub it directly into the wound, I thought.

But we often read our works-in-progress to each other. So I stretched out comfortably on Isobel's long velour sofa, anticipating the journey. I had no inkling then how riveting it would be.

"Chapter 1," Isobel began, settling back into her chair.

> *Alyssa gives her long blond hair a final pat in the mirror, shrugs into her black bomber jacket and leaves the apartment. She knows what she has to do, but she isn't looking forward to it. She fervently hopes she is making the right decision. She is going to Parker to tell him the terrible thing she has learned about Mari, his fiancé.*

An okay start, I thought.

Isobel read on, painting a picture of Alyssa, a young professional living in New York City. Alyssa discovers that her best friend, Mari, has a secret past – a truly horrifying one. She feels that the young woman's fiancé has the right to know who Mari really is.

And who is Mari, really?

The daughter of a serial killer.

Oh, god!

Isobel read on. She described how Alyssa discovers Mari's secret after snooping around in her bedroom. Below a tangle of underclothes in Mari's top drawer she finds a creased, slightly dirty manila envelope filled with old news clippings. Each one covers the same subject: the arrest, trial and conviction of one James Scott Carson. A serial killer sentenced to two life terms for the torture and murder of more than twenty-five young women in the San Francisco area a decade ago. His wife and daughter, who was only twelve at the time, assumed new identities and moved to another part of the country to make a fresh start.

> *There are photos of the killer's family, and Alyssa gasps. It can't be! But there is no mistake. The murderer's daughter, Kelly Carson, is Mari! Aside from looking older, of course, Mari's face has not changed a whole lot over the years. Alyssa can hardly take it in. Her best friend Mari is the daughter of a serial killer!*

At this point in her reading Isobel paused and looked up.

I immediately looked down. *Shock* doesn't begin to describe what I was feeling. It was incredible, *unbelievable* – but Isobel had based Mari on *me!* Suddenly Isobel's bright living room seemed to darken, the cozy fire just a faint blur in the background. It felt like the room was closing in on me.

I had never told a soul, even Isobel, about my past. Could I possibly be mistaken? Did she not know anything about it, my likeness to Mari just a coincidence? No – too many similarities. Like Mari, *my* father was a convicted serial killer. Like Mari, *my* mother had arranged new identities for us and moved us across the country. And again, like Mari, *I* had been twelve years old at the time of my father's trial.

Alyssa, the busybody protagonist, was a stand-in for Isobel. Somehow my best friend had stumbled onto my own hidden collection of yellowed news clippings.

Still, I had doubts – because of my past. Didn't I get paranoid whenever someone looked at me sideways?

Then Isobel sat upright. "A person can never escape her past," she intoned.

Her eyes bored into mine. I seemed to see a wicked gleam in them. She *knew*. And she was taunting me! But I couldn't let her know I was on to her.

Isobel gathered together the pages of her draft. "Well, what do you think?"

"Uh…your writing is great, as usual," I said quickly. "I really like the way you fleshed out the characters."

"Thank you," said Isobel graciously, like a queen accepting a compliment from a lowly courtier. "Of course, I read up a lot on serial killers and their families. My one question is, do you think the story is realistic? How likely is it that someone has a friend who's the daughter of a serial killer?"

She was twisting the knife in deeper.

I strained to keep my voice casual. "I guess it's possible. Have you shown it to anyone else?"

"No, you're the only one."

I had to get out of there, so I told Isobel I needed to get up very early the next day.

***

I was lying, of course. My fiancé, Matthew, was coming over at ten that evening.

Before he arrived, I lay face down on my bed in total darkness, thinking about the past. My father's trial was more than ten years ago, but I will never, ever forget that time in my life. How could I erase from memory the hordes of reporters closing in on my mother and me, shoving microphones in our faces as we mounted the courthouse steps? The ghoulish spectators inside the courtroom, staring with fascination at the accused killer's family? They should have felt sorry for us, we who had known nothing of my father's horrifying double life. Instead, I saw suspicion, even hatred in their eyes – we were guilty by association.

The news headlines were even worse: "Family of the murderer: *what did they know?"* And: "Do children of serial killers follow in Daddy's footsteps?"

It was a time of real darkness for me. Things got so bad that I even thought of suicide, though I never actually attempted it. But I knew that I would do anything to prevent the world from witnessing our family shame ever again.

Years went by, in my new life, and nobody discovered my true identity.

And now Isobel *knew.* And so would the whole world, as soon as her book was published. It might even turn out to be a best-seller. Vividly I pictured swarms of gleeful readers, deducing in no time that one of the characters was based on a real-life person: me.

At that point, which of my friends would want to remain pals with the daughter of a vicious killer? How long would I be allowed to keep the job I loved, teaching elementary schoolchildren?

Worst of all, what would Matthew, the love of my life, do when he learned about my father? No one in their right mind would swear eternal love to someone who may have inherited an unspeakable gene.

***

At last Matthew arrived. He was tall and lanky, with dirty-blond hair that always managed to look messy. His eyes were deep-set and hazel, a fact I appreciated each and every time I removed his glasses. He had a slightly crooked smile and was genuinely a nice guy, though hardly a pushover. He was adorable, and the best thing that had ever happened to me.

We indulged in a late-night snack of chips and salsa. Later, in bed, I brought up The Subject – indirectly, you might say.

"I heard the strangest thing today," I began, untruthfully.

"Whazzat?" mumbled Matthew, half asleep.

"You're not going to believe this. Turns out my cousin Ryan's fiancée is the daughter of a serial killer!" I had, of course, no cousin named Ryan.

"What???" Matthew bolted upright.

"The father of Ryan's girlfriend," I explained patiently, "killed, like, thirty women in the San Francisco area ten years ago."

"Wow!"

"After he was convicted, she and her mother changed their names and began a new life in another part of the country." The story rolled off my tongue.

"How did Ryan find out?" Matthew wanted to know.

"His girlfriend finally decided to tell him."

"Wow," said Matthew again, but this time less urgently. He lay back on his pillow and closed his eyes.

I wasn't done, of course.

"I wonder if she should've told Ryan?" I mused aloud, as though I were simply curious.

"Huh?" Matthew opened one eye. "Oh! Uh, yeah, of course she should've told him."

"But why??" My voice was rising dangerously. "They love each other. Her telling him is ruining their whole relationship!"

Now Matthew sat up again, fully awake. "Well—*I'd* want to know if my girlfriend had a murderer for a father!"

My heart sank. "But children of serial killers aren't necessarily evil themselves."

"That may be true, Jen," Matthew admitted. "But I'd still want to know. How could I ever trust someone again if I found out she didn't tell me something like that?"

It was time to cut to the chase.

"So…if *you* had a fiancée who told you that, what would *you* do?" I smiled to show Matthew the question was purely academic.

Without hesitation Matthew answered. "If we continued the relationship, things would just be too creepy. Any time we had an argument I'd be paranoid she'd want to kill me."

Oh, no!

"So, yeah…I'd definitely break up with her."

It felt like a knife to the heart.

***

After Matthew left the next morning, I called in sick. I had a lot to think about.

What should I do about Isobel? I knew, even if I got down on my hands and knees, she would insist on going ahead with her novel. She knew a great story when she saw one. She was ruthlessly running with it.

I could think of only one way to make sure she never finished the book. I'm sure you know what I'm talking about.

But I was no murderer like my father.

Your father killed for pleasure, a little voice inside me whispered. *You would never kill anyone for pleasure.*

This was true, but I didn't want to kill for any reason.

But when Isobel publishes her book, the little voice persisted, *the whole world will find out who you really are.*

And I would lose Matthew.

With that thought, Isobel's fate was sealed.

***

Two evenings later, around ten o'clock, I paid Isobel a surprise visit. Again the temperature hovered near zero. Again I walked the fifteen minutes to her house with feet and hands practically numb. Because of the weather, I didn't see a soul on the way. Tucked under my arm was a bottle of Ravenswood Zinfandel, one of Isobel's favorite wines. I knew she wouldn't mind the late visit – both of us were night owls. And we often dropped in on each other.

I knocked on her door. Silence. The door was unlocked so I just walked in. "Isobel?" I called from the hallway. No answer. But peering up the staircase I saw a glimmer of light.

No doubt her nose was in a book, as usual. Trying to get her attention would take more than just a call from the bottom of the stairs.

I went up. "Hey, Isobel. I knocked, but you didn't hear me. Brought something to celebrate your new book."

She was surprised, but gave me a big smile. "Jen, how nice of you. Is that my favorite wine?"

We went downstairs to the dining room, and I opened the bottle. Isobel must have had a strenuous day writing—she downed two glasses quickly. When she excused herself for a minute and left the room, I poured my untouched second drink into the pot of her Monstera Deliciosa plant. I needed my wits about me.

When Isobel came back I had her third glass of wine ready. To it I had added six grams of pentobarbital, a deadly dose that could work in as little as fifteen minutes. I knew that my friend would be too buzzed to notice the bitter taste.

Isobel plopped down in her chair and tilted it dangerously backward. She laughed loudly. “Hey, Jen, you remember the time we crashed that party on the Cape? And I told everyone you were Kim Kardashian’s college roommate?”

I remembered it, all right. Isobel had left the party first – but not before letting everyone in on our little joke. Leaving me to deal with a bunch of very annoyed drunks.

I stole a glance at Isobel. This time, maddeningly, she was sipping, not gulping, her drink.

She was becoming sentimental. “We’ve really had some fun times together.” She sloshed the wine around in her glass. “I’m so lucky to have you for a friend.”

I didn’t want to hear any of this. And why were things taking so long?

At last Isobel licked the last drops from her glass. “I don’t know why I feel so sleepy,” she mumbled, giving way to a huge yawn.

She barely managed to get up from her chair, and I saw that she could hardly walk. I helped her to her bedroom and even tucked her in. I think she was unconscious before her head hit the pillow. I went back into the kitchen, washed out our glasses, wiped clean every surface I had touched, and took the wine bottle with me.

I was actually pretty good at this! Where did I get this natural talent for deception?

I encountered no one walking home in the dark.

The next day, Isobel was discovered dead in her bed by the middle-aged woman who came to her house once a week to clean.

The police, of course, were all over it. They interviewed everyone she knew, including me, over and over. I imagined the forensics team turning her place upside down and performing numerous tests and analyses. I pictured the investigators going over her computer files with the proverbial fine-toothed comb.

Surely they must have seen the first three chapters of the novel on her laptop? But they must have attached no significance to it: on the third day after the murder, the police admitted they were no closer to identifying a suspect. They couldn't even come up with a motive.

I was safe! But then I began to be haunted by terrible nightmares. In one of them Isobel appeared before me, her black hair wild, tears streaming down her face.

Why did you do it? she wailed. *Why did you kill your best friend?*

During my waking hours, a huge weight pressed on my chest. I hardly ate anything. My eyes kept turning to the pretty, carved Russian box on my dresser that Isobel had given me on my last birthday. On my night table was a framed photo of the two of us smiling on a beach. I turned it face down, then face up again.

Once more I heard that little voice inside me.

You had to do it.

Did I? Maybe I should have waited for Isobel's book to be published and found the courage to face the consequences.

She asked for it, insisted the voice. *She was going to ruin your life.*

But – murder?

Sometimes it's the only way out.

I honestly didn't know what to think – everything was a muddle in my brain. Even so, one horrifying thought burst through loud and clear. Did I take after my father after all?

***

You're probably thinking that the right thing to do was to give myself up.

But I didn't.

I would sooner have put an end to my life than face the notoriety of a murder trial again.

Fortunately, it appeared I was not under suspicion. But there was one small matter I still needed to take of.

***

Whenever she began work on a new writing project, Isobel liked to jot down her preliminary thoughts in a small, spiral-bound notebook. I was afraid she might have written in it that she was basing Mari on me. If so, the police might eventually put two and two together.

No doubt they had already discovered the notebook. Thank heaven for Isobel's practically illegible handwriting! It would discourage even the most diligent detective from reading her notes in full. Likely they had merely skimmed through it, deciding it had no bearing on the case. Still, there was a risk that one of the investigators would peruse the notebook again, more carefully this time.

I had to destroy those notes.

A year ago Isobel and I had given each other spare keys to our homes. And so, about a week after the murder, around three a.m., I found myself for the third time taking a walk to her house. As before, I encountered no one. I let myself in and began the search.

The notebook was in the top right-hand drawer of the desk in her study. As I flipped through the pages, to my shock I started to cry. Seeing Isobel's familiar, endearing scrawl, it finally hit home that I would never see my friend again.

Don't get sentimental, I warned myself. You don't have time for that. Then I found what I was looking for. A preliminary sketch of Mari:

> *She has managed to build a decent life for herself despite always living in fear of people discovering her secret: her father was a convicted serial killer. No one, not her friends, not her fiancé, knows about her past.*

That was all. Thank goodness Isobel hadn't bothered adding that she was going to base Mari on me. The relief!

Suddenly I felt angry all over again. How cruel Isobel had been, willing to ruin my life like that! Sure, in most instances murder was wrong. But in this case I think many would agree that I had ample provocation.

Then I turned the page and saw Isobel's final entry. And froze.

> *Base Mari on the daughter of real-life serial killer Arne Johansson, who tortured and killed thirty women in Stockholm in the 1890s.*

They're Just Clouds

By C. Brian Moorhead

After four hard days of wind and rain in the spring of 1906, the weather finally broke, and James O'Rourke took advantage of the lull to survey the damage done to his farm. About half the corn crop had been washed out, but the apple trees seemed to have made it with no worse than a few downed branches. Three of his ten hens were gone, but both roosters made it. His goats seemed to have managed fine. He walked to the back edge of his property, where the meadow met the bottom of the hill, and began walking up to get a better view.

Edna Mae Howard, youngest daughter of the homesteaders across the river, sat on a rock at the crest of the hill, under the willow tree. Her nose was in a book, as usual. Trying to get her attention would take more than just a call from the bottom of the hill. O'Rourke chuckled. *To be young again and beholden only to a good book. I hope she grows up to marry a nice, educated man.*

He walked up the hill and tapped the spine of the book to get her attention. She chirped in surprise, then they both laughed.

"Whatcha reading there, Edna Mae?"

"It's a book about different types of clouds, Mr. O'Rourke. Got some real nice pictures. I wanted to see which type of cloud the rain came from. It says here they're… *cu-mu-lo-nim-bus* clouds!"

"Quite a mouthful for a raincloud! How'd you and your folks come through the storm?"

"We're all right, except our horse Barney got loose." Edna Mae said. "Pa is out chasing him down. Yourself?"

"It'll be a bad year for corn, for sure, but I think we'll make it through."

A thunderclap rumbled off in the distance.

"Brrr," Edna Mae shivered at the sound, "sounds like the riders haven't quit yet."

"What riders?"

"Ghost riders in the sky." Edna Mae held up her book with one hand and pointed to a cloud bank off in the distance with the other. "Every cowboy knows the story. On days like these, you can hear them running the Devil's cattle drive. Oh, I sure hope they ain't got Barney."

"You're serious?" O'Rourke laughed. "Child, my grandmother from Killarney used to tell me an old fairy tale like that. In those days, they called it the Wild Hunt. The stories said they were chasing angels through the heavens, snatching up little boys that don't finish their chores. Nobody believes that nowadays. It's just thunder off in the distance, Edna Mae. They're just clouds."

Edna Mae was nodding but looking past O'Rourke at the southern sky. From the southwest, a dark, grayish-green collection of rainclouds rolled in. O'Rourke could see the shapes of horses' heads among them, just as he had said, but he also saw the silhouettes of riders with stags' horns on their heads. Here and there, the shape of a sickle or a polearm's blade extended from the pack. He heard a low rumble that sounded an awful lot more like hoofbeats than thunder.

The shape of a broad, muscular man hoisting a javelin emerged from the cloudbank, and O'Rourke gasped. Did he just see glowing eyes? A lightning bolt leapt from the javelin tip across the sky, terminating right in the heart of a light, wispy cloud shaped just like a young long-haired girl no older than Edna Mae herself. A *cirrostratus*, Edna Mae's book would've called it. The thunderclap echoed like a war cry as the pack billowed forward, overtaking the girl. The storm front parted around her, and her arms spread and stretched just as if a pair of assailants on horseback had each grabbed her by the wrist and pulled.

"Pa?" Edna Mae croaked out. "Barney? That ain't you up there, is it?"

"What?" said O'Rourke. "Child, why would you think—?"

The arm of some high-altitude vortex extended out of the dark clouds on the right, looking eerily like the blade of a sickle, and swung across the gap, straight down into the girl's heart. A second flash of lightning burst out from the spot where nimbus met cirrostratus, and the thunderclap sounded nothing like thunder and everything like a young girl's dying scream.

The javelineer shifted, and again O'Rourke saw sparks from deep within the cloud that looked uncannily like glowing eyes. O'Rourke's spine tingled, and he began to smell hot metal instead of wet grass. A bolt of lightning struck again—this time, hitting the earth mere feet from the two of them.

O'Rourke awoke to the feel of the rain on his face. He heard the rush of blood in his ears, and nothing else. The burns on his skin and the grinding of broken bones in his right arm fought for his attention. His feet were uphill from his head. It took him several minutes to stand back up and wipe the rain from his eyes.

He was at least fifty feet downhill from his spot on the hilltop. He couldn't have been thrown the whole way by the lightning alone, could he? He must have rolled. The bolt had split the old willow tree, and half of it lay across the crest of the hill, already half-consumed by fire. From underneath the burning fallen tree, he could see Edna Mae's left arm, limp and blackened. The smell of burning flesh was unmistakable. Even if he weren't injured, he knew he could do nothing for her now.

Edna Mae's book lay on the grass, and as the wind and rain played with the pages, he shuddered as he saw in the illustrations the very same face he'd seen in the sky. Was that the same face Edna Mae mistook for her pa? What else had she seen that he hadn't?

They're just clouds, he said, no longer able to hear himself. *They're just clouds.* He staggered down the hill back to his farmhouse. *They're just clouds. They're just clouds. They're just clouds.*

The Innerverse

By M.J. Cote

I'm no saint—on purpose. I don't want to go to heaven. I'd be bored out of my friggin' head in a place where everything is always peaceful and sunny. And I don't want to listen to angels playing stupid harp music. That's *not* for me.

Of course, I don't want to be burning in hell, either. There's got to be another option. Maybe God will create a new alternative just for me—if I'm good—and if there is a God. Who really knows? I haven't spoken to him or her.

My daughter says my wife's death has soured me against everything good. It didn't help—that's for sure. I wanted her here, on earth, not some…other place.

She died of cancer.

My twelve-year-old daughter, Angela, was terribly ill. She had a tough time swallowing and had a raging fever. I was worried sick. If there was a God, why would he do this to such a sweet angel? To me? To us? I went to church when I was young. I was kind to everyone. I saved a boy from drowning in a lake when I was a scout.

I walked to the foot of the stairs and looked up at her room. I wanted to know how she was doing before going to the local pharmacy to get medicine. "How are you doing?" I yelled up. I knew her nose was in a book, as usual. Trying to get her attention would take more than just a call from the bottom of the stairs.

"Whatcha reading?" I asked when I peeked in on her. Her eyes were swollen and she looked horrible. "You should rest honeybun."

She put the book down. "I know."

"I don't think the medicine is working, dear. How about if I get a doctor to come here?" It would help if she would go to the hospital. But I knew she wouldn't.

She gave me an angry look—she can't stand the sight of blood or needles. The last time I tried to take her to the doctor's she locked me out of the car until I promised to bring her home.

I felt her forehead. Her fever was worse. Maybe the pharmacist would know of better medicine if I described the symptoms. "I'm going out to get you more of the naproxen I gave you last night and see if I can find something that might work better. I'll be back."

She gave me a thin smile. I glanced down at her book. *The Innerverse*, stared up at me, begging me to ask: "What the heck is an innerverse?"

She shrugged.

I could tell she'd only started reading the book. She loved books. All kinds. Mystery books. Science fiction. Romance. Nonfiction. She was just that kind of girl. She was all that was left of my wife. I could see my Mary in her eyes. It pained me deeply. Very deeply. Whenever those thoughts crossed my mind, I pretended Angela was my Mary. It might seem foolish to some but *some* hadn't loved my Mary the way I had.

Anyway—that's how I found myself driving down the highway heading to the pharmacy.

I was going around a sharp curve when something came over me. I felt woozy. I shook my head and things cleared up. Traffic was light. I rounded another curve and drove… straight into the cargo area of a starship.

Of course, I didn't know it was a starship when I drove in. I was inside a huge metal building lit without lights. There was no visible source for the light. I had smashed to a stop on the wheels of…a small jet—or at least something that looked like one. The airbag deployed and I think I must have been unconscious for a few minutes.

I shoved the bag aside and pulled myself together as best I could. I kicked open opened the door and fell onto a transparent floor of some kind. It was smooth and felt like glass. I stood and looked around. This place was huge! A tin metal roof arched overhead with a bunch of strange-looking aircraft scattered all over.

I couldn't figure out how it was I got here. Maybe I'd driven off the road and crashed into an aircraft hangar. But I didn't recall any airfield or hangers near the road. It was a good hour's drive to the nearest airport—so what was this?

Where the hell was I? Unfortunate use of words—maybe this was hell.

I saw a uniformed man next to a door. Door? Door was good. I looked back at my vehicle. The front end was smashed in, pretty badly. I shook my head and walked over to the man.

"Can you help?" I asked, desperate to get the medicine I needed for my little angel. The man had jet-black hair combed back against his head and wore a tight-fitting one-piece uniform that covered his shoes like booties. Only his head and hands stuck out.

"Who are you?" he asked, dubiously. "And how did you get here?"

"I was going to ask you the same question."

After looking me over for a bit he said his name was Captain Rackham and that I was aboard the starship Tin-Can-Alley.

"That's an odd name for a starship," I replied. I thought it was a stupid name, but I needed his help and didn't want to insult the guy.

"The Admiral named it." He pulled the door open and motioned me inside.

"I need help," I insisted.

"Let's see if we can find you some. Inside, first."

I walked into a most marvelous room. It was like being inside a giant transparent bubble traveling through space. The door disappeared behind me as the captain closed it. A variety of people walked around pointing at what looked like colorful star clusters, except they weren't like any I had ever seen. The clusters appeared three-dimensional. A woman put her finger on the bubble's surface and one of the star clusters turned into what looked like a mountainous scenery. A deer looked up at her and fled as she walked in and disappeared. The lady couldn't be that likable if she frightened a poor deer—at least that's what I got out of that—poor deer.

"Where the hell am I?"

"I told you, you're aboard a starship—of sorts," the captain said.

"Starship? Looks more like a glass bubble floating in space than a starship."

"Well, most starships travel through the universe. This one travels through the innerverse."

I furrowed my brows, and let me tell you, I furrowed them tight. “There’s that word, again!” Hadn’t my daughter been reading a book with that title? Maybe this was a dream brought on by that book. But if it was, why was I dreaming? What had happened to me? “What the hell’s an innerverse? And how do I get out of here?”

“It’s where you are right now. A place inside our minds where we imagine, dream, and exist. Every time you dream, you come here. You just don’t know it.”

“That’s because I’m friggin dreaming—inside my brain.”

I was angry. He was taking up precious time. I had to pause for a minute to remember what was so urgent.

“More like inside your mind than your brain,” he said, “but generally, correct. The difference on this ship is that we’ve linked up with others—”

“Ouch!”

“What’s wrong?”

“Nothing.” I’d pinched myself. I know it’s stupid and clichéd but how was I to know if this was all real or not? All I knew was that I felt pain when I tried to pluck a bit of skin from my arm.

“Think of this as a common dream among a few travelers of the innerverse.”

“And I’m one of them?”

“To be honest, I don’t know how you got here. I think we should visit the Admiral; she might know more.”

“So, this is a dream, then?”

“No,” he said. “It definitely *is not*. You can die here as easily as you can die in the physical universe—or outerverse if you prefer. A group of us created this ship—piece by piece. We call ourselves innerverse travelers for lack of a better term. We meet in this mass dream and have fun."

"I thought you said this *wasn't a dream*."

Rackham shook his head and sighed. "Let's go see the Admiral. I guess it's how you define dreams. If it's your mental creation and you don't meet any people who live in the physical world, I'd say that's a dream. A mass dream is where you meet up with others, what we call an innerverse, a place where we can experience whatever kind of—well—whatever we want."

I followed Rackham, who looked like a goddamn prince in some movie. I figured there were two alternatives: one, this was a dream, or two I was delusional. I tried to decide which was in my best interest: delusion or dream. My last memory was of driving my van down the road to get medicine for my daughter—wait!

"I need to get back to my daughter." I said as I stopped midstride, panicked by the realization that my daughter was deathly ill. She needed that medicine! "How do I get out of here?"

"I told you. We have to see the Admiral first," said the captain. He touched the glass wall, and a small staircase appeared.

"Stop," I said, distraught and starting to hyperventilate. "I have to get the medicine—my daughter is awful sick."

"She'll be all right. Time is different here," said the captain trying to calm me. "I'll do my best to help, but we need to see the Admiral first to find out how you got here."

"If I find out, does that mean I can get back?"

"I just don't know. What I do know is that you shouldn't be here. The Admiral is the one who got us together to construct this ship. We all met her in our dreams. How she got in there, I don't know. She said she dreamt and saw us doing this or that and she got curious. She asked if we wanted to build a starship, one where we could meet while orbiting the earth."

"Orbiting the earth?" I asked as I stooped down to touch the glass floor—just out of curiosity. Next thing you know, the floor it disappeared and I went swooping down a slide, one like you'd find at a waterpark.

"What the hell!" I slid on my butt back and forth until the slide ended at the top of my minivan, and I went through the roof—like I was a ghost.

And…I was driving down the road, again.

I blinked. This had to have been a delusion. Maybe early onset Alzheimer's. I gripped the steering wheel and pressed the gas pedal. I had to make it to the pharmacist to pick up her medicine. I could go crazy afterward.

Everything seemed fine for about a minute. Enough time for me to exhale—when it happened again.

I drove into the same strange metal building. This time I applied the brakes well before hitting the aircraft. I slammed my van door and got out.

"Over here!"

I looked up. It was the same Captain Rackham. He was becoming a pain in my royal ass. Finding myself in this giant building, twice on the same day, was no little pain, either. He waved me back to the door that led to that giant glass ball like he was frustrated with my antics. I might be frustrated but I was furious.

I ran over. "I need to get outta here—"

"This way," said Captain Rackham, courteously. "The Admiral's waiting for you."

Instead of the door opening into the glass ball, this time it opened onto a staircase leading up. It looked oddly like my staircase at home. I gave the captain a suspicious look. “Am I dead?”

“No. You’re definitely not dead—the Admiral will explain everything.”

“Quickly, I hope, because I have to get that medicine.”

“Just go!”

I started up the stairs. It felt weird. When I looked back down, I was at home. This was my staircase, and that pissant of a captain was gone.

I gripped the banister. It felt solid enough.

Everything felt real. I had no idea what was going on. I stared at my hands. No medicine. Maybe I was going crazy. I must have turned around and come back home without it. Well, I wasn’t about to go see my little girl without it. Determine, I turned around and started thumping down the stairs.

“Dad!”

I stopped. She sounded so much like my Mary.

“You have to come up here. It’s not what you think.”

I turned and slowly made my way up.

What I saw astounded me. Her nose was in a book, as usual, but this time she was at her desk. She looked up with a wide grin.

I relaxed—relieved. “You’re all right,” I said.

She shook her head. “No. I’m fine here, but not back on earth.”

“What do you mean?”

She nodded toward the window. “See for yourself.”

I looked out cautiously. White clouds floated over bright blue oceans and familiar looking land masses stretched out over a curved surface. Earth’s moon crested the horizon. “That’s the earth from outer space,” I said. “How did we get here, honeybun?”

"We're in an orbital city my friends and I created. It's quite a story, but the short of it is that I discovered I could meet people in their minds, or their dreams, or wherever this place is. It's kind of a spiritual place, Dad. All I know is that I can come here when I sleep. It's like being in a dream I can control." She smiled. "I can even come here when awake by closing my eyes and looking inside my mind—I call it the innerverse."

"How did *I* get here?"

"I don't know. But I'm still in my bed at home and unless I get that medicine you went after…"

"You'll die, or something."

"I think so. It's hard to know anything for sure." Her frown turned into a beaming smile. Would you ever believe we built this place if you hadn't seen it for yourself?"

I shook my head and bent over to hug her, tight. Tears eked their way through the corners of my eyes as I squeezed them shut. "I don't care how I got here. I just love you and I'm so glad I found you—alive."

"They made me admiral," she said as she hugged back just as tightly.

I pulled away. "How am I here, honeybun? I need to get you that medicine. You were awfully sick when I left."

She pressed her lips together. "I still am." Then she looked back up with a smile that crossed her face. "What do you think of this place? I never thought I'd see you here. Every time I tried to visit you in your dream, you woke up."

"Is it real?"

"Real enough for me to enjoy it."

"But honeybun, it won't be if you die."

She pushed a button and the captain walked in. "You need to wake up and find my dad," she told him.

"Where would I look?" the captain asked, a bit bewildered at the request.

"You live near my house." She turned back to me. "You were going to the pharmacy, weren't you?"

"Yes. I thought the pharmacist could recommend something if I explained your symptoms—I know how you feel about doctors."

She looked at me like I had ten eyes when I mentioned the D word. "Do you know where the pharmacy is located?" she asked the captain still staring me down.

Captain Rackham pursed his lips. "I'll ask my father."

That's when I started feeling woozy, again. I almost fell on my daughter.

"What's wrong Dad?" She put down that stupid book she was reading. Why was she always reading? I never read—except for newspapers and advertisements. Certainly not books. Suddenly, I was back in the glass globe with people walking into and out of scenes or movies or whatever they were, only this time I was more of a ghost. I gathered the scenes were places where they met others and did things—play cards, camp out, go boating, stupid things…

Someone had me by the shoulders, shaking me.

"Get up!"

I blinked my eyes open. "Where am I?"

"You ran off the road into a ditch."

I looked up to see a blond-headed boy wearing jeans, a plaid flannel shirt, and sneakers so worn they had holes in them. Couldn't have been more than fifteen years old. He slapped me again. "Mr. Jacob. Angela needs her meds."

"What meds?" I answered, still confused. Then I realized what he was talking about. "What happened?"

"Your van went off the road."

"How?"

"I don't know, sir. I just know that Admiral Angel needs those meds. The doctor won't give them to me."

"Okay, okay," I said pulling myself out of the van. It was going nowhere in this smashed-up vehicle. I started to cry. "How will I get them? Did you call the police?"

"My father's here. He said he'd help us."

"Thank you!" I grabbed him by the shoulders. "How did you know where to find me?"

"I followed the road to the pharmacy like the admiral told me to."

Wait a minute. "What's your name?"

"Ronny."

"What's your last name?"

"Rackham."

At that point, all I cared about was getting the medicine. I wasn't injured, just badly shaken up. Ronny's father graciously took me to the pharmacy and back to my house.

I rushed up to her room. She looked pale. No pulse. "Call an ambulance!" I cried out to Ronny's father.

An ambulance came.

Men dressed in white uniforms with patches on their shoulders arrived. One of them checked her out as I shook and cried. "Can you save her?" I asked.

One of the med techs shook his head.

I clutched at her, crying even harder. "No! My angel can't be gone! It's my fault."

Ronny stood behind me and tried to console me by putting his hand on my shoulder. I shoved it away. He didn't know her the way I did. She would have been like her mother when she grew up—a beautiful young woman, intelligent, and book-read. They both loved books. If she hadn't had her nose in her book like that, maybe she'd have complained earlier, and she'd still be alive. Or if he hadn't driven off the road. Driven off into that… that innerverse place.

I still don't believe in heaven or hell. It's been days since I buried my Angela and I'm trying to decide if I have anything worth living for. But dark thoughts have made me wonder: Where do we go when we die? Where was Mary? Was Mary only a memory to those who could remember? What will happen to me? Will I cease to exist entirely?

Poof—I am no more?

I fell asleep that night and found myself aboard that damnable starship. It was a dream and I took out my anger on one of the small ships in the hangar. Captain Rackham must have heard me and made his way to where I fell to my knees. Not praying. I still didn't know if I believed in God or not.

"Who's the Admiral now?" I asked.

"Come and see for yourself."

After much prodding, I walked behind him, numb and morose. We went up a flight of stairs until we reached her bedroom.

There she was. My Angela.

"I thought you were dead?"

"I am," she replied. "Turns out there is no heaven or hell, just here. Now that I have no body, I can spend all my time on adventures traveling across the innerverse."

"But you are dead," I said, a deadpan expression across my face—no pun intended.

"I'm dead to the world, but not in the innerverse—Mom's here as well."

"Mary?"

Mary stood beside Angela. I'm not sure why I hadn't noticed. I ran over and hugged her, and she returned the hug. After a long tearful reunion, we sat and talked for a long while. When it was time for me to return, she put her hand on mine. "I won't see you again."

"Why not?"

"I've decided to," she paused, briefly. "I want to reincarnate; I think you would call it. When my soul enters a newborn."

"So?"

"I will forget you until I die again. Then I'll remember all my lives."

"But I love you."

"I love you too. But I want adventure. I liked living on earth. I want to return, and this is the only way."

All I could do was breathe hard trying to think of a reason she shouldn't.

"You always said, you didn't want to go to heaven or hell. Neither do I. I enjoyed living on earth and I'm going back."

ROCKS

Writing Prompt

He peered between the rocks.

"What do you think?"

"I think you should shut up!"

The man listened for the slightest out-of-the ordinary sound. Nothing. But he knew they were out there.

Stories

Deportment Lessons

By Shayla McBride

Ted Ford peered between the rocks, listening for the slightest out-of-the ordinary sound. Nothing yet. He knew Benson would be out there sooner or later. Where the hell was he? Ted winced at a memory of their most recent encounter. His ordinary question, Benson’s contemptuous answer.

“So that’s my idea. What do you think?”

“I think you should shut up!”

As Ted waited, again he relived the humiliating exchange. He’d only asked for Benson’s opinion, not that he wanted or needed his input, and he’d gotten that gratuitous take-down. The whole office had heard, Benson had made sure of that!

Well, he’d pay for the insult. Soon, Benson would come this way. And then they’d see who’d shut up. He was done taking shit from a lying, conniving thief who stole others' ideas and passed them off as his own. Nobody in the department liked him, nobody trusted him, the only people who hung with him were suck-up losers like Benson himself.

Ted peeked out again. Benson was out there, he always came this way after his Saturday golf game. He went from the eighteenth hole through the tumble of rocks, and along the shore path to where his snooty mistress lived. A long way around, but very discrete. The affair had been going on for six months. A record for Benson as even his mistresses eventually couldn't stand him.

Another thirty minutes, then he'd leave. Maybe the mistress had already given Benson the boot. Nobody deserved it more. The man was pure scum. But he'd get what he so richly deserved.

The rock felt comfortable in Ted's hand. Oblong, rounded, smooth. Lethal. Easily tossed over the cliff edge, after Benson. Who'd miss him? The mistress would probably sigh with relief. His wife would turn cartwheels. The man was a boor. Everyone in the department would secretly cheer. Nobody liked him.

But where was he? His golf game ended hours ago. Benson was a cheapskate, never stayed for drinks even when he'd won. He probably cheated to win, moving the ball would be typical.

Maybe he'd changed mistresses? Maybe he'd finally stood his golfing buddies a round? Hah. Fat chance. Cheap, sleazy, arrogant bastard.

Whatever, no more time wasted waiting for the jerk. There'd be other chances. Ted tossed the rock down, dusted his hands, and strode back along the cliff path. He turned away from the sea, took the trail through the stand of trees bordering the fairway. Where Benson undoubtedly cheated. All that walking for nothing! But Benson'd get his, one way or another, it was just a matter of time and opportunity. Ted jingled his keys as he approached his car.

"Mr. Ford? Ted Ford?"

He turned. Froze. Two police officers approached. One tall and skinny, the other short and portly, both with narrow, pouchy eyes. Portly had a hand poised over his pistol. Teddy smiled, spread his hands wide.

"Relax, officers. I'm totally harmless."

The tall one, name tag was Appleton, asked. "You are Mr. Thaddeus Ford, sir?"

"Yes. What can I do for you?"

"ID?" He took Ted's license, nodded, returned it. "For starters, sir, you can tell us where you've been for the past several hours."

"What's it to you, if I may ask."

Portly, name tag Mazzini, spoke. "We ask the questions, sir. Where've you been?"

"I was…I was taking a stroll. Alone. Nice day for it."

"Anyone see you, sir?"

Not likely. "No, I don't believe so. What's this about?"

"You know a Mr. Warren Benson?"

"Yes. We work in the same office. Why—"

"Seen him today? On your walk?" Mazzini's scowl matched his tone.

Ted tried to disguise his whole-body shiver as he shook his head. "Not since yesterday at the office."

"When you and he had an argument."

"How'd—? No, we didn't argue, we just had a snappy exchange."

"A number of people are calling it an argument, sir." Mazzini came down sarcastically on the *sir*.

"Well, officer, a number of people would be dead wrong. We didn't always get along but I think overall we worked pretty well together."

Appleton stuck his thumbs into his wide black utility belt, fingers of one hand spread just above his pistol. "Not what we've heard, sir."

"Well, what the hell does it matter anyway? Are you the deportment police or something? D'you investigate every breakdown in manners, in deportment? So what if we weren't best buddies, so what if we had the occasional shouting match?" He barely kept his anger in check. Even absent, Benson was a colossal pain in the ass. "Benson has a terrible temper and a short fuse, nobody in the office hasn't exchanged words with him at one time or another. Or repeatedly."

"Sir—"

"And," he cut in on Mazzini, "he's a damned sneak, a tattletale, an ass kisser. And an ass pincher. What, did one of the women in the office file a complaint? *That* kind of deportment? Wouldn't surprise me, not one bit, Benson's a hound, a letch. He made a pass at my date at a Christmas party. He's—"

"He's dead," Mazzini said. "Someone took a rock and bashed his head in."

The irony! A high laugh burst out of Ted Ford. He knew at once it was a terrible mistake, but he couldn't stop. With a few steps, the cops bracketed him. Appleton had a pair of shiny handcuffs in his hand. But Ted couldn't stop laughing. His voice pealed over the parking lot, higher and higher.

"Oh, poor Benson," he finally choked out. "That is absolutely hilarious. Er, heartbreaking." He sobered, tried to regroup. "Poor, poor Benson. He'll be missed. Terribly. His poor wife—"

"Sir," Appleton said, "we'd like you to come with us to the station."

"Why should I? I didn't do anything."

"That's as yet to be determined. And it wasn't a request, sir. You will come with us to the station. We need your fingerprints, and a statement." Appleton flourished the handcuffs. "Wouldn't look so good we march you past all your friends with these on, would it, sir?"

He tucked his hands under his armpits. "They're not my friends."

"So if all these people," Appleton waved one hand toward the small group of onlookers at the edge of the parking lot, "aren't your friends, why'd you come out here today?"

"I told you, I went for a walk. Fresh air. I didn't do anything. Nothing. Nothing at all. Whatever you're thinking, you're wrong."

"We're not thinking anything. If you're innocent, we're in your corner, sir. All you have to do is explain exactly where you were and what you were doing for the past couple of hours. Tell us the truth, you'll be just fine."

"Where'd he die?" Premonition made his voice shake. The rock…why hadn't he tossed it into the sea? "I did nothing, I tell you. Where was he found?"

Mazzini smirked. "Not at liberty to say, sir."

"Wasn't me." Ted couldn't draw a full breath. "Leave me alone. Go away." He tried to step away from the officers, they were as bad as Benson. All his life he'd had to deal with losers like these two morons and Benson. He was so much better than all of them! "I've done nothing wrong! Hey! What—"

The cuffs were cold and hard. Appleton took his right arm, Mazzini gripped his left. And bent in to whisper.

"We're not the deportment police, sir, but we will assure you'll behave yourself. You have a reputation as having a nasty temper. So, deportment lesson one: always do what a police officer asks without argument. Deportment lesson two: stop lying to us, it really pisses us off. We know the truth, all you have to do is sign off on it. Let's go."

Peering through the Rocks

By Amira Loutfi

Ruwaymi was usually happy to serve his clan. It was the dogs they'd seen on the mountainside that changed his attitude from dutiful pride to one of wariness and hesitation. The bitch made disgusting sounds and had eyes that blazed, while its pups battled over its teats with an aggression unbecoming of puppies. He continued up the mountain with his scouting partner, but couldn't shake the awareness that something about the entire area felt wrong. Whatever that wrongness was, Ruwaymi was certain they were getting closer and closer to it. His hand hovered over the pommel of the curved blade that hung at his side.

Ruwaymi had also begun to lose confidence in his companion, Amaar, a mage whose personality he felt was needlessly contentious. Each man had been selected for the mission by his respective clan. Ruwaymi hoped that Amaar's clan had chosen wisely. He usually trusted tribal decisions, but the two clans had only recently begun to collaborate. As the two men ventured further up the mountainside, he grew increasingly nervous. His steps slowed, until he was several full paces behind Amaar.

The mountain side was dusty and dry, with sparse patches of vegetation sprouting from between cracked layers of earth and stone. Ruwaymi stopped when he found Amaar crouched on a relatively flat clearing. Amaar was examining a bush, but Ruwaymi's eyes were drawn to a small opening into the mountain. Its mouth was composed of a long straight slab of rock whose sides disappeared into the golden dryness of the upward slopes. The ground beneath it was smooth, as though something had passed through it numerous times. Ruwaymi squatted to look inside, and saw nothing but blackness. There was a faint smell.

"Are those bite marks?" Amaar asked from behind him.

Ruwaymi turned to his companion and the subject of his query. Two pairs of dark Bedouin eyes scrutinized a gundelia bush. It was half blown away and blackened. The other side looked fine—twiggy and dun-colored, covered in thick spiky leaves and a few pinkish flower pods.

The gundelia was known for its cleansing properties. Many used it as a medicine. Amaar twisted its stiff branches. Ruwaymi gently prodded its damaged parts, which were ashy and deformed. Two flower pods were completely black, and turned to soot-like dust in his hands. Another pod was partially peeled, revealing the gritty flesh beneath its casing. And indeed, as Ruwaymi inspected, the fresh side appeared to have been abused by a violent set of teeth.

"First that rabid litter and now this?" Ruwaymi said, looking around, "And this whole ledge smells like feces." He stood up. Then he noticed the faint outline of what must have been dried vomit covering the earth around the abused plant. He felt disgusted, "and vomit. We should go back."

"Go back!" Amaar said, "And what do we tell the caravan?"

"We tell them that there is something evil about this place."

"Why?" Amaar gestured to the mangled bush, "Because we found a stinky plant? Obviously there was just a desperate animal—maybe a wildcat—tasting the gundelia and puking it up. But that can't be what scared the shepherd! We have more scouting to do."

"Forget that damn shepherd. There is clearly a demon up here." Ruwaymi grabbed a handful of the wrecked bush, "What kind of creature emits vomit like this!"

Amaar stood to meet his eyes. "We still know nothing," he said, "we have no idea what spooked the shepherd. Maybe it was a demon. But there's clearly something living in that cave" he gestured carelessly, "I'm going further. With or without you."

"There is no going back to the tribe separately."

They crawled in through the mouth of the cave, until the ceiling expanded high enough for them to stand. Ruwaymi could barely see in the darkness. But he could feel odd little shapes littering the ground with his feet, some more brittle than others. After a few more steps, he realized he was smelling death.

"The ground is covered in little corpses," he said. "Let's go back."

Amaar didn't respond, but Ruwaymi could hear the sounds of his footsteps growing further away. His eyes adjusted, but his companion had already continued further into the cave. With each step his feet brushed against more of the objects.

Weak beams of light poured in through cracks in the rocky wall. Ruwaymi held up one of the dried things to the light, turning it over carefully. It was the head and torso of a dead rat. From its middle down, its body was missing. Ruwaymi tossed it and grabbed another dry brittle thing from the floor. He held it up to the beam of light.

At first he thought it was another rat. But it was a rabbit, its ears as hard as leather. Its eyes were dried out and sunken and its cheeks hugged its skull. Its front legs and torso were intact. But its body had been torn from the bowels down.

Then he picked up a smaller piece. It was a small foot.

He picked up another and another, and a pattern emerged. The cave was littered with only the top halves of little corpses and the occasional hind quarter.

He felt sick. What kind of creature only eats half of its prey and abandons the rest? He almost called out to Amaar, but stopped. Without knowing what lurked in the cave, he preferred to grab his partner and leave in silence. He could hear movement from above a jagged uninviting length of rock.

With a steep climb upwards through slanted sheets of stone, dust, and scattered corpses, Ruwaymi found himself bumping into something warm. It was Amaar. The man grabbed his shoulder firmly and shushed him. Within moments Ruwaymi could see what had captivated his companion. Balanced between slanted stones, and steadying himself, Ruwaymi leaned towards a formation of rocks that allowed for multiple peepholes. There was a cave within the cave. Together, they peered between the rocks.

"What do you think?" Amaar said.

"I think you should shut up!" Ruwaymi hissed.

Ruwaymi listened for the slightest out-of-the ordinary sound. Nothing. But he had a feeling that something awful was out there.

"It's a clan of some sort." Amaar said.

There were dull streaks of light pouring into the cave on the other side of the wall. It was just enough that Ruwaymi could make out shadowy shapes, flickering lightly as they passed between darkness and dimness.

In a maneuver that Ruwaymi had not predicted, Amaar was atop another rocky ledge, just a few feet above him.

"Amaar," Ruwaymi hissed, "come back!"

The man ignored the warning. His footsteps crunched gently on scattered pebbles and dry bones above. He was gone from sight. Ruwaymi felt a small panic in his stomach. Each one of Amaar's steps made a soft sound and was followed by a small trickle of sand and debris that cascaded down Ruwaymi's shoulders to the endless darkness below. He returned his attention to the peep-hole wall as he listened to Amaar's footsteps. Ruwaymi could feel a nervous sweat running down his body. For a moment the sounds and trickles stopped. He returned a shaky hand to the pommel of his sword, thoughts of running and fighting flooded his mind.

Through the rocks, Ruwaymi then saw little more than a blur of darkness tumble into the den. There was a loud scream and a thud. It was Amaar. Amid several more terrified shouts, Ruwaymi could hear loud squelches. Down below he could see shapes and shadows rushing about. Then Amaar was silent. The squelching sounds continued.

Ruwaymi rolled onto a ledge behind himself. He sprang up and sprinted towards the mouth of the cave. Then, something flew above him and landed on the ground.

He grabbed it. It was moist. And it had a knobby joint. And toes. Amaar's leg? That was when it clicked in Ruwaymi's mind. *Bowel-eater*. His breath caught in his throat. He'd heard of it before. It was a creature that feasted on animals and men, consuming only their bowels and leaving the rest of their bodies to rot. According to legend, the best way to escape one was to get to sunlight.

He came to the ledge before the steep climb, it was a signpost for his nearness to the exit of the cave. It was a formidable drop. Behind him he heard a slight creaking sound. He unsheathed his sword and spun around. The giant slabs of rock above him shook, dropping sand and pebbles in a blinding and asphyxiating shower of dust. He shook it off. Ruwaymi couldn't see through the cloud, but he formed a martial position, as any competent swordsman would. A strong stench wafted into his nostrils. He twisted his blade about in swift whirling motions, and he could feel it striking at limbs that felt thick and fast.

The beast was fast, but so was the swordsman. When his vision cleared, he thrust the sword straight into the breast of the shadowy beast. Instead of relief, he felt another hard limb graze his torso. He jumped. And then rolled across the bluff. This roll left him with an uncomfortable pain in his right thigh. He slapped his pants and felt the spiky gundelia branch. He didn't even remember harvesting it.

The creature continued to assault him. He leapt and rolled out of the way of its limbs. He could see well enough—it was shaped like a man, but also not like a man. And his curved sword protruded from the front of its chest, posing no inconvenience.

The bowel-eater cornered him against a rocky wall. It raised its arms above its head and heaved forward to deliver a harrowing smash. Ruwaymi bounced off the wall and the beast's arms slammed into the floor. He swung up the beast's arm, and thrust the gundelia branch into its face. The creature recoiled, stumbling backwards. Ruwaymi braced for another attack until he noticed that the stench was gone. The beast had left without a sound.

Ruwaymi looked behind himself. And then back down to the path for the exit.

He could hear rumbling in the cave and the sounds of millions of little grains of sand shifting and falling against rock. Clearly there were more of them. There was, as Amaar had said, probably a clan. This was a tribal country and, Ruwaymi admitted begrudgingly to himself, tribal law applied to monsters and demons as much as it did to human men. It was his duty to teach these monsters that there was a swift and painful consequence to harming one of his tribesmen.

He considered this, breathing heavily in the cool dank air. He was right. He *should* teach them a lesson. It would be best for everyone if he could send them a strong decisive message sooner than later. But how? He had just learned his sword barely worked against these creatures—and it had apparently disappeared with the beast. The gundelia branch had been effective in driving his opponent away, but it had also disappeared. He checked his pants and found there was nothing else there.

Deciding to give in to his initial instinct, Ruwaymi started climbing down. There was nothing he could do but return to the clans and let them know what he'd found. As he climbed, he realized his escape alone would be enough of a success. Because if he also died in the cave, then the bowel-eaters would certainly view his tribe, parked in caravans only a few hours away, as a fantastic feasting opportunity. Escaping was the least he could do for them. And it *would* help.

He finally dropped off the rocks to the lower level, landing in the pile of dried out little corpses. At the far end of the cave, he could see a small bit of light pouring in. The mouth of the cave. He made a dash for it, but slammed into something large and hard.

Ruwaymi's face crashed directly into the abdomen of one of the bowel-eaters. It seemed that the creature was stunned for a moment. Ruwaymi was not. He rolled backwards. In the compact space the two creatures swiftly engaged. Ruwaymi was mostly ducking and dodging, but then Ruwaymi saw an opening to land a strong kick. He missed. Instead, small beams of light shook as his foot connected with one of the stones in the wall.

He stood before the wall and noticed that the creature had paused. It was watching him in the darkness, leaning forward. Its oddly proportioned head and shoulders pressed forward by the ceiling of the cave. The swordless man leaned against the wall again. It did seem relatively delicate. Dust and sand streamed into the cave, as did larger and larger strings of light. The creature finally made a move—it thrashed at Ruwaymi from the side. He dodged again. The beast followed him and he jumped a second time. This time, he lurched, throwing all of his power and weight at the fragile wall.

The rocks fell down. The light poured in. Ruwaymi scurried into the light, the monster screaming behind him. It was a sickening sound. He stood in the sunlight and turned around. The mouth of the cave was now huge. Its rocky walls and smooth floor was now exposed to the mountainside. Shifting mounds of yellow sand and rock poured over it. Ruwaymi looked for the beast. To his relief, the bowel-eater was writhing helplessly on the ground. A stone had fallen on its legs and its face was covered in sand. Exposed to the light were its chest, arms, thighs, and what must have been its loins. Its pale purple skin sizzled, burning. Ruwaymi noticed the beast smelled more smoky than fecal. Was the smell neutralizing in the sun?

The sunlight made the shadows of the cave appear darker. A powerful stench heralded the arrival of several more of the beasts. They hid by the shadows of the newly formed stony structures. He could barely see them standing in the light, but he could hear them howling and growling.

It was clear they weren't going to enter the sunlight.

On the other side of the sandy rock pile, his sparring companion lay, as though dying. It was almost twice his size. He grabbed its legs under his arms and hoisted it out from under the large stone, dragging its entire form out of the shadows and into the hot sunlight. It burned under his arms, and he noticed the sensation increase, but he was a desert-dweller and was therefore accustomed to ridiculous amounts of heat.

He hated to touch it, but he heaved the creature up until it was completely exposed to the sun. The other bowel-eaters screamed as he worked. He tried not to look at them nor the thing he dragged. But he could feel its heels and the joints of its feet—tough, though slimy, and burning his body. When he felt he had satisfactorily perched the beast on the top of the pile he dropped its legs and peered at the group huddled in the shadows.

They looked like men, but also nothing like men. Ruwaymi planted his foot on the smoking body of their comrade. The beasts continued jeering. He glared at them. He didn't know what they were saying, nor did he entirely understand what he was looking at. He forced himself to hold his gaze on them, bellowing, “You think you can disembowel my tribesman without consequence? Do it again and we will come for you! We will come for all of you!”

Ruwaymi then released a victory cry. Mostly he was just happy to be done with the bowel-eaters. They disgusted him in every way.

As he made his way down the mountain, Ruwaymi felt conflicted. The mission was, technically, a success. He'd done his duty for the tribe. More than his duty, actually. He had both gathered valuable news *and* had granted swift vengeance for the death of his tribesman. As he continued it occurred to him why he felt dissatisfied. He wasn’t actually certain what any of it meant to the bowel-eaters. He hadn’t understood one utterance out of them. Yes, he had fulfilled the laws of the desert, but would those creatures understand?

At any rate, Ruwaymi had news for the caravan.

The Double Dare

By Marie LeClaire

"There's no such thing as fairies!"

"There is so."

"Is not."

"Is so," Brandon taunted his little brother.

"Is not!"

"Is so and I saw them." The claim was out of Brandon's mouth before he could stop it.

"You're a liar. You did not."

"Did so."

"Okay, where?" Damon challenged him.

Brandon had to think quick. "Out back of Old Kelsey's barn." It was an easy target. There were campfire stories told about Old Kelsey. No one liked him and most of the kids steered clear of his farm. Damon wouldn't doubt him.

"Nut-uh,"

"Yuh-hu."

Damon locked eyes with his older brother. "Prove it."

When Brandon hesitated, Damon took full advantage of the balk. "I dare you."

Oh, no. Now, it was *on*. "Alright. How?"

"Show them to me."

"They don't like being seen."

"Oh, sure. No surprise there. Cuz you're a *liar*."

"I am not!"

"I double dare you!"

There was no backing down now. "I'll show you. Tomorrow, after supper. Behind the barn." Brandon figured his brother, three years younger, would back down, too scared to go.

Damon stared his brother in the eye. Was Brandon bluffing? Would he really go to the old farm *and* at night? Damon's need to win the dare was too great. "Okay," he nodded.

"Okay!" Brandon spat back.

Brandon lay in his bed that night wondering how he got suckered into this. One minute he was heckling his brother, the next he was going out to Old Kelsey's farm after dark to prove that there were fairies out there. How was he going to pull this off? He'd have to sneak over during the day and set something up – and hope Old Man Kelsey didn't catch him.

***

Armed with the solar-powered daisies from his mother's garden, Brandon headed over to the barn after school. He was hoping the lights would glow long enough for Damon and him to get to the woods, get scared, and then run home. He was sticking them in the ground at the edge of the woods when Old Man Kelsey snuck up behind him.

"What do you think you're doing out here, boy?"

Brandon spun around. "Ah, ah," he stammered.

"Speak up, boy. Fast!" Old Kelsey was leaning on a long-handled garden shovel and looking down at him with beady eyes.

"I—I want to scare my little brother."

"And?"

"I told him there were fairies in the woods here, then he dared me to show him." Brandon was fast-talking now. "So, I'm thinking I could set these lights up and come back after dark." He paused to see Old Kelsey's reaction.

"You don't need them lights to see 'em."

Brandon looked at him, unsure if he was serious or not. "What do you mean?"

"The fairies, boy. You can't be messing with 'em," Old Kelsey said. "They ain't all nicey nice like in those bedtime stories."

"But—fairies aren't real."

"Course they are. Otherwise what the hell are you doing here setting up lights to see 'em?"

"But I—"

"Look! There's one now." Old Kelsey pointed into the woods past Brandon's left shoulder.

Brandon spun around in time to see leaves in the brush move but nothing more.

"Look, kid," Old Kelsey said, "We need to get out of here. They really don't like it when humans mess around at their door."

"You're making it up. Everyone knows fairies are nice—if they're real. But they're not." Brandon found a little bit of courage to challenge him.

"They *ain't* all nice. You remember that little girl Sarah, from down the street? She went missing last year?"

"She moved away," Brandon corrected him.

"That's just what they told you 'cuz you're a kid."

"What do you mean?" Brandon was hooked into the story now and forgot how scared he was of Old Kelsey.

"She was messing with the fairies."

"Nut-uh."

"Yuh-huh," he nodded. "She had this glass pickle jar with holes poked in the lid. She was trying to catch one. They didn't like it much."

"What did they do to her?" Brandon's eyes were buglike with fear.

"I don't know but she ain't come back, has she?"

Brandon was scared all right, but not enough to give up on a double dare. "My brother *double* dared me to show him one."

"Hmmm," Old Kelsey thought about this a moment. "Well now, a double dare, that's pretty serious stuff. Is he younger 'n you?"

"Yeah."

Old Kelsey nodded slowly, considering this. He liked to scare the kids every few years to keep them off his property. It made it easier for him to come and go through the Fae portal where he procured the most amazing moonshine, made from real moon shine.

"Tell you what. You bring your brother by tonight and I'll give you both a peek at the fairies. But I gotta warn you, they can be real mean."

"For real?"

"Don't push it kid. I could change my mind."

"No, sir, Old, I mean Mister Kelsey."

"Be here at dusk. That's when they are most busy."

"Yes, sir."

"Hide behind that stone wall over there." He pointed to an old wall along the edge of the field that ran into the woods. “Now get outta’ here. And take those ridiculous flowers with you.”

Brandon grabbed up the garden ornaments and ran.

***

The boys ate quickly and put their dishes in the sink.

“What’s gotten into you two?” their mother asked.

“We’re meeting Manny and some kids to play ball.” Brandon had his excuse all set up.

“Really? First I’ve heard of it.” She looked at them both trying to determine if this was true.

“We decided at school today. We’ll be home early.” The boys didn’t wait for an answer before they were out the door.

Making their way along the old stone wall to Old Kelsey’s barn, they found a spot where the stones had shifted, creating a gap. They ducked behind the wall and peered between the rocks.

“What do you think?” Damon asked.

“I think you should shut up!” Brandon sneered in a hushed voice.

They listened for the slightest out-of-the ordinary sound. Nothing. But Brandon knew they were out there, or he hoped they were.

Then, coming down the hill from the house, strode Old Kelsey carrying a camp lantern that swung back and forth as he walked making shadows dance around him. In his other hand he had an old pottery jug. He didn’t stop at the edge of the woods but took a few more steps into the brush. He lifted his hands out to his sides like a big Y and stood still.

As the boys watched, little balls of light appeared, first as small dots, then growing bigger, to the size of baseballs. Then they started pelting Old Kelsey. He ducked and winced as the attack intensified, then, in a bright flash of light he was gone, sucked in as the flash collapsed to a pinpoint before vanishing, taking the light balls with it.

Branon clapped a hand over Damon's mouth before he could scream, then grabbed him by the arm and both boys ran like lightning back across the field to home.

***

Kelsey was sitting in his kitchen using an ace bandage to wrap an old cast around his right leg. He'd already applied blue and purple makeup to his face. He wrapped his left wrist in gauze, grabbed the crutches and headed out the front door just as the school kids were going past. He made sure he could be seen, mumbling a few indiscernible words at the few kids that came too close to the house.

He stumbled back inside but not before Brandon and Damon got a good look at him. He sat back down at the kitchen table, removed the fake medical treatments and poured himself a tall drink of Fae moonshine. That should keep the kids out of his way for another couple of years.

Standing Stones

By Melody Friedenthal

The granite stelai were eight feet tall, with mottled gray surfaces and jagged edges. But Craig was less interested in their geometry than in their metaphysical location, their agency as delimiters between this world and some mystical *other*. His heart raced and he took a step back.

He half-turned towards Hailey, who was laying out a picnic lunch on the blanket that had been purpose-bought for this outing. The shop had wares in a hundred different tartans, or so it seemed, so Craig had chosen one affiliated with the clan of his distant ancestors. It looked cozy in this sunlit glade.

"It could be, you know," he said diffidently.

His wife said nothing, though the look she gave him spoke plenty.

"I don't think… all those stories…" He stopped, and tried again. "I think there's some kernel of truth in those legends we've been hearing. The details might have gotten muddled over the centuries but something happened here – don't you feel it?"

Hailey pursed her lips and wished she were back in New York. The center of fashion, the center of literature, the center of theater. The center of her world.

Craig reached out his right hand and touched the rough grain of the nearest standing stone. It was warm and, he had to admit, felt just like any other unpolished rock. The surrounding woods felt ordinary, too; some birds chirped, a squirrel dashed up a nearby oak, and the stream on the far side of the glade burbled. It was serene. He took a deep breath. No truck fumes. So different from the cacophony of their neighborhood back in the city!

Hailey had not been enthusiastic when he had proposed a fifth-anniversary trip to Scotland, but she'd gone along with the idea. He suspected she would have preferred Nantucket or Cozumel. Besides complaining about the mostly-rainy weather, she'd been uncharacteristically quiet these last four days.

"In Iceland they believe in gnomes or elves or something."

"We're here, Craig. What you wanted. I'm here. Let's have lunch." She handed him a roast beef sandwich on thick, crusty bread, and then poured each of them some wine, half-filling the plastic goblets the innkeeper had packed along with the foodstuffs.

They ate in silence. Every time Craig tried to catch Hailey's eye, he found her staring at the enveloping old-growth forest.

"If we walk between the stones, maybe we'll go back in time, like that Englishwoman on TV."

She rolled her eyes, and he tried again. "Ancient people put up these stones for a reason. I think they're markers of some kind. I feel like this is a sacred place, a portal."

Hailey sipped her wine. She'd been looking forward to lazing away on a tropical beach. Dancing. Mojitos. Getting a tan. "Give it up, Craig."

She missed her friends. Anya and Katya, twins who were elite dancers with the New York City Ballet. Suzanne, who was a bookstore manager. Rae, who earned a respectable income as an artisan. And Bronwyn, the perpetual philosophy student. They had all known each other since high school, been each other's supports, bridesmaids, confessors.

She lay back on the blanket, her petite form wiggling a bit to find a comfortable position on the uneven ground.

She thought about Craig. He was getting on her nerves. Elves, Spock-ears, crystal healing.... She had thought he was a sober and practical lawyer when they started dating. She'd just failed out of college and had been looking for a stable, responsible guy. One swipe right and the next thing she knew he was proposing. She was happy to accept. He provided certain things, respectable things, which her life was missing. But her closest relationships were still with the members of her female cohort. For secret-sharing she still went to Anya or Suzanne. For a taste of the divine, she went to Rae. For laughter she had all five.

It had been a shock when Craig admitted to an obsession with all things geeky. Suzanne said Craig reminded her of her cousin Eiji, back in Japan, who was similarly obsessed. The Japanese labeled people like them "otaku." What silliness.

Craig finished his meal and pulled his jacket a bit closer around him. The clouds had drifted in and the glade wasn't nearly the sunny oasis they had arrived at an hour earlier. He noticed that Hailey looked tense. The air wasn't the only thing that was chilly.

He sighed. Being a corporate lawyer paid well, but after a handful of years, all he could feel was the drudgery. He wanted, more than anything, to experience a scintilla of enchantment.

"Don't you feel it?" he pleaded.

She was tired of his childish fixations. Attorney mid-week, Trekkie on the weekends.

"Craig, they're just rocks." She closed her eyes briefly, gathering strength. "We should be heading back soon."

He wasn't ready to leave. There was something irresistible about those standing stones. His eyes kept being pulled back to them, or, more precisely, to the void between them. His viscera told him there was a portal there, or there would be under the right conditions. Maybe they needed a full moon. Or the right alignment of the planets. And on the other side? Maybe another century. Or an alternate Earth…

The two of them, wife and husband, experienced the moment in disparate ways. She saw the oak and alder foliage that hemmed them in, and the rockiness of their marriage. He saw the shades of the fairies he had hoped to encounter, and a rocky gateway to glamour. Elves, maybe. Or shape-shifters. Magic-wielders, for sure. He gave his full attention to the potent space between the stones.

"I think I see something!" he exclaimed, liminally aware of some presence.

He peered between the rocks.

“What do you think?”

“I think you should shut up!” She pressed her lips together. *Shouldn't have said that…*

Surprised at her vehemence, but distracted, Craig listened for the slightest out-of-the ordinary sound. Nothing.

Hailey started packing the picnic things. "Time travel is a cute science fiction trope. Elves were invented by Tolkien. Shape-shifting is ridiculous. Let's go."

He reluctantly tore his eyes from the stelai. He picked up the blanket and shook it to dislodge the forest detritus. Then he carefully folded it and placed it in the wicker basket.

Hailey thought, *Not much of an anniversary trip, but at least I have a tale to tell the coven.*

Fifth Dimension

By Lucy A.J. Tew

"I think… you oughta shut up, Commander!"

"CUT!"

Otto's voice came from the canopy where the camera crew had set up. Beside Nora, Mike cracked up at his flubbed line.

"Seriously?" she groaned. The rest of the crew hooted with laughter. The key grip hollered at the cameraman to save the take for the wrap party.

"Relax, *Commander*." Mike rolled his eyes. The makeup crew darted forward to touch up their fake wounds and sweat sheens. "I screwed up, no big."

Nora didn't say anything as Amani touched a sponge to the gash on her cheek, from the Vorack Beast in yesterday's shots. She'd gotten good at not saying anything lately. She was the first female, nonwhite actor to portray the titular Commander Chronostar in the show's decades-long history (a recasting feat achieved through the character's ability to Revivify in new physical forms). She was used to everything from unprofessionalism to racist diatribes strewn across the internet like Quatroleum Crystal particles across the starscape of the Tenth Dimension, the show's setting.

"Okay?" Amani asked, offering a Hydroflask. Nora sipped and nodded, returning it. Amani retreated to the shade. Mike finished slugging his water and tossed it to his makeup artist.

After a ratings dive when Commander Chronostar and Lieutenant Tasha Tomlinson had shared an onscreen kiss—two, actually, one under the influence of alien hormones and one purely character-driven—the producers had… *negotiated* with the writers. In the season finale, Tasha was sacrificed to a Fifth Dimension villain, but came back Revivified as… Taz, played by Mike Brenneman. That device had worked to introduce Nora Yang as the Commander—why shouldn't it be used to "reset" the relationship between the Commander and the Lieutenant?

A portion of the fanbase had expressed fury over the announcement, but this had dissolved when they saw the "chemistry" (courtesy of a crack team of editors) between the Commander and the new version of the Lieutenant.

Otto, the episode director, was now jogging up the sun-grilled alien hillside in Agua Dulce, California. "That's a funny bit you came up with, Mike. Try it again, and keep the blocking I gave you, yeah? Remember, we like the tension, 'cause it'll resolve nicely when we get to the cave scenes next week."

"Can't we just go as written?" Nora asked, dropping her fake American accent. "Nobody tells the Commander to shut up, especially not Tasha."

"Taz," Mike corrected her, tugging his uniform straight.

"Go with it, yeah, Nor? Hot as hell out here," Otto said. Without waiting for an answer, he called to the tent, "We're going again! Back to one."

Nora and Mike put their backs against the rocks again, lifting their rayguns to wait for the cue.

"Lookin' a little red there," Mike said, gesturing to Nora's forehead. She frowned at him. "Don't squint too much, huh?" He gave her a smile that came closer to a sneer.

She opened her mouth to ask exactly what the hell he meant by that, but Otto had already called the cue.

"What do you think?" she managed to say, just barely getting the cue line out.

"I think—"

"Cut! Airplane!"

That evening, as the team packed up, Nora stepped out of her trailer into a sunset of bleeding purple and gold. Walking down the rocky dirt road to her car, she passed a cluster of crew members hanging around the tailgate of a shiny white truck. Mike stood in the bed, beer in hand, holding court.

At that moment, the showrunner appeared at the top of the fire road and barked at the crew to get back to packing up the sound and camera equipment. Mike jumped down as they all scattered.

"Hey, Commander," he said, with a mock salute.

"Mike." Nora stopped a few feet from her car, gripping her script tighter. "Need something?"

"Nope, just checking in," he said, still grinning lazily. "Sunset's something out here, huh?"

"I guess," Nora replied. "Night, then."

"Wanna drink? I got a cooler."

"I don't drink and drive."

"Suit yourself," Mike shrugged, taking a sip of his IPA. "Uptight..."

Nora slapped her script, keys, and bag on the trunk of her car, and turned. "What the hell is your problem with me? Not enough that you beat my downvote on casting you, you've got to be an asshole about it, too?"

"Nope." He lifted his chin. "I just think girls like you, who take this type of nerd-saga bullshit serious as gospel, are a waste of a good rack. Think you're better than me because you've seen all nine thousand hours of this freakshow, or something? I've heard you at fan events, talking like this is some kind of elevated art form—"

"And *I've* heard you—you're perfectly happy to sing the show's praises when you've got a paycheck on the line," Nora snapped.

"God, you're a piece of work. I do that stupid crap because I'm not an idiot—"

"Oh no? Could've fooled me!"

They became aware, at the same moment, that silence had fallen over at the load-out up the hill. Nora was sure Mike knew as well as she did that a dozen beetle-black iPhone irises were already pointed their way, zoomed in on their granulated figures against the streaky sky. She could imagine the Tweets and message board headlines – which one of them would be the bad guy, at the end of it all?

It was already too dark to tell who'd seen or heard what from where Nora and Mike stood among the parked cars, looking up the boulder-adorned slope to the trailers. All the same, they peered between the rocks.

"What do you think?" Mike asked.

Nora looked at him. "I think you should shut up."

They listened for the slightest out-of-the ordinary sound from the load-out team. Nothing. But Nora knew they were out there. And as she started her car and drove away, she felt some small part of her snap off, hurtling into the Fifth Dimension.

Of Witches, Wizards, and Warlocks

By M.J. Cote

"What do you expect me to do?" asked the old woman. "She's dying of radiation poisoning."

Josh leaned into his grandmother, eyes begging, bloodshot and tired. "You're supposed to be a witch. Can't you cast a spell or something?"

Millie wrinkled her nose at Josh. "Girlfriend, is she?" His grandmother was plump and short; had sunbaked skin and a face with more wrinkles than a Sultana. Her hair was orange with purple highlights and she wore a navy sweater covering a ragged eye-popping chartreuse dress.

After more cajoling and ranting about how his heart would implode, she grudgingly agreed. They filled a small cast iron cauldron with herbs and water. But she said they needed a special ingredient and it had to be put in the pot immediately after picking. So, she convinced him to carry the cauldron as they trudged down a crooked path through the forest.

"You can cure her, can't you?"

"Don't get your pants up your crack," she said. "It's just radiation poisoning. I've cured worse."

“The doctors said there’s nothing anyone can do for her.”

“They’re idiots.”

“They’re doctors—they went to medical school.”

“And I went to Wicca school—trumps medical school, it does.”

“I’m only here because the doctors say there’s no other way to save her.” Josh panted, holding the cauldron by the handles, doing his best to keep up with Millie. He struggled to keep the cauldron of *whatever she had concocted* from sloshing over. But it hardly mattered. He tripped and the cauldron flew out of his hands.

“No!”

“Well, that’s it, she’s dead.”

Josh grabbed her. “We have to go back to make another brew.”

“No time.” Millie picked up the spilled pot and looked inside. “There’s enough left.” She handed it back to him.

“Why do I have to carry the pot instead of you?”

“Because it’s your lovey, not mine.”

“I’m tired and I don’t want to drop it again.”

“Thanks for sharing but—I don’t give a flying fig’s ass.”

Josh carried it for another hour before dropping the pot on an old stump and bending over trying to catch his breath. “I don’t see how carrying a pot out here will cure her—that’s all.”

“Quarks,” she said.

“Quarks?” He looked around. He’d walked miles carrying her cauldron to this small peninsula. Stone obelisks between five and six feet in height sprouted everywhere between sparse trees and patches of grass.

How *strange.* One was mushroom shaped. All were weathered and misshapen.

"She's got too many *strange* quarks," said Millie. "She needs a bunch of *charm* ones to counter them. Now, look around for a patch of bright orange mushrooms."

"Mushrooms aren't orange."

"No? Then you must have cataracts. No, that's not right either." She shook her head. "You're too young for that—must be a case of stupid-idis."

"I'm not stupid. Why do you say stuff like that?"

"Why do you doubt me?"

"Fine—I'll look." It didn't take Josh more than a minute to find orange umbrella-like mushrooms growing at the base of a tree. They were striped white and seemed to glitter and vibrate in the sunlight. He'd never seen mushrooms like these but grabbed a handful and rushed back. "Why are they screeching like that?"

She looked at him like he had two holes in his head. "They're *charming* mushrooms."

"So what?"

"You grabbed them."

"What was I supposed to do? Pick them one by one like they were dainty flowers?"

She shook her head and held up the cauldron. "Just dump them in the pot."

Josh threw them in and brushed his hands on his pants. "What is that icky stuff?"

"Soothing gentle lotion—"

"But my hands are turning purple!"

"Guess it isn't lotion then, is it?"

"You're the one that had me look for those stupid mushrooms."

"And you're the one that grabbed them when I told you to *find them*, not torture the poor souls."

"They're just mushrooms—"

"*Charming* ones," she replied. "Now, let me see your hands if you want to have any left."

"My hands!" he screeched when he held them out. "What's wrong with them?"

"Who goes grabbing and squeezing the bejeezus out of mushrooms like that?" She grabbed his wrists and held them tight. A soothing warmth flowed down his palms into his fingertips. The purplish stuff peeled off like the skins on a burnt potato. Underneath, raw flesh showed through as she blew off the dark flakes.

"Go do something like that again," she said, "and I'll squeeze the stupid out of your head. Do you hear me?"

That's when he saw blue conical hats bobbing up-and-down behind some of the stone pillars. Millie jumped him, knocking him to the ground. "Damn! They're not supposed to be here today. Hide behind a stone!"

"Who are they?"

"Them, that's who."

He peered between the rock pillars.

"What do you think—"

"I think you should shut up!"

Josh listened for the slightest out-of-the-ordinary sound. Nothing. But he knew they were out there. He'd seen those blue hats.

"Must be the warlocks," she whispered in his ear.

"Warlocks," he mouthed the word and peeked out again.

"Don't look. They'll see you," she said in an intense whisper. "Didn't you notice the stones?"

He shook his head and looked up at the one he was hiding behind. It was weathered with what looked like the rough outline of a face on the top. He stared back at Millie, who was busy studying the men dressed in blue robes and conical hats. "Are those pillars… men that got turned into *stone*?"

"Yes, and if you don't shut your mouth, I swear I'll stuff it full of crap and stitch it shut."

"Why are we here?" he whispered, squatting. "Why are those men—warlocks here?"

"Shut up. I might be a witch, but I'm still your grandmother, and if you want to save that lovey girl of yours—keep quiet!"

"I'm scared."

The men in conical hats circumambulated the mushroom pillar, humming and thrumming.

"Are they like Medusa? Look at them and you turn to stone?"

"Shut up."

The warlocks began chanting, but he couldn't recognize the language. The intonations reverberated in his head and made him feel dizzy.

"No, you don't," Millie whispered, grabbing his head to steady him. Whatever she did, made everything clear as day.

"They make my brain feel like jelly."

"Believe me, if it were jelly, I'm sure there wouldn't be enough to put on a toast. Now pay attention! We have to get the hell out of here. Now! Clear?"

Josh gulped to clear his throat. "How?" he whispered as low as he could manage. "We're on a peninsula. They're between us and the lake."

"Lake won't work," she said.

"Why?"

"Warlocks."

His jaw dropped. He lived in the modern world. Warlocks didn't exist except in books. Where in hell had she taken him and why? Carrying a pot of stew, no less. He'd never really believed his gentle and always mellow grandmother was a witch. "Can we leave the pot behind?"

"No."

"You have a plan?"

"No."

He held his hands palm-up in exasperation.

"No plan, just follow me. We're going to walk right through their little get-together."

"Walk through!"

"Just follow me." She stood and pulled him up with her.

Josh snapped his eyes shut. "They'll turn me to stone like the others who came here if I look at their eyes."

"You should've thought of that before you went grabbing everything in sight instead of doing exactly as I said. Now, open your eyes."

"No."

"Fine." Millie dragged him by the hand. He stumbled through the brush falling twice before the chanting stopped.

"Millie!" He heard one of the warlocks cry out.

"Millie yourself, Did Lamphere. Why are you skulking around these parts like caterwauling cats that don't have anything better to do?"

They all laughed. "Who's the one you're dragging behind you like some puppy dog?"

"Josh? Gotta sweetheart dying on him. Trying to save her."

"You didn't come for the warlocks, did you?"

"How else does a witch get charm quarks into a stew?" She looked at Josh who stood there with his eyes squeezed shut. "Open your damn eyes and say hi to Did so we can get out of here and save your girlfriend."

"Fiancé—I don't want to turn to stone."

"You won't turn to stone." Millie stuck her fingers in Josh's eyes and started pulling his eyelids open.

"Stop! What are you doing?" Josh tried to walk backward and fell over a stump and moaned. He looked up to see an old man with a blue wizard's hat crooked on his head, peering at him to see if he was okay.

He hadn't turned to stone.

Thank God! "I thought you said if I looked at a warlock, I'd turn to stone like those others."

"I said no such thing."

"You implied it."

Did shrugged. "Well, you would if you looked in their eyes. Everybody knows that."

"So, why didn't I turn to stone when I looked into your eyes?"

Did laughed. "Because I'm not a warlock."

"Damned idiot," said Millie. "He's a wizard."

"Oh."

"The warlocks are those orange mushrooms you grabbed and put in the pot. Now, go back and get the pot so we can finish what I need to do."

Josh went cold. "I could have—"

"Were their eyes open?"

"I—I didn't see any eyes."

"Probably sleeping, they were," said Did. "Those white lines open like eyelids. They hypnotize you first by sending out charm quarks. You start to feel woozy, then stiffen up from the quarks. Eventually, you turn to stone."

"Enough with scaring the boy, Did. We need to get going." She turned to Josh. "Get the pot."

Josh scurried back to where the pot lay. It was warm to the touch when he picked it up by the handles. "It's hot."

"Just the mushrooms doing their… thing," said Millie. "Now let's get going."

***

The night nurse said Sarah did not have much longer to live. She led Josh and Millie over.

"What do I do with it?" asked Josh, looking at her pale face on the bed.

"It's a cup of stew!"

"Yes, but it's a witch's brew. Do I let her smell it? Apply it to her face?"

Millie stared at Josh. "If you don't feed her a little, now," she started to say.

"But—"

"I'll smash it side of your head! Now, give it to her."

Josh took a spoonful and held it next to her lips. Her lips were pale, blistered, and bleeding.

"Don't look at it! Open her mouth and put a little in," Milli insisted. "And I'm a good witch, not a sorceress. Sorceresses are ugly, green-skinned hags that come out on Halloween."

"They call them witches—"

Millie grabbed the spoon, opened Sarah's mouth, and poured some of the orange goo into it. A slow glow began at Sarah's face and spread throughout her body.

"You see," said Millie with a smile. "The charm quarks in that mixture are reacting with the strange quarks to cancel out the radiation poisoning effects. They're bringing her body into what I call a *charmonium* state. She'll be fine after getting a good night's rest."

"Are you sure?"

"No. I have no idea what I'm doing. I made you do all this for nothing."

Josh stood stiffly, a grateful smile on his face, and a tear dribbling down a stony cheek. He saw his grandmother sigh as his hand turned to stone.

"You're an idiot—but my grandson. Must've had a warlock's eye on the spoon. I told him he'd turn to stone if he looked, but did he listen to me? No. Now I'll have to brew up a cure for him."

A Tale of the Gnolls and the Mountain

By C. Brian Moorhead

We imagine that we live in an age of scientific enlightenment, that we have conquered our forefathers' superstitions and folk legends, and that Science and Reason will explain the cause of any unexpected phenomenon we encounter, but I know that this is not the case. My friend Douglas Gnoll taught me that lesson well, although I doubt he understood it in his own lifetime.

I refer to him as my friend now, but I was more reluctant to call him that when he was still alive. Douglas Gnoll wasn't a particularly pleasant or well-liked individual, and I can't exactly say I mourn him, but the mysterious circumstances of his death will never let me fully forget him, either, for they taught me just how little I truly understand about how the world works.

He and I met when we attended Quinapoxet University together. Before I continue, I will tell you that the rumors and outlandish stories that have attached themselves to that school over the years are all exaggerations. Quinapoxet is a perfectly respectable school; its only real flaw is that it's in

Massachusetts and is thus unfairly compared to dozens of the most prestigious colleges in the country.

But I've digressed; Quinapoxet's only real relevance to the matter at hand is that it is a smaller school. Any two students of the same year and same major will undoubtedly cross paths often enough to become acquainted. So it was with Doug and I, and he decided that this was sufficient cause to ingrain himself into my social circle.

He frequently invited us to various excursions in the town surrounding the campus—lunch at the local diner, bowling, and the like. We attended, out of courtesy or boredom, but once there his personality flaws became apparent. He would interrupt others' sentences and show no interest in what they were speaking about. He was dismissive to the point of hostility towards anyone who disagreed with him, on even minor issues. He almost seemed to thrive on disagreement, as if his real reason for wanting our company was that he wanted someone to lose arguments to him. We tolerated him and learned to disengage from a line of discussion when it became clear that he was sniffing for an argument in it. I for one hoped that he would learn better social skills from our example. In hindsight, refusing to socialize with him at all for his poor behavior would have probably made a more effective lesson, but Doug never was of a disposition to learn.

This pattern continued for some years after university. I doubt any one of us liked Doug enough to invite him to a social outing, but of course it was always him who did the inviting. We considered his initiative and commitment to maintaining friendships after college to be his best quality; *he* considered his best quality to be his punctuality. I would often arrive five or ten minutes early to an appointment and find him already there waiting for us. Being on time was important to him, primarily because it gave him something to argue about with those who weren't. The second greatest lesson I learned from him is just how limited the value of punctuality really is.

"What good is showing up on time if there's no good in you showing up *at all*?" I'd imagine myself asking him at times when he'd try our patience. I never did call him out to his face, however, and to this day I wonder if holding my tongue was the right thing. His passing away at a young age has further complicated the question—my silence allowed him to live out his entire life content in his ways, but then again, he wouldn't have lived to hold a grudge over it if I had.

The final time I saw him alive was the first time I ever saw him late or behind schedule. I knew it meant that something was wrong, but to this day I'm not sure what.

It was early autumn, eleven years after Douglas and I had begun that semester at Quinapoxet. Doug's uncle, Tobias Gnoll, had purchased a dozen or so acres of land in a small rural town in the Berkshires, upon which he intended to build the secluded woodland cabin of his dreams. Tobias had cleared enough forest undergrowth for a driveway and foundation, but the actual construction had been delayed. Douglas had convinced his uncle, since they had no use for the land in the meantime, to let us pitch tents in the clearing and invite us for a long weekend of bonfires and revelry.

Fewer of our friends than usual showed up. A few of them told me beforehand that they didn't think they could handle being around Doug for more than an afternoon at a time. Out of the fifteen or so people he had invited, only six were there: Doug, me, and our friends David and Abigail, plus Doug's two cousins Kyle and Melinda.

Melinda had a part-time job in the valley and couldn't get time off, so during most of the day we were only five. Kyle seemed less interested in partying than in chaperoning us around his little sister and the site of his future house. None of our group were naturally raucous or boisterous anyway, so it was a quiet weekend getaway—a far cry from the wild party I suspect Doug had hoped for. Doug would have turned 30 that winter, if he had lived, and this trip would have been the last big party of his twenties, if more of us had shown up for it. His disappointment was palpable throughout the trip.

On our last night there, Doug proposed we make time for an early-morning swim the next day before we had to pack up and leave. We all agreed, though I remember quietly resenting that even on a vacation out in the woods, Douglas was insisting on a schedule.

By nine o'clock or so the next morning, it was only Doug who had not yet awoken. The other five of us had gathered around the coffee pot, picking over the last of our bacon and hash and quietly wondering what to make of it. None of us had ever once had to wait for Doug.

"Honestly, I'm glad for it," I said as I finished my plate. "I'm glad he's finally allowed himself to relax and not get so tied up in being on time. This is a vacation, after all, isn't it?"

"He's missing breakfast." I could hear Doug's typical irritation in Kyle's voice, but he at least was a bit more tactful about it.

"He can eat when he wakes up. There'll plenty left for him." We had cooked all the remaining food we had brought to avoid bringing leftovers home.

"Well, I have to be at work by 2pm," said Melinda, "so we either go swimming now, or I don't get to go."

"He's never been shy about leaving without us when we're late, has he?" said Abigail. "I'll get my swimsuit on."

I didn't enjoy doing it to him even if he would do it to us, but it was clear I'd lost the vote. Before returning to my tent to change, I found a clean container to put away the rest of the food so that the flies wouldn't beat Doug to it and left him a note. I noticed that the sun would be hitting his tent directly in less than an hour, at which point the heat would surely wake him.

It was almost noon when we decided that we had had our fill of swimming, and it was clear that Doug wouldn't be joining us. We headed back to our tents to dry off and pack up, half-expecting to find him sulking in his tent. Instead, we found him sitting on a stump, sweating and pale and staring off into the distance at nothing, a look of abject horror on his face. Next to him sat an older man, a stranger to me, trying to snap him out of his shock.

"Dad?" Melinda asked. "What's going on?"

"I don't know," said the man, evidently Doug's uncle Tobias, "I just got here a few minutes ago. I was just going to check in, make sure everything's okay, but Doug here looks like he's seen a ghost."

"I—I was," Doug started, "I mean, it was… was before dawn. The sky was just lightening but the sun hadn't risen yet. It was earlier than I had meant to get up, but I… I got up anyway. I don't know why. And when I came out of the tent, none of our stuff was here."

"What? Everything was still here when we got up." I said.

"No, I mean… just let me finish. All our stuff, our tents, our cars, none of it was here. It didn't look like it had ever been here. The clearing wasn't even fully cleared yet. I was definitely still on this land, I remember seeing that big tree there," Doug pointed, "and that rock. There was more brush here, and this stump I'm sitting on, it was… it was still a tree."

"How is that possible? It was cut down a month ago." said Kyle.

"I saw it with my own eyes! I saw it and I got up and I started walking and I—but it wasn't really *me* walking! I was… it was like an out-of-body experience, except it was an in-someone-else's body experience! I don't know who. But I could feel it wasn't my own body. Arms and legs weren't the same length as mine."

"Doug, I have a very important question for you, and I want you to answer honestly." David looked Doug straight in the eye. "Did you bring any party drugs out here and take them after we went to bed last night? You can tell me."

"No, damn it! Stop interrupting me! Just let me tell you what happened!" Doug was starting to go red-faced and hoarse from yelling, and he looked about ready to strangle the next person who spoke. The smug expression he usually got during arguments was nowhere to be seen. "Listen, there's a… a… some kind of a big sundial! Up on the other side of the mountain! Except it's like Stonehenge, with rocks and a big slab in the center, with some writing on it. Like it's carved into the mountain, right where the sun first hits it when it rises."

"What's that got to do with—"

"Be quiet! That's where I was walking to! Last night, when it wasn't me! It was fifty years ago, at least! It felt like fifty years ago at least!"

"*What.*"

"I walked up the mountain to the sundial when I was somebody else, and there were four other people there too. All dressed in old-fashioned leather and furs, and sitting around the big slab like they were waiting for me. And then they all got to chanting, and, and…"

"Chanting." I tried my best not to roll my eyes at him. "Do you remember what they were chanting?"

"I do! It was… '*We genuflect to the forces of the earth and the sky and that which lies beyond*'" Doug paused, as if shocked to hear the words coming out of his own mouth in his own voice. "There was more but that was like… the chorus? It wasn't a song. We all just kept chanting that for like 20 minutes. I could feel those words coming out of the other person's mouth. I could feel it was *his* tongue forming the words in *his* mouth, and I could hear *his* voice, not mine."

I looked over at the others. David glanced back at me, and we each nodded, confirming for the other that we were each just as confused. Abigail had worry in her eyes as she listened to Doug ramble, as if she knew something was wrong but couldn't think of what to do about it. Kyle had his brow furrowed in contempt, and Melinda had given up listening altogether and was hanging up her towel.

"Then I looked up, and everybody was… foaming at the mouth? And they had pulled a little boy out a sack!"

"A little boy?" said Tobias, "about how old?"

"I couldn't tell. No older than ten or so, maybe younger? I grabbed him and threw him over my shoulder and ran away. I don't know why though. Like I was saving him? From the other people there? I ran about halfway back here before I ran out of breath, so we hid in a ditch. They were chasing us. They wanted to catch that kid, I just know it! I must've saved him from… God knows what they would've done to him.

"So we were hiding in the ditch, and the kid looks up and says 'What do you think, Doug?' He knew my name! My *real* name! But I wasn't me! 'I think you should shut up!' I yelled back. He and I listened for any out-of-the-ordinary sound. Nothing. But we knew they were out there!

"Finally, we snuck back to the clearing here, and I got out my gun."

"Your *gun?!*" Abigail yelled. The whole group of us recoiled. Listening to Doug's frantic story was unsettling enough without imagining that the person telling it had access to a firearm.

"I don't own a gun, you know that!" Doug snapped. "Search my tent if it makes you happy, you won't find one. But there was one here! It was inside an old pickup truck. Like a *really* old pickup truck, like it was old fifty years ago. No way it's still on the road today, they don't even make that model anymore. But it was parked in this clearing, and there was a gun in a case in the truck's cab. Not a pistol, it was long like a hunting rifle." Doug held up his hands as if holding the rifle. "The kind you only load in one bullet at a time, and reload after every shot.

"I told the kid to hide in the truck where he'd be safe, and I went back out… to find the people who'd been chasing us. I got the drop on the first one, and got him in the chest.

"I never fired a gun or reloaded one, but I could feel the whole thing. The way the gun recoiled in my hands, the loud bang, and the way my fingers moved as I loaded another bullet in. I never knew how to reload a gun, but my fingers knew exactly what to do. It only took three or four seconds. If I had that same type of gun here right now, I bet

I would know how to reload it now." Doug pantomimed the action with his hands, complete with clicking noises with his mouth. It looked less like reloading a gun and more like he was having a nervous spasm.

"The others must have heard the gunshot. I started hearing more people move down the hill. One of them came from around a tree and I got him in the pelvis. But then while I was reloading again, two more came from around that big rock there," Doug turned and pointed, and stopped as if watching to see if the two fur-clad assailants really were lurking behind the rock, "and they both had guns too!

"They shot and I felt it! Right in my chest here!" Doug slapped the right side of his rib cage. "I tried to fire another shot but I was already dizzy and in pain, I think I missed. I felt the ground spin under me, and I started coughing up blood. I heard the two of them yelling, and I… I died."

"You *died?*" I said. "Okay, that's enough, Doug!"

"You shut your goddamn mouth while I'm talking, you goddamn jackass!"

"No, *you* shut your mouth before you talk your way into a straitjacket and a padded cell. You really want to try and convince us that you are now *dead*? Are you going to show us the bullet wound?" Doug had exhausted my sympathy. I looked at the others, expecting them to agree. Abigail seemed to, the other three just looked confused and irritated. Doug's uncle Tobias, however, raised a hand to shush me. He turned to look at me only briefly, but it was long enough. His face had blanched to an ashen gray from horror, and in his eyes, I saw tears he'd been holding back, as well as an unfathomable dread.

"I believe it. In fact I *know* it all happened," Tobias said, "because I was there. It all really happened, fifty-five years ago. This *same week too!* The second-to-last week in September! I had forgotten nearly all about it, but *I* was that boy in the burlap sack!

"My uncle Allen and a few of his friends had taken me on a hunting trip. I was… eight, I think? It was so long ago, and I hadn't understood what was going on at the time, but I remember being grabbed and shoved in the sack in the middle of the night, and I remember having to hide in the pickup truck all morning until my father got there, and… that chant you described! '*We genuflect to the forces of the earth and the sky and that which lies beyond.*' I thought your whole story was a dream too, until you said that! But I remember it now, clear as a bell. I remember hearing them all chant that over and over.

"And you said you were in someone else's body? I know whose! From what you described, I remember who it was! He was a friend of your grandfather's, and his name was Doug, too—Doug Long. He and my uncle both really did die of gunshot wounds on that trip! The story Dad had told me was that Doug Long murdered my uncle Allen and another man, and then the others shot him in self-defense. But somehow I never believed it."

Doug and Tobias looked at each other, both in sheer dumbstruck awe. Abigail looked over at me, and I shrugged.

"Doug, I've got some photos back at my house I want you to look at." Tobias said, and the two of them got up and made their way to Tobias's car. As an afterthought, Doug ran back and took the plate of food I had set out for him. He looked up at me.

"Thank you for this," he said, "I know you don't believe me. Not sure I would either but… well, I believe it. I'll come back later to pack up my tent and all my stuff.

You don't have to wait for me." Those were the last words he ever spoke to me, though of course I didn't realize it then.

Two weeks later, I was at the publishing office of the Crier on an unrelated matter when I happened to catch a familiar name in the obituaries:

Local resident Douglas Gnol, age 29, passed away unexpectedly last Saturday. The initial coroner's report suggests a lung embolism or other pulmonary aberration was the cause. His surviving mother Donna Goyette, 61, reports that he had seen a doctor two days prior to his death, complaining of a painful cough, but his complaint was misdiagnosed as a common bronchial infection.

After my initial shock at the news wore off, I went to speak with the editor.

"You knew the man?" she asked. "Oh, I'm sorry." This was not the first time I had received condolences for being acquainted with Douglas Gnoll, but it was the first time someone had said it sincerely.

"Yes, I had just seen him only two weeks ago. He seemed…" I couldn't bring myself to say he had seemed *fine*. "Anyway, one question for you. I had always known him to spell his name with two L's, but you spelt it with one in the obit here…"

"A typo," The editor's face darkened. "and a damn unfortunate one. When I spoke to his mother over the phone I had originally thought it was *Knoll*, with a K, and she blew a gasket at me. Spelt it out for me four damn times before she was satisfied I had got it, and now here's a new mistake. Our own fault, but I just know she'll be calling the office to pitch a fit when she sees it. I know her type. She went off for ten minutes about how she planned to sue the hospital and *demanded* we print that she was suing the hospital, even after I explained to her that'd open *us* up for a libel suit." The editor sighed. "God, now she probably wants to sue *us* over the typo!"

"I seem to remember Doug telling me that after the divorce, no lawyer left in the state still takes her calls." I said. "I wouldn't worry about it."

The circumstances of Douglas Gnoll's death will never let me fully forget him. The only explanation for any of it that I've ever found even halfway satisfying is that at some point in the past, some member of the Gnoll family must have told Doug the story of what happened to Tobias as a child, either before or after Tobias himself forgot it all (it may have even been Tobias himself that told Doug the story years prior) and Doug had been reminded of it during our expedition, causing him to have a vivid nightmare about it.

But this fails to explain much. How did Tobias Gnoll come to purchase the very plot of land on which he'd been kidnapped as a child without anyone in the family realizing it? Was there really a Stonehenge-like sundial built on a clearing somewhere on the southeastern side of that mountain in the Berkshires? If I were ever to find it, how much more of Doug's story would it prove? How accurate was Doug's incredible story, especially the parts that Tobias had not witnessed himself and couldn't vouch for? Who were those other two people who hadn't been shot that day, and what had they meant to do with the child Tobias on that mountainside? How much presence did they still have in the Gnoll family's lives? How had Doug dreamed of, or vicariously experienced, getting shot in the very same organ that would fail and claim his life two weeks later?

And could it really be pure coincidence that a typo in his obituary would render his last name as the same last name of the man whose death he had experienced, but spelled backwards—*Gnol* instead of *Long?*

Extracurricular Activity

By Dana Norton

It's not *my* idea of a date. But Nick's right—it *is* kinda nice out. May evening. Warm. A sliver of light from a crescent moon.

We make our way through the field behind the library then turn quickly onto the trail leading into the woods.

"Kaitlyn—hurry up!" Nick pulls my arm. "Someone might see us. What did you tell your mom?"

"The usual. I'm at Emma's. Doing homework."

Nick laughs. "And *I'm* working late at the market."

We head deeper into the woods. Branches hang low over the winding trail and Nick uses his phone flashlight to watch out for roots. Everything is quiet, except for the beer cans clanking in his backpack. I'm in charge of the blanket.

"Nick. What if there's somebody hiding in the woods? The principal said this morning—"

"Yeah, sure. He's just trying to scare us. They don't want us out at night." He snickers. "*'Kids—they're nothing but trouble.'* Anyway, there's no one out here."

Nick's really cute and I really, really like him, but sometimes he's wrong. Because I turn around and in the moonlight I see two shadowy figures way down the trail behind us.

"Nick!*"*

He looks back. "Relax—it's fine." But he frowns and takes my hand. "We'll just walk a little faster."

"Oww—you're pulling my wrist!"

"C'mon, Kaitlyn. Just trying to get away from them."

"So *you're* worried, too."

"I am *not*."

"You *so* are. What if they're what Mr. Harkness said? Y'know—*violent?"*

"Quit playin' with me." But Nick pulls me along faster.

After a minute I look back again. "They're getting closer!" I swallow my gum.

Nick rolls his eyes. But he turns around to see. "OK, we're gonna lose 'em this time." So now we're running up the hilly trail. I stumble on a rock and Nick yanks me up roughly. My legs feel like lead. And still I hear the sharp crackle of leaves behind us.

I peek over my shoulder a minute later. Is it two guys or what? I wish to God I was anywhere but here—even at Emma's doing boring geometry homework. "Nick, they're catching up!"

He pulls me along faster. "See that rock wall at the top of the hill? We'll hide behind it—see what these guys are up to."

Another dumb idea of Nick's! But I can't run much further. So we make it to the rock wall, climb over and crouch low.

I reach for my phone. Damn! Why'd I have to drop it in the bathtub yesterday? "Nick, call 911!" He tries. No reception.

We peek over the rock wall. The two dark figures are creeping, slowly, up the winding trail toward us. I hold my hand over my mouth so I won't scream. My whole body is shaking. Why did I ever listen to Nick's bright ideas? This is it, they're coming for us!

Suddenly we can't see them anymore. Are they hiding behind a bush?

Nick peers between a gap in the rocks. "What do you think?"

"I think you should shut up!"

We listen for the slightest out-of-the ordinary sound. Nothing. But we know they're out there.

Then we hear voices—very clearly. Though we still can't see anybody.

"I knew you'd like it, Marian," a man's deep voice is saying. "Let's spread out the blanket next to this bush. Much nicer than a stuffy motel room, don't you think?" He chuckles. *Where* have I heard that laugh before?

"Clever the way you managed it, George." The woman's high-pitched tones remind me a little of our school secretary, Ms. Kelly.

"High school kids—they'll believe anything," says the man. "You should have seen their faces at assembly this morning. Mouths hanging open, eyes wide as saucers. Right after I told them there's been reports of *extremely* violent hoodlums in the forest after dark."

He laughs again. "So no chance they'll be anywhere near these woods tonight. No one—not even my wife—will discover our little tryst."

I look at Nick. He looks at me. For the first time this evening we agree on something.

"Adults are so sleazy," he whispers in my ear.

"Yeah—nothing but trouble."

TREES

Writing Prompt

The trees in the dark wood seemed to wrap around her. Although it was almost sunset, no light shone through. The tree trunks looked midnight black. Bare branches twisted and twined around each other. She took the crumpled note out of her pocket and consulted it once more.

Stories

Ghost Story

By Lucy A.J. Tew

"It's a snow day," Lynn's voice sighed tinnily through the speaker, the moment Emily answered the on-call phone. "Well, it will be when Mike calls it. He's going to hold off on sending the email until the end of study hall so the girls actually focus on their work."

Em looked out her cracked kitchen window at the group of Gower residents currently playing in the rising drifts of snow at the base of the hill. "Yep. They're definitely focusing," she said, as she watched one hoodie-clad soccer player nail another right in the face with a snowball. "I'm watching half the Gower Hall girls run a physics study group down on the lawn."

Lynn chuckled, then stopped herself. "Wait a minute, it's after eight, who's on in there tonight?"

"No one who's done an actual study hall check-in. I'm pretty sure these girls have been out there since dinner." Em turned back to the stove and stirred her pasta. "But I think RJ is the dorm parent on duty."

"Oh, god," Lynn groaned, and it echoed funnily in the speaker, like her voice had been captured and muffled by a wineglass brought too close to the microphone. Lynn usually had a glass of wine in the evenings, and Em would've gladly joined her in this one if she wasn't working her third night on duty this week. Now, with a snow day, she would be continuing through the weekend.

"We've really got to talk to someone else about taking on some of these admin-on-duty shifts," she said to Lynn. "Not that I don't live to serve, but I feel like I haven't been off-duty since October."

"Don't I know it. I'm working on Mike, I promise. He won't up the stipend, of course, and—"

Em put the phone down on the counter and tapped the speaker button while Lynn got going; Lynn was her closest friend at work, even if she was forty years older. Emily was only too happy to let Lynn vent. She, after all, had taken *Emily's* hourlong phone call hollering about some other on-duty drama just yesterday.

Unfortunately, their cohesion as a team running the boarding program never seemed to reliably and consistently translate down to their picks of dorm parents – but then, when you were only able to offer cramped, awkwardly arranged apartments and a meager-at-best 'stipend' as compensation, you sometimes had to just take the warm body that showed up to the interview.

One such warm body—RJ, the perpetually delinquent Gower dorm parent—was just now walking across the lawn. She was gesticulating angrily at the squad of soccer-player juniors now building a snowman with suspiciously human anatomy.

"Hey, there goes RJ," Em mused out loud.

"What?" Lynn squawked.

"RJ is getting the Gower girls on the lawn. I don't have to put my boots on."

"Well, that's something," Lynn sighed. She paused. "Is that the wind? Is it really that loud?"

Em crossed to the window. "Yeah, my kitchen window is still broken so it sounds even worse."

"Oh, honestly, *still*?" Lynn exclaimed. "We've got to get someone on that, too!"

"Good luck with that," Em replied. Then, just as the wind rose to another howl, the lights in the apartment gave a soft *pop* and went out. "Shit," she muttered.

"What now?" Lynn asked.

"Power just went out," Emily replied. "I don't know if it's the whole building or not."

"Oh, you're kidding."

"Nope," Em muttered. "Gotta go. Maintenance is going to ask me to check the fuses when I call it in, so I'll save them the trouble."

"Call me with updates."

"Aye, Captain."

Emily hung up on Lynn. Once her eyes had adjusted a bit, she carefully lifted her pot full of pasta and drained it into the colander in the sink, shutting off the now-dead electric burner. She put on her coat, hat, and snow boots. Then she went to the cupboard and pulled out a canvas bag full of flashlights, and an old Post-It note where she kept the instructions on how to reset the circuit breakers.

Monmouth-Whitman Academy, formerly the Whitman School for Girls, had taken up residence in the Monmouth House Hotel, a Gilded-Age retreat for the wealthy, in the 1930s. Most of the endowment was gone even before the 2008 recession, when the school's day student population had gone co-ed to boost enrollment. The school now served as a pleasant, sleepy-eyed, slower-paced but winsome alternative to the Choates and Exeters of the world. Matriculation was all but guaranteed for seniors, with a healthy smattering of Ivy League acceptances in every class. The building was long and thin, laid out in an arc. It hosted four dorms stacked on the top floors of converted hotel rooms, with the two bottom floors, cellar, and ground floor wing extensions serving as classrooms, cafeteria, assembly space, and offices. Freshmen lived in Lyman Hall on the top floor, sophomores in the next level of dorms, Crosby, juniors in Gower, and senior girls on the floor closest to the classrooms, in Mendum Hall.

Every window in the old hotel building was strategically placed to allow as many guests as possible a view of the pond and the sprawling woods that embraced the grassy hilltop in a dense, dark crescent of trees. It was undeniably a gorgeous view in the spring, summer, and autumn. Tonight, however, the trees felt as though they were closing in from all directions as Emily fought her way through the snow to the breaker boxes in the maintenance shed just at the edge of the treeline. The trees in the dark wood seemed to wrap around her. It was long past sunset, and no light shone through. The tree trunks looked midnight black. Bare branches twisted and twined around each other. Em took the crumpled note out of her pocket and consulted it once more. It was a set of convoluted instructions that she feared had no real basis in applied science. Nonetheless, she went through the routine of on and off switches more than once.

But after flipping the breakers for ten minutes, it was clearly no use. The whole building was without power. Within the first five minutes of the blackout, Em had answered the on-call phone to what seemed like every resident and dorm parent notifying her of this turn of events—as if she might have missed it. She stopped answering after a while, more focused on getting to the fuse boxes than anything else—but there was nothing she could do if the power lines had failed. She attempted to get hold of the maintenance team, only to learn that they had all gone home and no one would be able to clear the drive and work on the problem until the blizzard let up. After an hour in the dark, the calls on the phone began again. Not only were the girls complaining of the lack of wi-fi, they were getting cold in their large-windowed rooms.

So, Emily convened a meeting of the dorm parents—all of them, on duty or not—and passed out flashlights with instructions to gather all residents, blankets, pillows, cushions, and lightweight dorm mattresses in the student center. The center was a ballroom-turned-relaxation space, with only a few high windows and enough open floor space for all the girls to sleep there.

By the third hour of the blackout, a large-scale slumber party had gotten underway, with girls sharing portable battery cells to keep their phones playing music. RJ had gotten into a closet full of camping supplies from the annual school trip, and portable lanterns and additional flashlights now dotted the student center, illuminating little clusters of girls all bundled up in their warmest clothes and blankets, their mattresses tucked in side by side.

Em was just pulling a fleece blanket around her shoulders when she caught a snippet of conversation from the nearest cluster of girls, a mix from Lyman and Crosby. "We telling ghost stories?" Em asked Molly, a hockey player from Rhode Island.

"Oh yeah, Ms. Bennett, I know a ton of good ones," Molly grinned. "Did you know this place is haunted?"

"Totally," Em agreed, squeezing in between Molly and her roommate, a Thai sophomore named Banyen. "I hear weird stuff all the time when I do my lockup rounds."

Banyen's eyes were wide. "You *do?"*

"Yeah, Ms. B," squealed Jess, another Lyman girl. "Tell us one!"

Em shrugged. "Well, I don't want to scare you…"

There was an immediate uproar.

"No, Ms. B, you *have* to tell us so we can be protected!" exclaimed Cherie, a sophomore from Beijing.

"Oh, none of our ghosts want to hurt you," Em assured them. She paused dramatically. "Well, *most* of them don't." Edi and Parla, a roommate pair of Crosby girls from Turkey, who were permanently glued to their phones and seated at the outer edge of this circle, both looked up at this. Em leaned into the theatrics. "You know that door on the staircase between Crosby and Lyman? The door that doesn't open?"

"The one that's stuck?" asked Molly. "It's got, like, cement or something behind it, it never budges when I try to turn the handle."

"You *touched* it?" Banyen asked, with a mix of horror and appreciation for her bravery.

"Just the one time," Molly said. "It gave me bad vibes."

"Molly, shut up and listen," Parla snapped. "Ms. B, tell the story."

Em blew out a breath and nodded. "Well, that door on the back stairs leads to the *real* sixth floor." The girls frowned at her, looking confused. She tried again and asked, "You know how when you're climbing up between the sophomore and freshman dorms, there's an extra set of stairs? Or when you're down on the soccer field, and you look up at the dorm tower, there're seven stories to the building?"

"No, there's not," Molly said, frowning and clearly racking her brains. "Wait—behind the flags, you mean?" She pointed at the nearest window, to indicate she meant the neat row of heavy wood panels mounted near the top of the building, painted as the flags of every country represented in the student body. The student center was nowhere near the row of flags, but Molly's meaning was clear enough, so Emily nodded.

"Those flags are covering up a row of sealed and painted-over windows. See, there *are* seven stories, but we only *use* six," Emily said. "We skip one and call Lyman the sixth floor.

"Why?" asked Edi.

Em shrugged. "Well, when Miss Whitman got here with her students, she took one look at the real sixth floor, and she had it sealed off for good. She had it written into all the school records that the construction was just to make the stairwells safe—but actually, she was scared of what she found there."

"What did she find?" Cherie whispered, her eyes wide.

"Some pretty weird stuff," Em said, trying not to sound like she was stalling. "Witchcraft stuff. Signs of spells and summonings. And in the apartment that the hotel manager lived in, she found a trapdoor that hid a chute, just wide enough for a person, that dropped straight down into the boiler room."

"A—shoot?" Cherie asked, frowning as she made a finger-gun.

"No, a chute like a slide," said Jess. Cherie looked even more confused. "Like a chimney, kinda?"

"Oh!" Cherie said, bursting into laughter. "Chute, like C-H-U, not like a gun!"

The other girls all giggled with her. Em had lost a little momentum in the story—Edi and Parla were drifting back to their phones. "But you didn't ask the most important question, Cherie," said Em, trying to restore a little mystery to the moment.

Cherie frowned again, and Em dropped her voice to a whisper. "Why would anyone need a chute like that in a private apartment?"

"Laundry?" Jess giggled. "Hello, it was a hotel!"

"It wasn't connected to the laundry," Em said, without breaking character. She wanted to keep them going, however, so she invented another little detail on the spot, courtesy of the last spring musical, *Sweeney Todd*. "But it *was* streaked with blood."

"Ew!" squealed Jess, as the other girls gasped.

"So, Miss Whitman had the doors to the whole floor locked, and kept just one key for herself. The records of the floor were hidden away, for good," Emily went on quietly. "But even when the work was done, that didn't stop the strange noises and the things the students and teachers noticed."

"Like what?" asked Edi, drawing her long legs up against her chest and leaning forward into the pool of bluish-white lantern light.

"Like the reports Miss Whitman got from the girls, saying that it felt like something was always just behind them—watching them—hovering in the corners, every time they passed by the old sixth floor." Emily lowered her voice to a whisper, and the six girls leaned in closer. "They tried everything. When they padlocked and deadbolted the door in the back stairs, people would smell cigarettes and hear faint music on the other side. Once, one girl even heard someone knocking on the door—from the inside. Finally, one night, five girls decided to steal Miss Whitman's key and see the old sixth floor for themselves."

Em paused for drama—even other girls from nearby circles of juniors and seniors were falling quiet, turning to listen to the story. This, after all, was the only part Emily was not inventing—embellishing, perhaps—but the story of the five girls was a verifiable fact. Every Monmouth-Whitman girl eventually heard the story, passed from one generation to the next.

"Maybe they were investigating—maybe they wanted to work some spells themselves. Who knows? But whatever the reason was that they went in there, only four of them came back. They said that they'd seen a blinding green light, and the fifth girl had *disappeared*. The other four left the school the very next day, and none of them ever spoke another word about what they saw, as long as they lived. The only thing they ever told Miss Whitman about was the green light. They swore they had no idea what had happened—but that they didn't believe their friend was really gone. And maybe she wasn't… because every once in a while, she would be seen, climbing the back stairs… trying to lure other girls to follow her."

Banyen shuddered. "A ghost."

Em nodded. "The strange experiences in the stairwell got so bad, Miss Whitman had the doorway bricked up, and the door cemented shut over it." Emily sat back, looking around at the half-lit features of her captive audience. "But they say you should never, ever take the back stairs by yourself—just in case you see the girl, or the green light from behind the door, and you're the next to vanish."

Molly smiled and shuddered, and the other Crosby and Lyman girls looked simultaneously impressed and nervous.

"Nice one, Ms. B!" whooped Cam, a Mendum girl sitting a few feet away with a pack of her friends. "Gets better every year!"

The tension broke, and all the girls started to giggle.

"Don't worry," said one Gower girl to a very nervous-looking Banyen. "She's been telling that story since she started as my sister's dorm parent, and *she's* a freshman in college now. It changes every time. You'd better write it down, Ms. B, so you remember all your edits."

Banyen tried to smile. "But how do *you* know it, Ms. Bennett?"

"Oh, Ms. B knows pretty much everything about this school," said Molly with a shrug, before Em could answer. "Cause she spends all her time hanging out with Mrs. Winters in the boarding office. Mrs. Winters went to school here, so she *actually* knows everything."

"Yep, hanging out, that's what we do," Emily agreed, rolling her eyes. "It's just such a breeze being the thirty-something parent of a hundred hormonal teenage girls, Mrs. Winters and I just kick back in the office and swap stories all day."

"You're *thirty?*" Molly gasped.

"Okay," Em called, grinning and standing up with her blanket still wrapped around her shoulders. She raised her voice to carry across the whole room. "Ten minutes to lights out! Dorm parents, make sure you've got a good head count of your kids—I've got an emergency roster if you need it."

Banyen came and touched Emily's elbow, her dark eyes wide in the gloomy student center. "Ms. Bennett, your story—I don't like it."

Em felt a little rush of guilt. "Oh, honey, I'm sorry—I didn't mean to scare you. Honestly, I made almost all of that stuff up. Seriously, I was just messing with you all."

"But the back stairwell *does* have bad vibes," Molly said with a mischievous grin. "Watch yourself, Ban!"

Banyen blanched, and Em said firmly, "Knock it off, Molly. Get ready for bed."

It wasn't a comfortable sleeping arrangement, but the student center and its ancient radiator system, which took the longest time to cool down, was still infinitely warmer than the girls' rooms would have been. Outbreaks of whispering and giggles rose over the whistling, howling wind every few minutes, punctuated by hisses to quiet down from students and dorm parents alike. Em drew her sleeping bag and cushions to the ramp by the doors to the bathrooms—just to make sure none of the on-campus couples got any ideas about sneaking off for some privacy. Around one in the morning, the girls were quiet and still enough that Emily finally fell asleep.

She jerked awake a short while later, to a long-haired someone leaning over her in the darkness. She jerked straight backwards and hit her head on the drywall.

"Ouch! What—what do you need?" she groaned, rubbing her head and trying to make out details in the intense darkness. She could only see the vague shape of the girl.

"I left my book upstairs," the girl whispered. "I need it back."

Banyen—it was Banyen, Em was almost sure. It was hard to tell, as the girl was speaking in a raspy, soft whisper, trying not to wake anyone around them.

Emily checked her smartwatch, bleary-eyed. “Not right now, honey, just—try to get some sleep.”

The girl shuddered, like she was cold, or like she was physically shaking off Emily’s rejection. “No. I need it tonight.”

Em sighed, still fighting to see in the darkness—the battery-powered emergency lamps above the exit signs had faded long ago, so the only light in the student center came from the moonlight beyond the windows—the snow clouds had broken up. “Okay, you can go get it. Go ahead.”

There was a long pause before the girl finally spoke. “I’m scared,” she whispered, her voice even quieter than before.

Emily sighed and rubbed her eyes. “Okay—okay, fine. I’ll go. Wait right here.” She picked up her flashlight and got out of her sleeping bag. The girl remained motionless, but Em could feel her watching as she got to her feet. She shivered and went to the doors to the main hall, which was freezing. Em picked the nearest stairwell to the dorm tower and climbed. She’d made it all the way to Crosby when she remembered that she had forgotten to ask Banyen which room she and Molly lived in on Lyman, and which book she’d even needed.

Half-asleep and freezing cold, she felt inside the kangaroo pocket of her hoodie for the crumpled emergency roster. She found the room number just before her flashlight flickered once, then died.

“Oh, come on,” Emily groaned, smacking the handle. The cheap pharmacy flashlight flickered again, and then gave up, plunging the cold stairwell into near-complete darkness. The only light was the filtered charcoal of the sky outside, dashed by snow flurries swirling past the windows on the landing. The trees closest to the building were midnight black silhouettes—thorn hedges closing around Sleeping Beauty's castle. The windows flickered with the shadowy movement of the branches. Em put a hand out for the railing and started up the stairs again, keeping her eyes on her feet as best she could.

It took her a moment to notice the echoes—the faint scrape of footsteps that seemed to shadow her own. She stopped and looked back down into the yawning darkness of the stairs below. "Ban?" she asked, her voice not much louder than a whisper. It was lost to a particularly sharp howl of the wind past the dormitory tower, which made Em jump.

She tightened her fingers on the cold metal rail, frozen for a moment. The thread of a chill, one that had nothing to do with the freezing cold of the stairwell, unspooled down her back. It had been a very long time since she'd scared herself with her own imagination—in fact, the whole reason she'd even invented half the ghost stories she told the girls about their school was that she'd spent so much time walking the halls alone, late at night. After a moment, she managed to recover herself, and started up the stairs again, a little more quickly.

That was when the stairwell began to brighten. At first, it seemed to Emily like the light in the windows was shifting. Was it closer to dawn than she'd thought, or was another snow cloud drifting past? Then, she realized that the landing she was approaching had no window—only a door. The light now spilling down the stairs grew brighter as it swung silently open.

October 24th

By C. Brian Moorhead

It was Iezabel's birthday—her *original* birthday, the one she had celebrated when she was still alive.

This was her first birthday as a vampire. She hadn't planned to celebrate it, then she got the message from Felix. He had made it sound like there would be a party.

Now here she was, alone and ankle-deep in the middle of a swamp. The trees in the dark wood seemed to wrap around her. Although it was still twilight, no light shone through. The tree trunks looked midnight black. Bare branches twisted and twined around each other. She took the crumpled note out of her pocket and consulted it once more.

Hope you haven't made birthday plans. Come to the marsh where I dumped your corpse. Follow the smell of blood. Get there as early after sundown as you can. You don't want to miss a moment of this. -F.

Iezabel sneered at Felix's hand-drawn smiley face. What could possibly happen out here that she wouldn't want to miss a moment of? He'd gotten her hopes up for an orgy. Now she'd already lost a stiletto in the peat, and her fishnets were ruined. A human in her place would have leeches between her toes by now.

Felix himself had been nowhere in sight when she had arrived at the marsh's edge. He had left a wheelbarrow and an empty burlap sack for her by the embankment, with no explanation. She had thought at first that he had meant for her to help bury a body. Then she remembered he hadn't bothered to bury *her* properly. She had been winding herself up to tell him off when she caught a whiff.

Felix hadn't lied. There *was* a smell, or some sort of intangible force, that she could feel guiding her through the swamp, beckoning her deeper in. It didn't quite smell like fresh blood, but it made her the same kind of hungry. She could practically see the vapor trail.

It led her to a candlelit gazebo, enshrouded in moss and creeping vines as if the swamp threatened to swallow it. Iezabel couldn't differentiate between the individual trees, but in her gut she could feel that this was the same spot where Felix had left her drained and desecrated body months ago. She had seen no man-made structure when she awoke under that first full moon, yet the gazebo looked ancient. The peat and humus around its base looked recently disturbed. She wondered if it had somehow risen from below the surface.

Inside a ring of candles and profane geometry on the deck of the gazebo squatted a grinning imp, skin shriveled and scabbed over, teeth like splintered wood. A wooden trunk, a stack of books, and a pewter goblet and pitcher sat next to it.

"Felicitations, Iezabel." it hissed, "Come, and claim your birthright. All you see before you are gifts from your… patrons."

Iezabel paused only to shake the muck from her feet, for fear of smudging the profane inscriptions. She then stepped into the circle. Her eyes were drawn to the goblet. It was full of blood.

"Drink your fill." The imp said.

"What do you ask in return for all this?" she asked.

"A day shall come when your patrons demand a favor from you," the imp said, "but not today. This is a day of jocularity. Take what is offered to you."

Iezabel took the goblet and drank. The blood was still hot, practically steaming in the cool night air, as if fresh from the vein. The taste was familiar, but never before had she been able to drink without having to pierce skin or hold down a squirming victim. The experience of gulping down mouthful after mouthful so effortlessly was a sinfully luxurious indulgence she had never dreamed of.

As she tilted her head back to drain the last of it, she felt the imp place a second goblet into her free hand. She sloshed that one down even faster than she had the first, but not faster than the imp could refill the empty goblet. She was halfway through her fifth—sixth?—serving when the rip of fabric snapped her out of her frenzy. She looked down. Her stomach had swollen to the point of tearing open the seams of her dress.

"How much have I drunk?" she asked, still dizzy from euphoric intoxication.

"About eleven pints." The imp said.

"What?! Eleven pints? That's imp-p-p-" A heavy belch interrupted her sentence.

"Only for a human," said the imp. "How do you feel?"

"Like I ought to drink like this every night." Iezabel rubbed her stomach in awe. "How many victims would I need?"

“At least a dozen,” said the imp with a grin, “if you intend them all to survive. Seven or so if you really wring them out. With a grinder and sieve, three may suffice. Are you quenched?”

“For the moment.” Iezabel sat down on the creaking gazebo boards, crossing her legs to give her swollen belly a lap to rest in.

“Good. There is more than blood on offer tonight.” The imp lifted the lid of the trunk. It was full of gold coins, gems, and other treasures. Iezabel reached in and picked up a pearl-handled dagger.

“This is all for me?” Iezabel asked. “All of it?”

“Your benefactors are exceptionally generous,” said the imp, “and wish for you to aspire to a high position in society that can only be obtained through coin. And to be most grateful to them for it.”

“Okay but seriously, why give me all of this? My ‘patrons’ must want something from me in return.”

“They do indeed. There are plans that have been set into motion centuries before your living form walked this earth, and yet they include you as one of the agents of implementation. This benefaction is your compensation for your future service but know you this: that for which you are being compensated shall be easier to accomplish with the benefit of wealth. You would do wise not to squander it.”

“Standard investment advice, really.” Iezabel said. “I guess this explains why Felix left me a wheelbarrow and an empty sack. To carry it all in. Not that the wheelbarrow would have made it this far into the swamp anyway. Still, I probably shouldn’t have shat in it to spite him.”

“You may take the trunk, along with the treasure,” said the imp. “And the goblets, should it please you.”

"I'm guessing the goblets don't endlessly refill with blood after tonight, do they?" Iezabel took another sip. Her dress was already ruined anyway, what sense was there in holding back now?

"Alas, they do not. But they are still rightfully yours."

"He's waiting at the edge of the marsh to jump me and steal it all, no doubt."

"He is not." The imp's brow furrowed and its tone grew harsh. "No vampire may steal another's birthright, or else be reduced to ash on the spot. He knows this." The imp paused to regain its composure. "And more so, why should he do such a thing? He too has received his own benefaction, and knows he shall do so again, when his own season returns."

"His own season?" Iezabel asked. "You mean every vampire receives a gift like this, every year?"

"Each year, for your first one hundred and one years in this world." The imp said. "You are young yet even by human standards. Able-bodied. *Nubile.*" The imp broke eye contact briefly. "But ill-equipped to comprehend the relative ephemeralness of a century and a year. Tonight you imagine it equivalent to an eternity. But you shall soon recognize the finite extent of your… stipend. And upon its maturity, you are expected to be well-heeled, and well-versed in the *ghifhtagresch*."

"Gesundheit." Iezabel said. "But seriously, well-versed in what now?"

"Apologies." The imp said, its expression betraying frustration. "It is an esoteric term, with no etymological root in any human language, much as a language of cattle should contain no adequate translation for the semiotic implications of the terms 'porterhouse' or 'ribeye'. I believe your sire translates it as 'haemotheurgy'."

"Haemotheurgy." She repeated the word, trying to remember when she'd heard Felix use it.

"A neologism constructed from what remains of a dead language. The synecdoche of it pleases."

"Is that the power you gain over someone when you've drunk their blood? Felix has mentioned it a few times, but I could never get any details out of him."

"What has he elucidated to you so far?" The imp leaned in, intrigued.

"He talks about it like it's magic, that uses our victims' blood as a fuel source." she said. "He said it's the real reason we feed, to tap into its power. He suspects that it's that same power that keeps us up and walking despite the fact that we're all technically corpses."

"A succinct explanation, if simplified."

"He also said there's a ritual that's like a… a beacon to anyone you've ever fed on who's still alive, calls them all to you or sends them a hypnotic message of some kind. But he says he can't get the hang of it yet."

"Felix has... related the truth, insofar as he understands it, but he is yet a neophyte." The imp pushed the stack of books towards Iezabel. "This is your true gift, and you shall reap its benefits most richly, as long as you are able to keep yourself quenched." The imp patted Iezabel's swollen stomach. "Your voracity shall be your greatest asset."

"So these are like… spellbooks? Will they teach me how to do blood magic?"

"The books, and I as your tutor. The ritual of the 'beacon' is but one of myriad invocations I can teach you, but as I said before, you will receive one hundred and one visitations in total, no more. Whatever aspects of the haemotheurgy you have yet to lucubrate by then shall be forever obscured to you. And upon that night, you will be presented with your patrons' obligations. Obligations that you may find require every available advantage, both occult and pecuniary, to fulfill. If, after one hundred and one years, the advantages your patrons have bestowed upon you are insufficient to satisfy what is demanded of you… well, would you like to speculate?"

"This is Hell I'm dealing with after all, isn't it?" For the first time since her death, Iezabel felt real fear. "I knew there would be a catch."

"You inferred more quickly than Felix did on his first birthday. Your patrons have greater esteem for you than for him. And despite my exhortations, they do yet intend to exalt you. These gifts are not to be squandered, but they are still your gifts. Come then. Sunrise is yet distant, and until it breaks, you may ply me with questions."

How It Really Happened

By Melody Friedenthal

One day, years later, while I was accompanying my sister to the market, I overheard an old man relate an almost-unrecognizable version of our story to his grandchildren. It had warped in the retelling—he said the cottage in the deep woods had a roof made of confections and was decorated all around with gum-drops. What nonsense! There were only the pea tendrils, but his little listeners were riveted to his tale, so who am I to judge? I might have corrected him, even so, but I was not speaking then, nor had I for years.

My sister was almost two years younger than I, yet everyone knew, even when we were small, that she was cleverer than me, and more courageous. If I climbed a tree, she climbed higher. If I balanced on a rickety log that had fallen over a brook, she ran across it, giggling.

I think our parents actually liked me better, though, because they spent a good deal of time sighing over Gretel, chastising her, or wearily ordering her to go to bed. In my last clear memory of them they were demanding that she come down from a walnut tree she had clambered up to steal its fruit. That tree was always a favorite of ours and had only recently become crucial to our larder.

She risked her neck for those walnuts because the crops had failed yet again and every day we grew a little bit hungrier. My father and stepmother, I realized eventually, were less concerned with Gretel's safety than they were that she'd eat her harvest before they could raid it.

Meals were reduced to a mouthful or two, and we grew thin and snappier with each other. Only Gretel retained her sunny disposition and liveliness. I barely had enough energy to finish my chores, of which there were many.

One morning, I woke before dawn to hear Papa and Mama whispering to one another. Papa's voice sounded tense but his wife's voice sounded strident, persistent, and demanding. She spat out, "We have little enough food for ourselves." I thought nothing of it, but only wished I could huddle in my bed for another hour. Gretel slept on, undisturbed by our parents' argument.

Papa called to us to rise then, so I nudged Gretel with my toe. She smiled sleepily at me, and we started another day with thin gruel and sharp words from our stepmother.

I saw her and Papa exchange a look, then Papa announced that we'd be going into the forest that day to hunt and perhaps, if we were lucky and the animals hadn't found them first, to forage more walnuts.

Gretel was her usual cheerful self but I hung back. The forest was gloomy at the best of times but on this unseasonably cold and overcast day, it was foreboding. I just barely remembered the folk tales my real mother had told me, before Gretel was born, of ogres and witches and wood sprites who loved nothing better than to snatch up small children and use them in their evil plots.

We walked for some hours, or so it felt to me. Papa didn't stop anywhere but led us ever deeper into the overgrown woods, stepping over enormous, twisted tree roots, pushing aside the dank foliage. The tree canopy was so thick that the leaden sky, last seen near our cottage, was invisible.

I smelled rot and mud and the fungus that sprouted everywhere near the towering oak trees. I was scared but tried not to show it. Gretel chatted happily as we made our slow progress—nothing seemed to bother her. She led the way, with me following close behind her, to help in case she tripped or got lost. Sometimes, Papa called out instructions:

Go down the left trail, children, or *Boy,* l*eap over the brook and continue along that line of rocks.*

We found no walnuts or anything else edible, and I wondered if Papa had some destination in mind in this trackless wilderness. Our stepmother was, for once, silent, hanging back. When I glanced at her, I saw her eyes darting back and forth. But, besides the ever-present prickly undergrowth and the towering trees, there was naught to see.

My stomach cried for food. I said nothing, knowing we had nothing.

And then, it happened… Gretel's apron caught on some thorns and I stopped to help extricate her. This took some minutes, and when she was free I turned around and saw that we were alone.

Puzzled, I searched the forest round-about. The terrain was tortuous and visibility was quite limited. I saw neither our Papa nor our stepmother, and my heart raced. Gretel was still, taking her cues from me, I supposed, so I tried to keep calm, or at least appear to be so.

I called out, "Papa!"

There was no answer.

I climbed atop a boulder of gray-streaked basalt, being careful not to slip on its moss-covered, uneven surface. I turned slowly, scanning the forest. It was very quiet. I couldn't even hear the birds whose chirps had accompanied us earlier in the day.

No one was within sight.

I called again, "Papa! Mama! Where are you?"

Gretel then shouted out her own plea for help.

No one answered.

I looked at Gretel, and she at me. Her eyes were wide.

"All right, sister-mine, we will go home and I'm sure we'll find Papa there, happy to see us, with apples and a bit of hot stew for our lunch."

She nodded and gave me a small smile. We both knew there would be no stew, hot or cold.

"How did we get separated from them, brother-mine?" she asked.

"I know not, little sister. But surely we will be reunited soon." I was not a good actor.

We tried to find our way back but nothing looked familiar, the land in all directions wild, confusing, damp, and densely grown.

I soon tired, but Gretel found again her usual optimism. She moved jauntily through this rough landscape, chatting about butterflies and her best friend, about the doll which I had carved for her, and about our real mother, who of course Gretel had barely known, as she had died in childbirth.

I attended with half an ear, focusing mainly on placing my feet on level surfaces, and listening for some sign of

Papa or even of wood-cutters who found their trade deep in these ancient woods.

Real fear came to me soon enough. We were lost. We were alone. We were hungry. And, despite calling out for help every few minutes, no one came to our aid. Dusk was approaching.

There were wolves in this vast forest. So many of the stories we heard, while sitting in front of our meager fire, were of wolves tearing the flesh from travelers.

We were lucky—no wolves encircled us, but I soon learned that there could be wolves in human form.

After another hour—or was it two?—Gretel called out, "Look!"

I saw a neat stone cottage, smoke rising from its chimney, nestled in a clearing. We hurried toward it, my heart lifting at what I thought was our salvation. Its oaken door was studded with rivets, and a pea vine grew over the cottage's old stones. There was a well nearby, and also drying racks, and an old loom. Crocuses bloomed to one side. It was all very picturesque.

We threw ourselves onto the pea vine, and, in our hunger, forgot our manners. I ate peas as quickly as I could shell them, and Gretel did too.

The door creaked open and a crone came out. Her back was bent and she moved slowly. She wore a ratty old gray shawl over her head, which hooded her face, and a threadbare brown home-spun dress that looked as ancient as she did herself. Spectacles made of thin wire rested on her nose.

"Come in, children. Are you hungry? Is that why you steal my peas? Well, I am hungry too—come in, come in!"

I was still anxious about our travails and could barely allow myself to think that Papa and Mama had deserted us on purpose. But we followed the old woman into her cottage. It was warm inside and I felt my body release some of its pent-up tension. Gretel wandered around the single room, examining the drying herbs, cauldrons, and various odds-and-ends, and ending up near the fireplace. She started to hold out her hands to the dancing flames but turned abruptly when the old woman secured the oaken door, sliding over the massive iron bolt with an abrupt strength that I wouldn't have thought she had.

"What are your names, children? And how do you come to be in my forest?"

Gretel told her our story and our names. "We've been looking for Papa," she said, "but we never found him, nor Mama, his wife."

"Poor children! And so skinny!" She cackled.

I was about to ask the old woman for directions back to our hamlet when, with a whirl of fabric, she threw off her hood, stood tall, and showed herself to be a man in disguise. I took a step back in shock. This man grinned at us, then he grabbed my arm and lifted me up. I screamed and Gretel did too. He shoved me inside a wrought-iron cage that sat, unnoticed by us, in a corner on the floor near the fire.

Gretel rushed at him and tried to hit him with her still-chilled hands, but he laughed at her efforts. Then, as with the oaken door, he swung over a bolt on the cage, locked it in place with a brass key and returned the key to some hidden pocket.

My heart pounded in my chest. What evil was this! The cage wasn't tall enough for me to stand, so I knelt and shook the door with all my might but it didn't budge. It was all too much and I admit I cried a little. Gretel scowled at the man and shouted, "Release my brother! Now, you awful monster!"

He turned toward her and sneered, "I will fatten up your brother and eat him, and if you don't want to join him, little girl, you will do exactly as I command!"

Gretel was set to spinning yarn and raking coals, feeding the chickens and washing the dishes. I was given food, but not in a dish, just crusts and scraps pushed in between the rigid bars of the cage, to land on its filthy floor. I knew my imprisonment was as much of my mind as my body—I felt debased. Quaking, I wheezed and trembled. Would this man really eat me?

Oh, cursed day. To be abandoned by parents in servitude to their own stomachs, only to be captured by a fiend.

That night, when our jailor went to his bed in a blanket-covered alcove, I whispered to Gretel that she should leave me at dawn and try her luck again in the forest. Perhaps she would cross paths with some merchants or other cottagers. I almost suggested that she might find Papa, who would certainly be desperately hunting for us, but I held my tongue. I didn't believe it.

In any case, Gretel refused to seek her own safety at the price of mine. She had courage, that girl.

She tried to slide the bolt but simply didn't have the strength.

I didn't sleep that night. Gretel, having nothing else, curled her body around the cage and fell asleep holding two fingers of my left hand, which I had stretched in between the bars.

When the man pushed aside the hanging blankets in the morning, I saw him retrieve his thick spectacles from the mantel, don them, leer at Gretel, then, finally, unbolt the oaken door.

Every day he set Gretel to new tasks. I watched through the open door. She no sooner finished one chore when he found another for her to do: pluck a chicken for his dinner, stuff a pillow-case with its feathers, wash his clothes in the trough outside…

Gretel was exhausted but she never gave in to despair or let herself be subjugated. She was feisty and refused to speak to this villain—just glared at him whenever he addressed her.

He addressed me too. "Going to grow fat soon, aren't you? Then you'll make a fine meal, yes, a fine meal." He grabbed my arm and squeezed it, to see if I was plumping up.

On the third night, well after he had taken to his bed, Gretel made eye contact with me and then looked up toward the spectacles where they rested on the mantel. Due to the angle, I couldn't actually see them, but Gretel signaled her intent. Moving slowly and quietly, she tilted a chair onto one leg, and pivoted it so it was now close to my cage. Centimeter by centimeter she lowered the three floating legs back to the floor. She scrambled up onto its seat and from there onto the top of the cage. From that vantage she could grab the spectacles. She put them in the pocket of her now-dirty apron, and reversed the whole process.

She held them in her hands, eyes burning and randomly shooting a glance at the alcove. We held our breaths, but we heard nothing except explosive snoring.

Gretel shooed me backwards in the cage with a wave of her hand. Then she grabbed a pewter spoon from the table, and using all the might in her little body, pushed on the top of the cage. One edge rose up—it was only a centimeter, but it was enough—and she stuck the spoon under the cage, its handle sticking out. She retrieved the spectacles and shoved it under the cage, one lens next to the spoon. Next, she jerked out the spoon. The cage came down with a thud and I saw her smiling. The lens was covered with a fine tracery of cracks.

We both looked fearfully at the alcove. Or, to be honest, I looked fearfully, Gretel just appeared defiant. She placed the spectacles on the floor near the end of the mantel at the opposite end from where I sat, desperate and afraid.

In a quiet, breathy voice she said to me, "Careless man—his poor glasses have fallen! Now, here is a chicken bone. When he comes to test your readiness for the pot, let him feel this instead. He won't be able to see the difference."

I nodded, amazed at her ingenuity and composure.

Our jailor was furious when he found his damaged spectacles but he didn't suspect us. After all, I was encaged and Gretel was a slip of a girl—he obviously underestimated her.

The chicken bone tricked him every day for three weeks. Gretel took satisfaction from that, but I withered and sank further into despair. He never let me out of that cage that entire time.

Eventually, he had enough delay and announced that today was the day he would feast. He ordered Gretel to ready the fire.

She played the fool. "I don't know how, sir. Please show me."

He huffed and cursed our mother for not teaching Gretel the proper domestic skills girls her age should know. Gretel just stood there, her head down, the very picture of demure and modest girlhood.

The man—we never learned his name—muttered to himself as he built up the flames. I could feel the intensifying heat and shrank back as far as I could. Gretel, however, scrunched up her face and stepped backward a few paces. Then, with all her might and strength and will, she released all the emotions she'd been unable to express during our captivity. Adrenaline, I later learned they call it, some power emanating from her deep well of anger, and she ran at the man and thrust him into the fire.

He shrieked and shrieked, and when he was dead, she picked his pockets and found the key to my prison. She dunked it into a pail of water to cool it, and then released me. I sobbed.

Gretel ransacked the hut and took bits and bobs of whatever food she could find, and many small treasures to sell. The man had gold and silver aplenty and she took it all. I watched, unable to throw off my anguish and depression. Gretel helped me limp to the well in the yard, where I washed as best I could. Then she ran back into the house and reappeared a few moments later with some kindling and a cook-pot containing live coals. She ruthlessly set that wicked cottage on fire.

We chose a direction and began the journey home. Gretel's eyes flared the whole time. We met up with travelers and she handled the conversation and negotiations by herself, for it was many years before I spoke again, except, rarely, in a whisper to my sister.

When we arrived back at our hamlet, we learned that our stepmother had died during our absence. Papa had gone to live with his brother and his wife in another village. We took over the house and lived well enough on the money we received from the sale of the jewels. We never saw Papa again, and that was all to the good.

About once a year we traveled to a far-off town to sell a jewel, a different town each time. We lived well enough, and quietly. I slept poorly all those years, with my memories of my ordeal birthing nightmares. I would toss in my sleep and Gretel told me later that I whimpered.

On one of those selling trips Gretel met a handsome carpenter named Gottlieb. She was eighteen. She agreed to marry him only if the marriage contract stated he would include me in his household for all my life. Gottlieb readily agreed; we got along well.

I enjoyed working side by side with my brother-in-law and, eventually, playing with my nieces and nephews. When times were good Gottlieb built furniture for newlyweds and when times were bad, he built coffins. We survived.

Gretel was very ill during her sixth pregnancy. Gottlieb and I each held one of her hands during the birth. The midwife did her best, I know, but turned to us in sadness and shook her head. The child lived but we buried Gretel in the back garden on a late afternoon filled with rain and mist.

Gottlieb handed me a note. "She said to give this to you if she… if she…" He could not go on. I just nodded.

I had taught Gretel to read and write, and everything else I could think of, one halting whisper at a time.

Unfolding the coarse paper, I read. I was to go to the walnut tree we had climbed when we were young and innocent. I wasn't sure I could find my way… but I set out, resolutely. The trees in the dark wood seemed to wrap around me. Although it was almost sunset, no light shone through. The tree trunks looked midnight black. Bare branches twisted and twined around each other. I almost turned back. But I overcame my paralysis and took the crumpled note out of my pocket and consulted it once more. Yes, I was at the right place. I reached into our secret hiding place behind a burl. There I found an ornate, chip-carved cherry-wood box.

I recognized Gottlieb's work, but the note inside it was in Gretel's hand.

Be strong, Hansel, she said. You can recover, she averred. I have faith in you. Build a new life. I will always be with you.

In the months that followed I began to talk to Gottlieb, then my nieces and nephews. They were amazed that their silent uncle could tell stories. And, eventually, I spoke also to our neighbors and the merchants on market day.

A year later I found my own handsome carpenter and went to live with him in the big walled city on the other side of the mountain, far from the dark woods. I took with me only the cherry-wood box and Gretel's note.

Escape

By M.J. Cote

She'd had enough of living underground, in a room the size of a coffin, eating food fertilized with bat dung, and living with the same ten people, day in, day out. Rocks and darkness surrounded Marie as she pulled herself up onto a rocky ledge.

The upleading passage scraped her back as it narrowed. Her head-torch flicked along the rocks as she crawled up, hand over hand.

She rested, sucking another breath from her oxygen canister.

"Where are you going?" her brother had asked.

"Getting away from you and the awful things that happen in this place."

"You'll die." It was all he's said.

Her ancestors had predicted humans living on the surface would die when oxygen levels fell low enough. Below 16%, nothing burned and creatures suffocated. Politicians worried about carbon dioxide, not lack of oxygen.

And so, her survivalist ancestors had moved underground.

She *hated* the confinement, the monotony, and most of all, her stupid brother.

Movies from their small library showed what the world used to look like. They played them over and over on a flatscreen television in a living room barely large enough to fit ten people—more like a dying room. Watching made her angry and bitter. Oxygen generated from electrifying water supported ten people at most. Their family had survived for 246 years in these dungeons below the earth. Ten bedrooms, a kitchen, exercise rooms, a library—that was it. Their underground home opened out onto an enormous cavern. Fake sunlight from solar panels outside allowed them to grow just enough to survive—baked bat was the only meat.

According to her parents, they were saving humanity—but she'd rather die.

She pulled herself onto a slate shelf, wet from water dripping down the passage. Her head-torch wavered over a large circular door. This had to be the hatch leading to the outside world. She inhaled oxygen from her canister, then strained, pulling at the metal crank.

It wouldn't budge.

After a repeated inhaling between tugs, it let go. The crank creaked and after a push the door swung open. He head-torch flicked along a small metal chamber with another rusted door at the other end.

As much as she strained, she couldn't budge the other door. She fell back against the cold metal wall crying—something scratched at the door.

She went silent.

The outer door slammed open. She stood ready to fight only to hit her head against the metal ceiling. A cool draft filled the chamber as she rubbed her head.

This was it. Beyond—that door—was the outside world—supposedly bereft of enough oxygen to keep her alive. She stuck her head out and took a breath.

She panted—her chest quickly rising and falling—but there was enough.

Fresh air wafted over her as she climbed out onto land—real land!

The aromas were deliriously sweet compared to those in the caverns. The trees in the dark wood seemed to wrap around her. Although it was almost sunset, no light shone through. The tree trunks looked midnight black. Bare branches twisted and twined around each other. She took the crumpled note out of her pocket and consulted it once more. She'd sketched a map from the Exit Book in the library—instructions on where to go and what to do upon emerging.

Her pocket oxygen sensor read a little over 16%. Plankton in the oceans had finally released enough oxygen. She knew her parents would say that the air was borderline and that she needed to wait a bit longer. But she'd had enough.

She put a compass to her crude rendering and began walking.

She often wondered if anyone else survived fossil fuels burning until decreasing oxygen levels killed everyone off—except for her ancestors. They'd long ago descended, deep underground, where machines created oxygen from water.

She gasped when she stepped out of the forest and saw the ocean. Waves washed against a moonlit shoreline. She trembled at the beauty and the shock of seeing it was real.

A growl caused her to stiffen.

She turned slowly.

The creature crept forward. Its face peeked through bushes at the forest's edge. She froze, terrified. Her first thought that some sort of cat had survived.

Whatever it was, it skulked out slowly. Tree shadows covered the creature as it emerged into the moonlight revealing an oversized chest and enormous nostrils—probably to cope with scarce oxygen. It was at least six feet high. Furry hair obscured its shriveled face—different from any pictures she'd seen of lions or cats from books in her library.

She shuddered, tiptoeing back into the forest, then trying to find her way back. The creature's footsteps matched her pace, crunching and scraping against the forest undergrowth.

She started to run.

She heard it growl and careen in her direction. She screamed and then sucked as much as she could inhale from her oxygen canister.

A paw sent the tank flying out of her hands.

She held her breath and sprinted away, hoping this was the right direction. She felt herself weakening and growing faint. She finally breathed as she rounded a tree—too little oxygen for running. She stumbled. Her only chance was to find the hatch.

She glanced back.

It ran on two feet.

She had no idea what type of mutations could have occurred since her ancestors had gone underground, but this had to be one of them.

She reached the door. The creature jumped in front of her—fangs out—ribs on its enlarged chest plainly exposed. But the eyes—the eyes that said it all. The creature was human, or whatever it was that humans had become.

Terra Forma

By Marie LeClaire

"It's truly miraculous," Mirabyi said softly, eyes wide, as she looked out of the Domes' porthole window at the small forest growing on the lunar surface. At 28 years old she was already considered the most accomplished soil scientist on Earth and still, the sight of trees on the moon took her breath away.

"I think so too, every time I look at it," Tim replied, standing beside her. "You should walk through it. It's even more amazing,"

"Oh my god, when can I go?"

"Not right away. You've got lots of onboarding to do." Tim took her by the elbow and guided her further down the corridor. "First, let's get that suit off."

He took her to a locker room where space suits hung neatly in cubbies adjacent to lockers. Names were printed out on small plaques above each suit.

"Earthbound suits are kept here. You'll also have a Moonsuit, designed specifically for the lunar surface. You'll get one when you have clearance to be outside the Domes. But you already know this, right?"

Mirabyi had just completed the six-month training required for her post on the Moon's surface. "Yes and no. It's one thing to know something, and another to actually be here." She was still wide-eyed with excitement as she looked around the locker room.

He continued to talk as Mirabyi desuited. "I'll be your government-issued shadow for the next thirty days. I'll answer questions, show you around, and keep you out of trouble."

"Will we be working together?"

"Not exactly. We're both assigned to Biome Development. You're fungus. I'm trees."

Tim was equally accomplished in Botany, with a specialty in species that grow in harsh Earth environments. The lunar forest consisted of hybrid plants from the most inhospitable Earth environs. The Suguaro cactus from the Sonora Desert, the Polylepis tree from the Andes Mountains, and Himalayan Moss. The result was a tree approximately twelve feet tall, thick around the middle, with thousands of short branches and small, waxy leaves.

Mirabyi hung her suit on the assigned hooks and smoothed out the orange cotton jumpsuit she was wearing underneath it. "I feel like a prisoner." The bright color was intended to make her stand out as a newcomer so people could help her steer clear of restricted areas. At any given time, there were a dozen government agencies and a few private ones assigned to the Domes, all working on their own classified projects.

"You'll lose the orange after thirty days," Tim flashed her a smile. "And the shadow too – but I'll get to all that later." He guided her further down the hallway. "Which brings us to step one, the security office to activate your badges and clearances. Then to your quarters."

“The dorm? Please tell me I got a semi-private.”

“You’re in luck, sort of. You’ll be sharing with a woman from DOD research and development. Unfortunately, there won’t be too much you’ll be able to talk about.”

“What do you mean?”

“Her security clearance is three levels above yours. My advice? Don’t ask her anything more than directions to the dining hall. And even that she might not tell you.” When he saw her expression sink, he added, “You’ll get a more appropriate roommate when one comes available.”

“Great.” Mirabyi tried not to be discouraged. She had known it would be difficult. Her training on Big Blue—what the Moonies called Earth—had been rigorous. The psych eval itself had lasted for hours. But the worst part for her had been the *accompanied isolation* training. She was put in a room with three other people for three days. They were not allowed to talk to each other. They said it was to prepare her for keeping secrets from other lunar residents. It felt like torture and left her heart heavy for days.

She distracted herself from the memory by turning her attention to her attractive host. She felt an instant connection to him. Was the feeling mutual? Or was she just imagining it? Time would tell. And she had plenty of it. Three years with an option to extend for three more. She was already calculating her chances of making it through the first round.

Tim continued his rote delivery. “I need to remind you that the entire base, inside and out, is monitored 24/7 by video and audio surveillance.”

“Check.” Mirabyi checked an invisible box in the air.

“The only rooms not visually monitored are the bathrooms and bedrooms.”

“Check.”

“No communication with Big Blue for 120 days.”

“Check.”

“You’ll eat three meals a day with me for 30 days.”

“Mmmm. Check, check, check,” she flashed him a smile.

Tim deviated from the routine long enough to return her smile and nod.

They stopped outside a metal door with a large window with *Domes of Galileo Security Inprocessing* stenciled on it. “I’ll leave you in capable hands with Sergeant Chang,” Tim said as he opened the door and gestured her into the office. “He’ll let me know when you’re done and I’ll be by to pick you up.”

***

Mirabyi fell easily into the daily rhythm of the Domes. After a few conversational faux pas, she picked up on what could and could not be said and where. She was still getting used to the stilted, indirect language patterns people used in common areas to adjust for the various security levels, and also to accommodate for the constant surveillance of personal conversations.

Restricted areas were easier to navigate. The security points were indicated with thick red lines painted on the floor, up the walls and across the ceiling, with the number representing the level of clearance needed to go further. So far, she’d not crossed any, but she had seen one unfortunate soul face down on the floor with a security guard standing between his spread legs with his weapon drawn. Another guard searched his pockets and a third was on the radio talking to the command post. It was enough to keep her hypervigilant.

When she commented about it to Tim, he had laughed her off.

"It's not as bad as it looks. I've been taken down a few times. It's easier than you think to cross the lines. Especially after you've been here a while. You can get a little complacent."

"I will *never* be complacent," she insisted. Fortunately, work areas were well separated and the likelihood of her wandering across a red line was small but not zero.

"The worst threat is being DnD'd." He was referring to being Deleted and Deported, the unsatisfactory discharge of staff. Employees deemed unfit for duty were hypnotized so that they forgot everything about the moon and then were sent back to Earth.

"That does sound worse," she agreed. "Have you ever known it to really happen?"

"Not specifically, but I have noticed someone missing."

***

Her lab was her safety zone. There were no limitations in her work area and she was free to run whatever experiments she wanted. It was a scientist's dream job. Her fascination with fungus and its possible benefits to agriculture had won her grant after grant until she came into the sights of the Space Force. They were particularly interested in her work around the patterns of exchange of electrons over large areas of fungus. They hired her directly into the Domes project, which was almost unheard of.

She loved her work. Every day held some new experience or understanding of the fungal ecosystem. To be able to push her research into creating a living environment on the moon was beyond most researchers' imagination.

Her work had started out as she expected with the acidic lunar dirt being tenaciously inhospitable. Fungus, with a short lifespan, decomposed and regenerated quickly without needing much sunlight, easily accommodating for the sixteen-day cycle of light and dark. Still, it was taking much longer than she expected to convert even a small sample of moondust into viable soil. She hadn't yet been cleared for a visit to the trees, so her experiments at modifying soil content used samples brought back and forth by the Forest Manager, Tim. Although they were both assigned to Biome Development, he worked in tree monitoring and she in soils development, so they hardly saw each other during the work day.

In the past few days things had turned a bit sideways. Twice now, she'd received a noticeable jolt from the fungus that she could only describe as an electrical charge, but not really. It had a warm soothing feeling to it. She thought maybe something had gone wrong and set the sample aside. But when she recreated the same experiment, she got the same gentle jolt.

When she brought it up with the chief scientist, he quickly dismissed her.

"Just static electricity, isn't it?" he scoffed, and walked away immediately, without waiting for a response.

But it continued to bother her. She didn't know what to make of it. And she didn't know why her boss would be dismissive of it. She'd try to talk to Tim at their next meal.

Through their limited communication, she had gleaned that Tim's contribution was something called heavy COx2, a carbon atom that was weighted to remain close to the moon's surface under the lighter gravity. It created a fog-like mist around the grove. She got the impression from Tim there was more to it than met the eye. She wondered if it was connected to her shocks.

***

She had just seated herself in the dining hall when she saw him approaching the table.

"Happy Day 30." Tim greeted her for dinner with a cupcake decorated with a smiley face.

"Already? Hard to believe," she replied, even though they were both well aware of the date. She reached out for the sweet. "Thanks."

He took a seat beside her. "You know, not everyone makes it this far."

"No. I didn't." She was surprised. "I'd think, after all that grueling training on Earth, people would be more prepared."

"I think it's the accompanied isolation that gets to people the most."

"Yeah. That's been interesting for sure. Now that you're officially released from shadow duty, can we still meet for meals?" She feared there might be some prohibition about it.

"We can if we want to." He looked at her with a coy smile.

She blushed. "I could, you know, want to?"

Despite her self-cautions, she had grown quite comfortable with him over the past month, and she thought he felt the same way. Although interpersonal relationships were discouraged, they were tolerated among those with the same security level.

"I'd like that. Both our time will be allocated differently now though, so dinner is probably all we can manage."

"That would be great."

Now she tried to ease into her question.

How is that beautiful forest going? she wanted to ask, but last time she had attempted shop talk in the dining hall, a buzzer had gone off, indicating that someone had breached protocol. Everyone had to stop talking until the second buzzer sounded, indicating that the transgression was minor but everyone should be more careful.

Instead she asked, "How are you liking your job?" (How's your project going?)

"I'm liking it quite a bit right now." (Getting lots of positive results.) "How's the dirt business?"

"Not as dirty as you'd expect. It's shocking, really."

At her use of the word, Tim's face flashed a split-second recognition.

"Research can be like that. Nothing for days and then, one night, a light goes off."

He was trying to tell her something. She was sure of it.

"Maybe we can play cards tonight?" he said in a hushed voice. Code for *Meet me in the bathroom for some unsupervised alone time*—Moon parlance for asking someone on a date.

The invitation was a little unexpected but she was game. "Sure. Where?" she mumbled, hiding her mouth with a forkful of mashed potatoes.

"Bay C. 30 minutes," he said, wiping his mouth with his napkin.

She nodded.

He got up a few minutes later and said goodnight. She watched him as he left the hall, waited a few minutes, then made her own exit.

They met in the bathroom in Bay C. 'Bathroom' wasn't exactly accurate. The community restrooms were well appointed, more like professional team locker rooms. This one had four small rooms: a sitting area with bench seats and mirrors, a room of lockers, a room with shower stalls, steam room and sauna, and toilet stalls in the last room. She was waiting in the sitting area when he arrived.

He immediately put his finger to his lips to shush her before she could say anything. He turned and locked the door. Then, out of his pocket, he pulled a Tuner/4 player and tiny speakers. He set them up on the nearby shelf and turned them on. The equivalent of elevator music quietly filled the room. Then he reached into another pocket and pulled out a notepad and pencil.

They can still hear us. No visual feed. Just don't rustle the paper when you write.

Mirabyi nodded and took the note paper. *Okay. This is a little weird. Not what I was expecting.*

I know. I wish my intentions were more romantic than they are. Under other circumstances they would be. He shrugged an apology and gently touched her cheek.

She took the pencil again. *Sounds serious. What's wrong?*

He hesitated, looking at her and then down at the paper. Finally, he began to write.

It's the forest. It's changing. What are you doing to the soil?

She made a quizzical expression. *Just playing around with different fungi. Why so secretive? We could be talking about this at work.*

Work doesn't know I know. It's above my clearance.

Know what?

The trees. I think, Tim hesitated again, looked into Mirabyi's eyes and continued, *THEY THINK.*

She held her hands out, palms up, needing more information.

He tapped the words with his pencil for emphasis then wrote, *Sentient.*

They think. Sentient.

She looked at him for a long moment before taking the pencil.

Why do you think that?

When I go out there, they react to me. They move toward or away depending on what I'm doing.

She stared at him in disbelief. Was this some kind of prank?

He wrote again, his words becoming more jagged and unevenly spaced as he tried to convince her. *It's happening more often every day and more distinctly.*

That's crazy.

I thought so too but it's been happening more every day. It started when you got here with the fungus.

She thought about this for a moment then took the pencil. *There's a theory that fungus has a biochemical kind of consciousness, communicating fundamentally with itself through electrical pulses.*

Like electric shocks? Tim wrote. Their eyes met as an understanding clicked into place for both of them. She nodded.

I've gotten them too, Tim continued. *What does it mean?*

Mirabyi thought for a moment. *The theory says that large colonies of fungus are actually one organism. Not proven.*

I think we just proved it.

That's great, isn't it?

Josee went into the forest to cut samples 4 hours ago and hasn't come back.

What does that mean?

I don't know. Last time I was in there, I couldn't help thinking of you (more than I usually do). He stopped to share another apologetic smile and shrug. *Like it wasn't my thinking, like it was coming from the trees.*

Mirabyi sat back in disbelief.

He continued writing. *I think the bosses are on to me. I think I might be D&D'd.*

She inhaled sharply. She opened her eyes wide and mouthed a silent *nooooo,* shaking her head.

Tim wrote, *I've seen them do it before. People just suddenly go back to earth. If I go, you have to get to the forest to see what's happening. I'll leave a final message taped under the seat here.*

This is CRAZY.

If I get D&D'd, I won't remember you. Find me when you get back to Earth.

She put a hand on his, wanting to say of course she would,

He circled the word *promise* and tapped it urgently.

She nodded.

Satisfied, he put the pencil away, tore the paper up into tiny pieces and flushed it into the composting toilet, confident that no scraps would survive. He returned to the powder room, took her hands in his, looked her in the eyes and kissed her.

The next morning, she arrived at work to hear that Tim had taken sick overnight and was on his way back to Earth. No mention was made of Josee.

As soon as she could, she slipped out of her office and made a circuitous route to the bathroom in Bay C. After retrieving Tim's note, she went directly to the Moonsuits stored at the hatch that led most directly to the forest. With trembling hands, she sorted through the suits until she found Tim's, which hadn't been removed yet. As quickly as she could, she donned the puffy oversized suit and locked the helmet in place. She was barely breathing when she approached the panel by the door which flashed green with Tim's clearance. She pushed the button that read Depressurize and Open. The doors slid open to the silence of the moon's surface.

She made the slow moon run for the forest's edge and was more than halfway there before the security lights started flashing inside and out of the domed village. She knew sirens sounded inside but she couldn't hear them. She was under cover of the forest before security left the dome.

As soon as she stepped into the woods, she felt it. An undeniable sense of wellbeing, of welcoming. Did the trees just close in around her? No light shone through the leafy canopy. Unusual, since the sun wasn't setting for another three earth days. The tree trunks looked midnight black. Branches and vines twisted and twined around each other adding to the dense undergrowth. She took the crumpled note out of her pocket to read again the cryptic clue Tim had left her.

Go to the trees. They will know what to do.

She lay down in the dense foliage as roots emerged and wrapped gently around her. “Mother,” they whispered.

The Comprehensive Skills Test for the 3rd Cohort of the Academy of Young Mages of Socotra

By Amira Loutfi

When Nusaiba broke the crest of the bluff, she saw her classmates sitting still: chins tilted up, eyes glazed over. The space was mostly clear but over a dozen birds' nests had collected between some boulders and sparse trees that surrounded her classmates. Several more island birds twittered and hopped about the bluff. *These all seem like normal birds*, Nusaiba said to herself. Looking at her classmates she made the connection, *my classmates must've already flown over the forest and now it's my turn to take possession of one.*

She paused with bated breath, looking about the scene timidly. Beyond the bluff was the canopy of the Dragon's Blood Forest. Crossing it from above was part of an examination for Nusaiba's cohort in the Academy of Young Mages of Socotra. She'd known that something like this would be on the exam, but there was still a chance that she could fail. Her mentor had warned her of the consequences of failure—she'd have to go home. The idea terrified her.

The proctor, a stern bearded man in a plain wrapped cloak, watched her silently. It was time for the animal possession spell, but her mind was blank. What was the incantation again? Her hand itched towards the note hidden in her skirt pocket.

If I can't do it they're sending me home, Nusaiba said to herself, *but if they catch me cheating I'm also going home.*

In spite of her determination to pass the exam, Nusaiba was immature for her age and had not yet developed the discipline to independently practice her craft. She didn't know how the other kids did it. But she had prepared her own solution. She was hiding a note in her skirt that contained every incantation the test might demand.

The proctor eyed her blandly. Nusaiba's hand itched towards the right side of her skirt again. She dropped her hand and furrowed her brow deeply as she gazed over at the birds. She tried to look like she was examining them, and not inventing a way to cheat.

She leaned over the side of the bluff. It was only a few hand spans above the succulent green leaves of the Dragon's Blood forest. The canopy was so thick it looked more like a furry green blanket than the top of a forest.

She sat down sloppily, and pretended to twist her ankle. She yelped in pretend pain and tumbled off the side through the treetops below. Hopefully her proctor would think it an accident! The swollen tube-like branches of a Dragon's Blood tree caught her in bare, hard arms. The canopy above was so thick that she could barely see, but she heard the rustle of little creatures fleeing the area and could feel the stickiness of the Dragon's Blood sap.

The trees in the dark wood seemed to wrap around her. Although it was almost sunset, no light shone through. The tree trunks looked midnight black. Bare branches twisted and twined around each other. She took the crumpled note out of her pocket and consulted it once more.

She stretched it out and tried, between the twisted branches, to catch a tiny ray of light on it so she could make out the incantations.

s - t - b - d - aa - l

That was the one. She shifted on the thick branches until she was able to straighten herself out and sit cross-legged as her classmates had above. She tilted her chin and eyes upwards and muttered the incantation—first with her lips, then with her mind, and then with her heart.

An exhilarating woosh of magic charged through her veins. With a mystical burst, her spirit flew out of her body. It shot straight up through the trees in a sparkling, dizzying blur. It anxiously sought another vessel. The first animal Nusaiba's spirit saw was a large-beaked grey-bodied petrel hopping on the bluff. She immediately took it as her host.

She blinked the wide black eyes, and fluttered the thick broad wings, tripping over the fleshy feet. She steadied herself in this new body and tilted the head, peering at the proctor. He was running down the bluff to look for her. Petrel-Nusaiba raced to get to her human body first. She still *needed* something from it—the cheat sheet! It contained another incantation for the next part of the exam, which she knew she was expected to complete while in possession of an animal's body.

She hopped off the bluff and dove down through the canopy. She was fast as a bird. Faster than the old man. Nusaiba could hear him clambering down the cliff between the branches, a loud and sloppy climber. Petrel-Nusaiba landed lightly on her human body's lap. Her bird head snapped about, but she didn't see the proctor. He probably didn't even know that she was already in possession of the bird.

With her large hooked beak, she pecked the note out of her fingers. She crumpled and rolled the note over and over in her beak. When she felt it was safely concealed in her mandible, Nusaiba prepared to fly.

She burst through the canopy of succulent green leaves and continued across the forest to the next part of her exam.

A Friend Indeed

By Dana Norton

The first silly limerick arrived this morning.

If ever you heeded my call,
Answer now the most pressing of all.
To find me, a clue
Down a hole in plain view
Resides in an object so tall.

What?? The verse came in the mail, with no return address, just a smudged postmark: Knoxville, TN. Pretty far from my home in Fairfield, Massachusetts.

I didn't know a soul in Knoxville, but I had no doubt about the sender.

Nikki!

Who else would bury a cry for help inside a silly poem?

Nikki—my best friend in high school, a lover of limericks. So smart, so literate—and so perpetually in trouble. So ready to turn to me to extricate her from the mess. But why was the envelope postmarked Knoxville when she lived just two blocks away?

I called Nikki immediately. No response. I tried her roommate next.

"She just kinda took off, Abby." To my annoyance, Emma didn't sound very concerned. "Lemme see. It was, like, a week ago. She didn't tell anyone where she went. She just texted me saying she had to take care of something."

"But what?"

"Hmm. Maybe something to do with Sean?" Then Emma excused herself, saying she had to get back to her stack of dirty dishes.

I didn't like it. I was sure Nikki was in some kind of trouble. And I wanted to help—just like I did back in high school eight years ago.

***

Clouds of smoke greeted me as I walked into the GIRLS bathroom at Fairfield High. Over in the corner by the full-length mirror, a little knot of my sophomore classmates surrounded a thin, mousy-looking girl named Nikki.

One of them pointed at Nikki's stringy brown locks. "Hey, forget to do your hair today?" Everyone laughed loudly.

"Love the baggy pants," teased another. More raucous laughter.

"Hey! Leave her alone!" I strode toward them. "Only cowards pick on others."

Startled, the bullies began muttering and turned away.

Later, Nikki thanked me over and over. "You're like my protector," she said, eyes shining.

"It was nothing," I assured her. But I couldn't resist slipping in a bit of advice. "Nikki, don't you think you should pay a little more attention to your looks, try to be more like the other kids?"

"I will, Abby," she promised. From that day on we were friends. From that day on I tried to help her with everything, from choosing the right clothes, to making friends, to fitting in.

***

I got almost dizzy trying to figure out that dumb limerick. Maybe a walk would clear my head. I put the paper with the verse in my pocket and headed to Fairfield's town common. Both Nikki and I had moved back to our hometown after college, and the woods beyond the common was a great place for some uninterrupted thinking.

It was May and unseasonably warm. I sniffed the air —lilacs. Everything was so quiet and still. As I made my way toward the entrance to the woods, I finally began to relax.

Abby!" A harsh voice shattered my peace. I turned around and saw Sean, who had suddenly come up behind me, hands on hips, scowling. Uh-oh.

In his mid-twenties, Sean was of medium height and a bit stocky. His sandy hair was already receding quite a bit. Nerdy glasses made his eyes look tiny. Most of the time he was quiet and reserved, but apparently not today.

"So, Abby—you happy now? You ruined things for us!"

I began to walk faster but he kept right up beside me. "I did the right thing, Sean."

He sneered. "The right thing for *who*?"

"For Nikki, of course. She knows I gave her good advice. And she agreed with me."

Sean's snort could be heard a mile away. "Of course she agreed with you! She always agrees with you. If you told her to jump off a cliff she'd do it."

I tried to sound understanding. "I know it's only been a month, Sean. But soon you'll see it was all for the best."

What Sean replied I can't remember. I was suddenly mesmerized by the sight of a towering oak tree, which stood in the woods a few yards away.

I forced my attention back to Sean. "Hey, do you know where Nikki is now? Haven't heard from her in a week."

"How the hell should I know?" Sean turned and stomped away.

Oh, well. I didn't have time to think about him. What *was* it about that tree? I was sure it had something to do with Nikki.

***

We sat in the woods, leaning against the broad trunk of a towering oak. On the ground between us lay a huge, almost empty, bag of barbecue chips. The brisk spring wind whipped our hair in all directions. Nikki and I had been friends for a couple of years now, and we were looking forward to our high school graduation soon.

"Who's your favorite mystery author?" Nikki demanded suddenly.

"Uh…."

She didn't wait for an answer. "No one can touch Agatha Christie."

"Sure—if cozy mysteries turn you on," I sniped. "You know—quaint English villages, nosy neighbors, conniving heirs, a gazillion cups of tea."

Nikki ignored this. "She was an expert on poisons. And pretty smart in her personal life, too."

"Oh yeah?"

"Agatha's husband told her he was having an affair, and she was so shocked she decided to 'disappear.' She hid out in a little English town somewhere. They couldn't find her for eleven days."

"She shouldn't have run away," I said. "She should have stayed and faced her problem. I don't think that was smart at all."

"Oh yes, it was." Nikki leaned back against the oak with a dreamy look on her face. "Agatha fooled everybody."

***

Of course! The huge tree I was staring at was the very same one Nikki and I used to sit under in high school. The "object so tall" in the limerick!

I stepped up closer to inspect it.

By now, in my mind, it had assumed an air of mystery. The other trees in the dark wood seemed to wrap around me. Although the sun hadn't set yet, no light shone through. The tree trunks looked midnight black. Gnarled branches with glossy leaves twisted and twined around each other. I took the crumpled note out of my pocket and consulted it once more.

Where was the "hole in plain view?" I walked slowly all the way around the tree and discovered a jagged opening in the trunk. Suddenly I remembered. Nikki and I used to leave each other little notes in there. I reached in my hand and fumbled around in a detritus of dead leaves and broken acorn shells.

Nothing. I stuck my hand in deeper this time, hating the thought of what else might be in there. Spiders? Worms? This time my fingers touched something distinctly man-made. I pulled out a wad of paper and unfolded it to discover… another limerick.

Why did Nikki have to play these games? I remembered that in high school she had loved concocting little puzzles for me. Once, after a particularly silly one, I informed her that her time would be much better spent getting ready for senior prom.

***

Lights sparkled on the girls' pretty dresses and their escorts' rented tuxedos. The scents of perfume and aftershave mingled in the air. As my date, Jordan, and I walked in, "One Dance" by Drake was playing.

Where was Nikki? I had finally convinced her to attend prom, though she didn't have a date. Then we had a fight over what she would wear. We went shopping together, and I urged her to buy a certain form-fitting mauve dress with a pretty embroidered neckline.

At first she resisted. The next day between classes she silently handed me—you guessed it—a brand-new limerick:

There once were two friends you might say

Who were different, as night was to day,
Nikki was meek
Thus ten times a week
Abby ended up getting her way.

And I did! I couldn't wait to see Nikki in that sexy mauve dress.

Then she walked into prom, and I was taken aback. Why hadn't I noticed that the slinky outfit only called attention to her flat, angular figure? Why hadn't I realized that the four-inch heels I encouraged her to get would make her totter so ridiculously? Hair and make-up she had done all by herself. The former looked okay, but her eye makeup seemed more suitable for a raccoon wedding.

I practically dragged her onto the dance floor, to dance with another girl. On the sidelines Jordan and I soon found ourselves in a small group of kids, including some of the meaner ones. A couple of them were pointing at Nikki.

I looked over at the dance floor. She was jerking her legs backward and forward while waving her hands high in an odd circular motion.

"Oh my god," shouted one of the bullies, whose face was pitted with acne. "She looks like a skinny pink stork on drugs!" He took a few dance steps to imitate Nikki—and nailed it. Everyone laughed uproariously.

Nikki looked over, saw what was happening and ran off the dance floor and out of the room. She didn't come back.

***

It was getting chilly in the woods. I looked again at the limerick I had pulled out of the tree. Better to grapple with it at home. An hour later I sat hunched over a bowl of clam chowder at the kitchen table, with the poem in front of me:

I don't want to cause you a fright,
But I truly need help with my plight.
Like 10 graceful Swans
Keep gliding along
To where Agatha vanished from sight.

Oh, Nikki! Why couldn't you tell me where you went in plain English?

It was clear she had foolishly taken a page (so to speak) from the book of her idol, Agatha Christie: when things get unpleasant, just disappear. Was she still upset about the whole thing with Sean? The second line was clear. Nikki needed my help, and fast. Unfortunately, the rest of the poem made no sense to me at all.

What did Nikki mean by "Swans"—with a capital "S"? And what about "where Agatha vanished from sight"? Did my friend actually intend for me to fly across the ocean and seek her out in the English town where Christie had taken refuge? If so, why did the first limerick come from Knoxville, Tennessee?

I racked my brains for hours. I googled one thing, then another. I read up on the details of Christie's disappearance and found out that she had fled to the English town of Harrogate. There she had remained incognito for over a week at the Swan Hydropathic Hotel.

Next I pulled up a certain map and studied it minutely. Finally, I was done. I felt exhausted—but exhilarated.

My plane landed at Knoxville Airport at noon the next day. During the flight I became increasingly worried. My instincts told me that Nikki was in serious trouble.

I rented a car and drove for an hour to the town of Harrogate. Swan Road was a dirt affair on the outskirts. As I drove along, I saw mostly woods, only rarely someone's home. By the time I arrived at No. 10, I hadn't seen a house for miles. Nikki obviously had chosen the place for its wonderful peace and quiet.

No. 10 was a small cabin, which she had likely rented. A couple of sad-looking shrubs on either side of the door provided decoration, and tufts of grass poked through the cracked slate steps of the walk. For some time I hesitated on the doorstep, then made myself knock.

A whole minute went by. The ruffled curtains in the front window twitched. Finally, the front door swung open.

And there was Nikki! Her mouse-brown hair was as stringy as ever and she was wearing clothes even more shapeless than those she favored in high school. For some reason, this felt reassuring.

"So you found me." Nikki was surprisingly calm. She had a strange look on her face that I couldn't understand.

I gave her a huge hug.

"I'm glad you came," she said.

I followed Nikki into a tiny living room that would have felt claustrophobic if I hadn't been so distracted and happy to see her again. She excused herself to make us some coffee.

When she came back, she handed me my mug and sat down across from me. Then she tilted her head to one side and looked at me in a kind of speculative way. I didn't pay much attention to it, though. I was too focused on what I wanted to say.

I had planned to ease into things. First I would tell her how worried I had been and how glad I was to see her. Instead, I found myself scolding her.

"Why'd you go off like that suddenly? Why didn't you stay, face whatever trouble you had?"

"Trouble?" Nikki opened her eyes wide. "I didn't have any trouble."

What? "I don't understand." I took a sip of coffee. Nikki, I had to admit, made a very good cup. "Why did you have me come here if you didn't need my help?"

"Because I had something else for you in mind." Nikki was smiling, but her eyes were cold.

What had gotten into her? She was sitting on the very edge of her armchair now. I didn't like her tone at all, but I reminded myself that I was the mature one in this friendship. It was up to me to take the high road and get control of the situation.

"Nikki." I made my voice as firm as I could. "What is this all about?"

"Abby." Nikki mimicked my commanding tone. Then her voice rose about an octave. "It's about how I'm sick and tired of you playing know-it-all advisor to my poor helpless self." Her blue eyes bored into mine. "I'm not the least bit helpless. And you're not fit to give advice to a *dog*."

Then she said, almost too casually: "By the way, Abby, does anyone know you came here?"

"No. I assumed you didn't want other people to know."

"Quite right, no other people—o*nly you.*"

She stood up. Her voice rose again, and her face became flushed. "You're *never, ever* going to give me advice again, Abby. And I'm going to make sure you never again give advice to anyone else either." She grabbed my phone, which was lying on the coffee table, walked over to the door and threw it into the hall. The resounding crack made me jump. Then she slammed the living room door shut.

"Nikki, take it easy," I said, with a calmness I didn't feel.

"You remember how I used to love murder mysteries?" Nikki looked smug as she surveyed the tiny living room in her cabin that was miles from nowhere. "Well, I think I've done a pretty good job setting up our little scene, don't you?"

"What do you mean?" I heard my voice shake. I drained my cup, hoping the coffee would steady me.

"No one knows you're here. If you were to somehow disappear, nobody would be able to find you."

Oh my god, she was planning to kill me! She was genuinely, certifiably crazy. Desperately I looked around for something to defend myself with.

"Don't bother," Nikki said, reading my mind. "Soon you won't be able to hold onto a pencil, let alone a weapon."

"What do you mean?" I could hardly breathe.

Nikki looked almost gleeful. "I put something in your coffee. In a short while you'll start to feel sleepy. Soon the only ones forced to listen to your idiotic advice will be the poor suckers in heaven—or more likely, hell."

"I don't understand!" I cried. "Since high school, I've tried so hard to help you in every way. I gave you good advice about prom, I helped you avoid a disastrous marriage."

"Wrong. And wrong again." Nikki sat down once more and now the calm manner was chilling. "I listened to you about prom. It was the worst night of my life."

"Oh, come on!"

"And then you got me to break my engagement to Sean. It was a huge mistake—we would have been happy together." She leaned forward in her chair. "You need to pay for what you've done to me."

I felt like I was losing my hold on reality. The coffee must already be taking effect. I started to cry and laid my head in my hands.

They say that sometimes, under great stress, a person can experience a startling moment of clarity. In my case I suddenly caught a glimpse of what I was in Nikki's eyes: a poisonous meddler who had ruined her life. In Nikki's eyes, I was her worst enemy. Could she possibly be right?

A sudden movement made me jerk up my head. Nikki was now standing over me.

"So now we're cool," she concluded. "And now you won't be giving hideous advice to anyone ever again."

"I'm so sorry," I sobbed. "If I could undo it all, I would. *I am so very sorry.*"

Nikki went back to her chair and sat down. And laughed!

"Good. You may go now. There was nothing in the coffee."

That Was Then, This is Now

By Shayla McBride

The trees in the dark wood seemed to wrap around her. Although it was almost sunset, no light shone through. The tree trunks appeared midnight black. Bare branches twisted and twined around each other. She took the crumpled note from her reticule and consulted it once more. The heavy paper crackled faintly as she held it where the rising moonlight would make it legible.

Mama had cautioned her so many times about squinting, but squint as hard as she might, the letters were still too faint to make out.

"Drat," she muttered, "why do people not write legibly? What a nuisance!"

In the distance, a dog howled. Another answered. Her skin prickled with unease. Was it dogs she heard? Or was it a more ominous noise, a…a wolf? More than one? There were still reports of them in this corner of Derbyshire. A brisk breeze swept through the trees, making them creak and the underbrush whisper with menace.

"Oh, tush," she chided herself, "if you are this missish, how can you be a successful spy?"

"I have asked myself that several times, my dear," a deep voice drawled from the darkness.

With a horrified gasp, she whirled in the direction of the voice. "W-who is there?" How faint and tentative she sounded! Self-doubt possessed her; she shook it off. Much depended on her courage. She picked up her voluminous skirts, stepped forward resolutely. "Who are you? Answer me at once, sirrah, and do not insult me by using endearments."

A sardonic chuckle answered her. A tall, broad-shouldered form stepped into the wavering moonlight, swept off his hat and made a leg.

"Lady Daphne," he said with a faint touch of mockery. "Again I must ask myself, is the tool—no matter that it comes most prettily packaged—up to doing the task?"

"How dare you—"

"Pish," he said with a wave of one long-fingered hand, "you were right to worry about being too missish. This business is too dangerous for those with faint heart."

"My heart is not faint. My brother is held captive, I will do all I can to effect his release." She raised her chin, daring the man to dismiss her. Missish, indeed! When it came to dearest Jamie, her brother and protector, she would dare anything! She held out the note. "Did you write this?"

He twitched it from her fingers, held it to a shaft of moonlight. Frowned and shook his head.

"When did you receive this, my lady?"

"It was in my room this evening, as I went to dress for dinner. Tucked under my jewel box."

Another frown. "How did you leave Oakley Hall without being seen?"

"As you can see, I dressed in dark clothes, used my maid's cloak, and slipped out the servants' entrance."

He turned away, throwing up his hands. "How can I be lumbered with such naiveté?" He turned back to face her, his frown now one of extreme annoyance. "There is no such thing as a discrete departure from that door, there is always someone on guard. In the kitchen or sculleries. Or in the kitchen garden, or the walk to the stables."

She smirked. "Not this night, sirrah. I know my maid and the footman have a tendresse, and I gave her permission to walk out with him for a bit. Rose enticed him from the door and took him to the kitchen garden." A realization struck her. "How do you know so much of Oakley Hall?"

His right hand rose, fingers splayed across his heart. "I am wounded, Lady Daphne, that you have not yet recognized me."

The dim light, her weak eyes! Should she confess to her ocular shortcoming? Not a chance! She would not give him any more ammunition for his coarse accusations.

"I do not recognize every man who chances to visit," she said airily. Two could wave a hand in cool dismissal…take that, whoever you are!

"We do not have time to exchange pleasantries, Lady Daphne. Show me your shoes, if you please."

What colossal nerve! "I most assuredly will not! How dare—" She stifled a shriek as he went down on one knee, flipped her skirts up and grabbed one boot. She felt his fingers caress the leather, then the warmth of his palm as it smoothed its way to her calf. "Sir! Unhand—"

"Good," he said, springing to his feet. "Sturdy shoes. You can run. You'll need to, I fear." He tweaked her skirt into its proper folds and grinned, his teeth flashing white in the dim light. "Unless you're too missish, that is."

"Why—"

He held up a hand. "I fear that note was a trap, set to expose you and, of course, me." He cocked his head, turned in a half circle. "Do you hear them, Lady Daphne?" He whirled and grabbed her hand, tugging her along as he headed deeper into the forest. "Come, we must leave."

"Stop! You cannot—"

"Cease your yammering. I most certainly can." Around a venerable oak, through a gap in the thick underbrush, up a rise. "You wish to be a spy? To rescue your brother? I applaud the desire." Down a slope, roots grabbing at her feet. "And this is an essential part of spying."

"Running," she gasped, feeling her coiffure come partway down as a branch caught at it. She brushed the heavy lock of hair from her eyes. "Running away?"

"To live and fight another day." He scooped her into his arms and stepped over an ancient log, then deposited her without ceremony or apology back on the uneven ground. "Come, come, Lady Daphne, move those prettily shod feet, else you may become sport for either the dogs or the men who pursue us."

The distant baying she'd once heard now sounded much closer. She'd seen what a pack of dogs could do to their quarry once caught and her heart leaped to her throat at the thought of foam-flecked teeth tearing into her own flesh. She shook her hand free from his hard grasp and hauled her skirt higher from the spiky brush.

He laughed. At her? Never! No man would laugh at her, regardless of circumstances. She'd endured a lifetime of denigration and was done with it. She picked up her speed, feeling the jolt of her boots on the ground. He shot a glance over his shoulder, again grinned as he seemed to approve of her exertions.

"Are you wearing stays, my lady?"

"No," she panted, "but running like a milkmaid chased by the herd is not something to which I am accustomed."

"We will lose them in the stream," he said, hauling her around a dense group of saplings and down a rocky slope. She heard water rushing but couldn't see far enough to discern its location. Shadows jerked by, the sky whirled above. Once again, he grasped her hand, this time yanking her off her feet. Suddenly, terrifyingly, she was airborne.

"What—"

Her flight ended with a splash. The impact drove all thought from her mind. Instantly, she was submerged. Shockingly cold, running hard, driving up her nose and filling her mouth. Panic surged through every muscle as she slammed into something huge and unyielding, tumbling headlong into an uncontrollable spiral, her long skirts threatening to become her shroud.

She flailed to the surface, coughing and spitting, at once submerged again. This time, she was hauled into the night air by a brutal hand twined in her hair. What a ridiculous time to fret about her coiffure!

Another hand clamped over her mouth, a hard body behind her. He shook his hand free of her hair, an arm like a band of steel slipped around her torso. Under her bosom! A hand under the fullness of her bosom, a broad palm on her midriff, muscled thighs churning beneath her own.

She fought her attacker, twisted and contorted to no avail. Once more she was under water and frantic with the need for air.

Dogs howled and barked close by as her head broke the surface. Her shoulder scraped against rock. Her captor eased his brutal grip over her mouth and she whooped in air. The hand clamped down once again.

"Silence," he hissed, "or we die."

The wild clamor came nearer, and moments later terse words from above. The clink of a bridle, the stamp of hooves. A voice, in French.

"Where are they, Dumont?"

"I would expect in the water, sire. As you can tell, the dogs have lost their scent."

"Downstream, then. The current will take them. We'll find them and end this chase."

A third voice broke in. "Below this stretch it widens out. There's a water meadow there, they could easily come ashore, m'lord."

That third voice. Rough, rumbly. Did she not know it? She shook her head and the imprisoning hand slacked off but stayed close in warning. Above, the familiar voice continued.

"She won't last. She's but a flighty chit, interested only in ribbons and ruffles and such. Easily caught."

"But he's another story," the Frenchman said sourly. "He cannot escape. He knows and can thwart our plans."

"Perhaps we'll find their bodies, sire." Dumont, the servant.

The voice was bored, the French pure Parisian. "That would be a disappointment, particularly Bannerman, but at least we'll know he will no longer be a thorn in our sides. Come, we can't afford to miss them. We've many scores to settle. And if she lives, she'll provide amusement as well as another hostage. A marquis's daughter, like a son, is a prize worth keeping."

The dogs, set on a new course, bayed eagerly. The clink of the horse's tack sounded, then grew faint. Had they all gone or was someone posted there, silent and watchful?

Suspended in the icy bath, shivers coursing from top to toes, she willed herself to lay within the muscled arms of…Bannerman. Clive Bannerman! How had she not recognized her brother's best friend? True, the Bannerman she'd known had been a gawky and spotty schoolboy, prone to violent blushes that made him appear ready to combust. She had been casually dismissed from their rough and tumble games—"You're but a girl, Daffy."—and spent much of her time sulking inside as they endlessly fought noisy battles and captured hillsides and careened on horses under the blue, blue sky.

"Lady Daphne, we must move now," Bannerman whispered. "Upstream. The waterfall?"

She managed a yes through chattering teeth. She recalled that the stream raged through a narrow, rocky defile and debouched into a deep, turbulent pool, then shot into a long, rock-strewn passage. How did he propose to get them through it unscathed? Perhaps unscathed was too optimistic. Was alive a better hope?

Molded to her body, his arm still wrapped around her middle, he propelled them around rocks, inching along the edge of the fast-streaming main channel. Water broke over her head, lapped at her mouth and nose. She had strolled the path along the mossy verges, never imagining she would be in it, battling for her life. But, she realized with chagrin, she was a mere passenger, Clive Bannerman was doing all the battling.

That would not do. Missish she was absolutely not. She would not be cosseted as if ribbons and ruffles were her sole concerns.

"Let go of me," she blurted. "I can swim."

"In this?"

"You can't carry me the length of it, Bann," she said, using the nickname her brother had dubbed his childhood partner in mischief and mayhem.

"Ah, so you do remember me," he said. "Very well, Daffy, but hold onto my jacket. The hard part is ahead of us and I never want to explain to Jamie that I'd somehow mislaid his baby sister."

He forged ahead, breaking the flow, and she struggled in his wake, one hand clutching a fistful of sodden but very fine wool. The cold had seeped deep into her and she wondered how long she could control her muscles, could keep up. Could not be missish. As long as it took, she vowed to herself.

Far away, over the rush and gurgle of the water, she heard the hounds. Did they return? Fear gave her a spurt of energy and she all but climbed Bann's back.

They angled into a backwater where the stream shallowed, the pebbled bottom slipping under her ruined footwear. Rose would have a conniption when she saw the boots! If she ever did see them. Bann angled back out into the water. A deep roar echoed from ahead, rising and falling like the ocean during a storm. He turned to her, pulled her into his arms. Warm, he was so warm. She curled into him, her arms around his waist, hands pressing against his broad back, her face against his chest. His heartbeat pounded and skipped.

He kissed the top of her head, eased her away from him. "Ten minutes, no more." He peered at her. "You're trembling, Daff. But exertion will warm you and you'll soon be safe, I swear to you. I won't let anything happen to you. My life on it. Are you ready?"

No, she was not ready. She wanted to be home, in her bed, a cup of hot chocolate between her hands, her cat Delilah snuggled at her side and Rose in the boudoir trying to repair the boots. She looked up, into his eyes. How did she remember they were the blue gray of a summer storm?

Impulsively, she stretched up, brushed a kiss on his chin. As far as she could reach. She covered her blush by looking down, fumbling under her skirt and untying her slips. And blushed even more. She worked her legs until the water-soaked fabric fell and she kicked it free.

"Yes," she said, hoping he didn't hear the lie, "I'm ready."

The water was a live, malevolent presence, determined to batter them into insensibility. Daphne made it personal, hated the water and vowed to defeat it. Never would she succumb to its force. She had overcome other forces who wished to negate her, to stamp her down, and she would this as well. She would triumph, she would find Jamie. She had defied society's restrictions and her family's opposition, she would defy the water, the French, anything that tried to keep her subdued, ignored, subjected. Bann tried to protect her but she hissed at him.

"Make your own way. I'll follow or, by god, you can let me drown."

To her amazement, the water along the edge of the defile was shallow and almost docile, the pebbly bottom gently shelving. Bushes had found footholds in the rocky wall and they went overhand from one to the next. The boulders marking the bottom edge of the turbulent pool nearly ended their journey: the rocks were smooth and moss-covered, high and treacherously slick.

"Take off your skirt," Bann ordered. He narrowed his gaze. "No argument. Give it to me."

"It really isn't your style," she quipped as she worked the heavy fabric free. "Here."

He slung it over his shoulder, grabbed her by the waist and hoisted her up onto the huge rock blocking their progress. She scrambled the rest of the way to the top, feeling the moss give way under her grasping fingernails. Spreadeagled, she caught her breath, then sat up. Cool air made her skin pebble with gooseflesh.

"What do you see?" Bann's low voice brought her out of a shivering trance.

"Not very far," she admitted, staring across the rock-strewn pool. "Close, all is turmoil. Running fast at my feet. But to the left there's a long rock with a flat top."

"You have beautiful legs. Here, take the hem of your skirt and slide down the other side until it's taut. I'll shimmy up if I can."

He could. From the long, flat rock on the left, they hopscotched from rock to rock and suddenly were on the upstream end of the pool. From around a curve, they could hear the thunder of the waterfall. Bann wrapped her skirt around her hips. His fingers were icy.

She shivered, leaned into him. "Ugh. It's clammy."

"Better than nothing." He took her in his arms. It didn't help as much as last time. His voice was deep but had lost its resonance. He sounded as weary as she felt. "We're at the most dangerous part, Lady Daphne," he warned with formal urgency. "Not from the water, but from cold. We can't stop, if we do we may never start again. But our goal is a mere ten minutes away."

"What happens when we get to the waterfall?" She couldn't stop shivering. "It's just more cold water, and dangerous. I have heard people have died there."

"But not us. We'll be fine." He hugged her, kissed her forehead. It was an atrocious liberty but it seemed so natural. And felt so good. "Just follow me," he said, "no matter how dangerous you think I'm being. Remember Miss Peebles?"

Her governess. Flighty but strict. "I do recall she deplored your daring exploits."

His teeth flashed in a grin. "But we survived, Jamie and I both. I know this pool very well."

He gave her a final hug and slid into the water, making for the side of the wide pool. She forced herself to follow, staying as close as she could to Bann. The torrent feeding the pool was narrow and treacherous. On the far side of the dark water, spume exploded on a tumble of rocks. Far above, white froth marked the edge of the precipice. He held out his hand, beckoned. Nodded: *you can do it.*

No, I can't, she thought with despair. I am done. The water has won. Again he beckoned, this time mouthing t*en minutes more.* Numbly, she followed him into the treacherous cold.

When she reached him, he pushed away, stroking along the edge of the pool, skirting rushes and jumbled rocks. She felt drowsy, uninterested in effort. Pausing, she took a deep breath. The sandy bottom shifted under her feet, then settled. Her eyes drifted shut.

Pain exploded on her face, driving her head into a rock. She sputtered awake, saw Bann staring at her with anguish, his hand still raised. She rubbed her face, felt a swelling, stared at him in outrage. "I have never been so insult—"

“I am sorry, I had to do it,” he said, “you were going under. Come on, Daff, it’s only another ten feet. You can do it.”

“No, I can’t,” she sobbed. “I’m n-not cut out to be a s-spy. I am missish. I’m weak and f-foolish and I j-just want to sleep for a little while. Leave me alone!”

“You’re not giving up. I won’t let you,” he said through clenched teeth. “You won’t fail, I promise you that.”

“…Please…leave me—”

“To die? I think not!”

He grabbed a hank of her hair, hauled her after him as he struggled toward the falling water smashing and foaming against enormous boulders. She fought him for a few minutes, furious at his presumption in striking her, abusing her. He pulled her to him and she struck out, raking her hand across his shoulder, feeling his skin rip. He laughed, pulled her to him and kissed her with blazing passion. Hugging her tight against him, she on top, he pushed off a boulder and slipped into the wildly frothing water. She fought to stay away, but he pushed them through a narrow gap in the tumbled rocks.

Water blasted down on them. Instantly, they were submerged, but Bann kicked and kicked and suddenly the brutal pound of the waterfall was gone and only its deafening, echoing thunder was left. The surface was almost calm, little wavelets lapping at their shoulders. One of his was dark with blood. He caught her dismayed look and shrugged.

“This way,” he said, heading into impenetrable darkness. “Ten feet.” He took her arm, pulled her along.

Sand shifted under her boots. After a few uncertain steps she was waist deep, then thigh deep. The air was dank and chilly, pressing against her. Her teeth chattered. Lightheaded, disoriented by the dark and the noise, she staggered, fell to her knees.

Strong arms gently picked her up; Bann cradled her against his chest. For a long, luxurious moment, they stood in the dark, skin on skin, taking comfort if not warmth from each other. With a resigned sigh, he pushed through the water. Soon, she felt he was walking unimpeded.

"Ten feet," he murmured.

"You've said that before."

"I don't think you've ever been here," he said almost conversationally. "Jamie showed this to me. We made it our secret hideout. Didn't you ever wonder where we'd got to?"

"Of course. But I was only a girl and had no business playing with wild, grubby boys."

He stopped but didn't try to set her on her feet. "That was then, this is now. I think playing with a wild, grubby boy might now be a good idea." He bent, set her gently down. His fingers closed over hers. "Over here."

"Only ten feet," they said in unison.

Around a corner. Six steps; she counted. And six more. They halted. The waterfall was muted. She could hear Bann's breath in the still air. He released her hand; she almost clutched at him.

"Stand still," he whispered. "I'll be right back."

Rustles, clicks, mutters, a sibilant curse, more rustles. A sharp exhalation of triumph.

"Where are you? I can't see." Her voice seemed muffled, as if the space devoured her words. She reached out, groping for contact, any touch. "Bann?"

"Here." At her shoulder. Something enveloped her: warm, scratchy, smelling faintly of lavender, the scent of

Oakley Hall's linen presses. His arms stayed around her. Fatigue swept in; she felt boneless and sagged against him. For long minutes they stood, pressed close, his heart thudding against her back, her heart pulsing against his palm where it held the blanket against her. She drifted as warmth grew. Her knees gave way and she straightened with a lurch.

"Brave, wonderful woman," he murmured. "Not another woman in England could have done what you just did. If anyone dares call you missish, I'll call them out. Now take off those wet clothes." He slowly released her, making sure she could stay upright, then moved away. "There's dry ones here. I'm sure they're a bit musty, but better than what you've got."

In the dark, she dropped the blanket and untied her sodden shift, let it flop to the ground. Pulled her chemise over her head. With numb fingers, worked her drawers down her hips.

Nearby, a light flickered to life. A candle in a brass holder, the metal gleaming, the flame limning Bann's face and muscled arms, his naked shoulders, the hard planes of his chest. A blanket slung around his lean hips. She squeaked in alarm and pulled her own blanket up. He looked up from the candle, squinting at her. Smiled.

"There isn't an artist alive who wouldn't want to paint you, my Venus."

She blushed. "You take liberties, sir."

"Do I?" He stood, hoisting the blanket as it slid down. He should've looked ridiculous, wrapped in a tattered scrap of wool. But he looked magnificently disheveled, like an ancient Greek god just rising from slumber. Or dalliance. "Lady Daphne, do I take liberties to which you object?"

She shivered at his tone of voice. Deep. Dangerous. Delicious. Did she object? "No."

His gaze narrowed. He dropped his gentlemanly wrap, slammed his hand over the flame. And then he was upon her, dragging her to the ground, his hand over her mouth. His body along hers, hard muscled and tense.

"Someone is here," he whispered against her ear. "When I release you, crawl forward until you reach rock, then turn right. You'll reach the bed, get behind it." A quick brush of his lips. "A down payment, Lady Daphne. More will come, my word on it."

Hampered by the heavy blanket, she slowly crawled forward, fingertips questing for the promised wall. Her ears strained to hear a sound other than the water's muffled roar. How had Bann discerned an intruder? How—

An animal roar froze her. Grunts and curses, the scrape of blades, more shouts.

She turned, began the laborious crawl toward the tumult. Impatient, she got to her feet, Flung the blanket over her bare shoulders in a missish nod to propriety and groped forward, hands outstretched. Her left hand brushed the wall. She snuggled next to it, inched ahead. A foul curse sounded, and a spray of sand hit her legs. Where? Which direction? How many?

"I'll take your bloody body to the Frenchies," a man panted, "and collect the reward. No more bowing and scraping to toffs what don't know what it's like to spend your entire life on yer knees watching them live high while we struggle down below."

The voice sounded off to her left., toward the entrance. She crept that way, delicate steps on the rock-strewn sand.

"You can try, Lassiter," Bann said calmly.

Lassiter! Footman at Foxwell Manor, the neighboring estate. Proper, silent, always-present and always-helpful Lassiter. But big and brawny, and one of the fisticuff champions of the shire. A man with a merciless reputation in the ring.

She smelled him. Sweat and pipe tobacco. She heard him breathing heavily, spout curses as the two men stalked each other in the dark. Drops of sweat peppered her face and neck. He was mere inches from her!

"And the wench," Lassiter said with vicious intent, "will be my playtoy for a while. The gel has a nice turn of ankle, does she not? And her udders—"

With a cry of rage, she heaved the blanket forward, as high as she could manage. Lassiter roared in surprise.

"Bann! Strike now! I—"

A fist like a hammer struck her, flinging her into the rough-hewn wall. Blackness descended.

Months later:

The parish church at Oakley Hall was filled: flowers, music, friends and family. Everyone on the estate had been invited to the wedding of the year. Lady Daphne was to marry the hero of the hour, Sir Clive Bannerman, recently created Earl Poole by a grateful sovereign in thanks for saving crown and country from the depredations of the vile French. More importantly, after defeating the treacherous Lassiter and taking her to safety, Bann had gone on—at great personal cost—to rescue her beloved brother Jamie.

His title was taken, he'd written her in one of his many courtship missives, in memory of their perilous crossing of the pool below the waterfall.

Daphne stood in the vestibule of the ancient church. Her sister Chloe peeped through the doors, gave an oooh!

of delight. "Daff, your Clive looks so…so handsome! The eye patch gives him such a dangerous, dashing air! And Jamie, my word if he wasn't my brother I'd set my cap for him!"

"You'd have to fight every girl in the shire and half of the misses in London as well," Daphne teased. She flexed one booted foot: Rose had rescued the bedraggled footwear and, in honor of the perilous adventure that had begun their romance, Daphne now wore them one last time to walk to her beloved.

The string quartet ended its Mozart. Music boomed from the organ in the loft above their heads. Chloe came to her sister, gave her veil a few unnecessary tweaks.

"Perfect," Chloe pronounced. "Are you happy with the results of your whirlwind courtship, my sweet, daring sister?"

Bann had charmed her mother, disarmed her stern father with his new title and estates. And wooed her with the singular focus that had saved their lives in the waterfall cave. In truth, she had chafed at his thorough, methodical courtship. She had seen the man she wanted as they fought for their lives. His subsequent injuries, the livid slash across his handsome face, was to her a badge of honor.

"I am less a man," he'd mourned at first.

"No, you are more," she'd said, tenderly kissing his savaged eyelid.

Now Daphne kissed her sister's soft cheek. "Yes, kitten, I am. And I will be happier yet when I am Bann's wife."

The old oak doors slowly opened fully, revealing the crowded church, the satins and laces and feathers, the crow-dark attire of the men. And the smiles, so many smiles. The strains of the wedding march filled the ancient church. Her stern, rarely-smiling father stepped into the aisle, smiled at his oldest daughter and cocked his arm.

The scent of roses floated on the air. Heart racing, Lady Daphne went to her father. But her eyes were on the tall, broad-shouldered man waiting for her at the altar.

Moments later, a mere instant it seemed, she and Bann faced each other. Rings on fingers, lips curved in smiles. He took her in his arms. After a kiss that brought a few gasps of surprise—or was it envy?—her new husband brushed his lips against her temple. Whispered.

"Wife. Lady Poole. My countess. As always, as forever, you take my breath away." Another kiss, lingering on the corner of her mouth. "There is not an artist alive that wouldn't want to paint you, my Venus," he said.

About the Authors

The contributing writers are participants in To Tell A Tale Writers' Group. TTAT used to meet in-person in Worcester, MA, but Covid drove us online where we happily continue to meet. The silver lining is we are at capacity, with members in several states.

M.J. Cote

Mike is an adjunct Professor at Northeastern University, where he received his Doctorate in Law and Policy. He holds a Master's in Business Administration from Nichols College and received his undergraduate degree in Psychology from the University of Vermont.

He spent the bulk of his career in management at various high-tech companies, most recently with Philips Healthcare. He has traveled to Stonehenge, the Temple of Apollo at Delphi, Machu Picchu, and to the Uluru in Australia, in search of ancient lore. He has written articles on leadership and is now an aspiring science fiction and fantasy writer—the culmination of a "wishening" he made as a teenager.

Melody Friedenthal

Librarian. Chocolate lover. Pythonista. Science fiction reader and leader. Editor of MetaStellar, an online magazine of science fiction, fantasy, and horror. SFWA member and chief bottle washer at To Tell A Tale Writers' Group.

Melody's stories have been published in Eldritch Science, MetaStellar's *Year One* anthology, Bardsy's *Love is Blind* anthology, and, coming in late 2023, New Myths' *The Cosmic Muse*. She's had two articles published in Information Technology and Libraries (ITAL) and is an ITAL peer reviewer. Under the business name Friedenthal Writing Review, she provides copyediting services. She's currently splitting her "free" time between writing a cozy mystery and writing a space opera.

Marie LeClaire

Marie LeClaire started writing a novel in 2011 just for fun. It turned out to be more fun than she expected, so she wrote four more. Her short stories have appeared in three anthologies and on her own website, MLeCLaire.com. She edits for a popular speculative fiction magazine, MetaStellar.com, as well as being a contributor of short stories and reviews. Most recently, she has turned her hand to writing screenplays.

She is a member of Science Fiction and Fantasy Writers of America, Women in Film New England, and To Tell A Tale Writers Group. You can find her books on Amazon, Barns and Noble, and Kobo. She currently calls Massachusetts home.

Amira Loutfi

Amira Loutfi is on a mission to craft excellent fantasy fiction inspired by late antiquity Arabia and Bedouin culture. Her stories often feature powerful warriors, eccentric mages, desert politics, and duties to family in a harrowing environment. You can learn more about this project if you join her newsletter (www.amiraloutfi.com).

Shayla McBride

Shayla McBride once thought she was a romance writer but she kept killing off the hero or heroine. Now she's happy killing off any one she fancies as a suspense and thriller writer. An award-winning non-fiction author (*Writing Your First Fiction: A Beginner's Guide to Genre Writing*), Shayla prefers to not write to prompts, but these really were fun.

C. Brian Moorhead

C. Brian Moorhead first honed his craft in the scholarly halls of western Massachusetts, and occasionally they allow him back in. He primarily plies his trade in Worcester County, and hasn't quit his day job.

Dana Norton

In a past career life Dana Norton wrote feature stories for a variety of news outlets, winning an award from the New England Press Association. She dealt in facts, but soon discovered she preferred the wide-open spaces of fiction – specifically mystery. She is a member of Sisters in Crime and lives with her daughter, a recent college graduate, in a suburb outside of Boston, MA.

Lucy A.J. Tew

Lucy A.J. Tew is a writer, director, performer, and professional cat herder (teacher of middle schoolers). She's Los Angeles born and raised, but has nurtured a lifelong love of New England and its many secrets and stories. She currently has three English degrees, a job as a theater teacher and director, an on-campus apartment at a New England boarding school, and two debatably sweet and cuddly cats.

Made in the USA
Middletown, DE
27 October 2023